SCAVENGER HUNT

DANI LAMIA

This book is printed on acid-free paper.

Published by:
Level 4 Press, Inc.
13518 Jamul Drive
Jamul, CA 91935
www.level4press.com

Library of Congress Control Number: 2019943901

ISBN: 978-1-64630-004-4

Printed in USA

Other books by Dani Lamia

The Raven

Demonic

666 Gable Way

Hotel California

Younger

1

t is 1987. I have never been drunk before because I am an eleven-year-old girl. I haven't yet done a line of cocaine off a glossy board game box top or screwed one of our summer interns just to watch them squirm when I make them get me coffee afterward.

My entire family is fucking terrible, and so am I. It is Scavenger Hunt Day in Ditmas Park, Brooklyn, where we have one of our weekend homes.

Alistair and I are partners again this year, which is probably frustrating for him, on account of the fact that I have basically no interest in winning or even participating in this game. I don't know what I was thinking, not demanding that our father partner me with Pomeroy Egan (who we currently all call "Pom-Pom"—later in life, he will be "Roy"). Was I hoping Dad would somehow read my mind? That he would somehow know what I want in my secret soul and help me get it?

I know that I was protecting my heart by not telling him. I don't want Pom-Pom's affections to be something that can be purchased like a new Nintendo game and delivered to me instantly. I want to earn his affections with my deserving heart and deserving body. I want to fascinate Pom-Pom Egan on my own, beyond my father's money and power and beyond all the fear and desire that the name Nylo strikes in the Pom-Pom Egans of the world.

Where I went wrong tactically on this summer afternoon was not at least insisting that Pom-Pom Egan be separated from Bunny Applewhite. All I can think about now is them together. In my head, I see them giggling, not trying to win, having fun, spending the whole weekend together, hands brushing hands, braces grinding against braces. My heart flutters with bruised despair every time I see them traipse across a cul-de-sac together, arm in arm, prosecuting this dumb scavenger hunt with maximum disengaged irony. My partner is my own splotched and anxious brother. What could be worse?

"So, these sprinklers," I mutter.

"We need one of the kinds that slowly and silently waves back and forth like a fan," says Alistair, studying our list. "You know, the kind that sits on top of the grass and you can run through it? We also need one of those sprinklers that is just a spike you stick in the ground, and it shoots out water on a ratcheted spring at a ninety-degree angle."

I usually don't mind his fussy precociousness, but today he is getting on my nerves something fierce. I try to remind myself that he can't help the way he is.

"Yep," I say, looking down the block. Pairs of kids are moving around all over the neighborhood. Our father spends all year coming up with this stupid scavenger hunt checklist. I close my eyes and imagine stamping down into hell like Rumpelstiltskin. I try to remember all the times I enjoyed the scavenger hunt before, the times I marveled at the specificity and cleverness of our father's game-making ability. This game is his attempt to give back to the neighborhood, to devise something personal and fun for all of us.

Gabriella, Bernard, and Henley are all too young to play without help from an adult, so they are being shepherded through the streets of Ditmas Park by Angelo Marino, our father's long-suffering confidant, attorney, and attaché. Angelo Marino is very good with our younger siblings: he is patient while never losing his old-world charm. I can see the four of them rummaging through the field house of the Egans. There is a sheet of red construction paper on its door, signifying the building as fair game for ravaging.

Alistair and I already turned the field house inside out, but we found nothing. He insisted that somebody must have gotten there before we did, but honestly, who cares? We are woefully behind, and I don't give a shit if we win or lose. This isn't even a proper game. It is a zero-sum struggle for resources. There is no real strategy here. It is more like a sport.

The fact that there is no strategy means that all the other kids in the neighborhood have as much of a chance to win as us Nylos. But I am annoyed by Alistair treating this game with the same respect and competitiveness as he would a game of Diplomacy or chess.

"What's the third kind of sprinkler?" I ask, trying to contain my misery and irritation. It isn't Alistair's fault that Pom-Pom Egan isn't my partner today. It isn't my father's fault that Pom-Pom and Bunny are running around like free-spirited nature sprites in bathing suits, with their perfect matching tans on their long loose limbs revealing how compatible they are with each other. Neither of them has brothers or sisters. I try to tell myself that they must each be very lonely and that it is actually good and fine that they have found each other and that they will now get married and grow old together.

"What's wrong?" asks Alistair. "Are you sick? You look like you're going to throw up."

"I'm fine," I say. "So what's the third kind of sprinkler on our list?"

"I actually don't know what this means," says Alistair. "It says we need to find a soaker hose. Have you ever heard of a soaker hose?"

"Yeah," I say weakly. "Look, I even know where we can find one."

"Oh yeah?" he says, perking up now that I am showing a minor sparkle of interest in this stupid contest for babies. "What is a soaker hose?"

"It looks just like a regular garden hose, except it's black and rough all over, like Lava soap. Water just sort of seeps out of it."

"That seems stupid," says Alistair. "So it's just a broken garden hose?"

"Yeah, but maybe you just want to water a flower bed without messing up the soil," I say. "I don't know."

Alistair and I are Irish twins. Born within a year of each other. I am older, but he is bigger. He is smarter, but I am in charge. Someday this is going to result in sexualities for both of us that require the perpetual mediations of good therapists.

"The Bountys have a soaker hose," I said. "They use it for the tomatoes in their back garden."

The Bountys are annoying hippies who are intent on growing their own food in the middle of Brooklyn. They are always leaving baskets of anemic brown tomatoes and shitty malformed squash on people's doorsteps with little notes. Everybody hates the Bountys. First of all, they actually seem happy together in their self-contained world, and second, no one can figure out why they won't leave everyone else in the neighborhood alone or at least join us in prosperous despair. Of course, the Bountys love days like this when the whole neighborhood is out and about.

We cut across two yards and hop the chain-link fence on the side of their house, behind the large bushes meant to keep dogs from digging up their precious vegetables. Their house is one of several on the block that is all the way open for the hunt. I'm worried that the Bountys are waiting here somewhere, ready to corner children and read their auras and tell them all about the healing powers of yoga and high-fiber cereal.

Their garden shack is closed, which I think is kind of weird. There is definitely a sheet of construction paper duct-taped to the aluminum siding. Alistair and I look at each other and then I push open the door.

Bunny Applewhite and Pom-Pom Egan snap around in the darkness. Bunny is slightly taller than he is. They are holding hands. They both smile at us sheepishly, dropping their hands and blushing. Obviously, they have been making out.

"Hey, it's the Nylos!" says Pom-Pom Egan. "You guys are the real threat. The power team. Nylo means fun!"

The worst part is the expression on Bunny Applewhite's face. I know exactly how she must feel. It is how I want to feel. How I have been anticipating feeling ever since Pom-Pom Egan announced that he would be participating in Scavenger Hunt Day this year since he wasn't spending the summer at computer camp.

"Sorry," I say, shutting the door to the shed. "Didn't know you guys were in here."

It is hard to look at Alistair. He looks so full of sympathy and pain that I can't meet his eyes. He looks at me, pursing his lips, worried as hell. Why does he look like he is about to cry? Doesn't anything belong only to me? I am so tired of my family. Of how big and sprawling and needy it is.

"I have to use the bathroom," I say. "I'll be right back."

"Where are you going?"

"Back to our house."

"You can probably use the bathroom at the Bountys'," he says.

"Nope," I say, running away. "Go back to the shed and get that soaker hose. I bet nobody even knows it's in there."

I run as fast as I can down the street to our summer house, a gabled bright blue Victorian with a turret on top. These massive suburban houses are so different from the rest of Brooklyn, but they're near the beach, and it's usually nice to be around all these other kids, unlike the rest of the summer when we're trapped in Nantucket.

There's a loud noise just as I head up to the front door, a flat crack like a tree getting hit by lightning. Everyone stops what they're doing up and down the street and looks at our house. It sounds like somebody slammed a door and broke it right off the hinges. Like they fucking destroyed it. I run up the porch stairs.

Even though I have lived in New York City my whole life, this is my very first gunshot, the very first data point on a dotted line. I don't know to recognize or be afraid of gunshots yet.

Somebody shouts my name, but I don't stop. I am going to cry my damn eyes out about Pom-Pom and I don't want anybody to see. I fling open the front door.

I nearly slip and break my neck on the blood pooling in the foyer, soaking past the carpet. I see Mom in the living room, the room where we aren't allowed to play on account of all the nice white furniture. She picked out the furniture and carpet herself. She calls it the White Room. White curtains, white carpet.

Now the white curtains and white carpet are covered in blood and brains. A mean, snub-nosed pistol is on the floor. The pistol is very far from her hand. Did her hand jerk when her brain was perforated?

Where is my father? He is supposed to be in the house. Is he still upstairs, coordinating the game with a bunch of walkie-talkies, waiting for the winners to return and claim their prizes? I begin screaming. I'm nearly knocked over as everyone in the neighborhood floods in behind me to see the carnage.

2

I t is 2019. My office is on the top floor of the Nylo Building in DUMBO. "NYLO MEANS FUN" proclaims the billboard out front. The family used to have real estate in Midtown, but we wanted to be a bigger fish in a smaller pond. Ideally, we would be the only fish in a pond exactly the same size as us. So we sold our suite of offices next to Times Square and were able to purchase an entire office building right on the water.

The sale of the building was profitable, like everything we do. The secret to becoming rich on a massive scale is to always do things that make you rich on a very small scale. At the time, I wanted to be closer to my husband, to my children, and to their school. This was before the divorce.

The Nylo Corporation makes games, first and foremost, but we have tendrils in all sorts of entertainment. What makes a game good? What makes a game substantial and rewarding versus merely entertaining? What makes it deep and nutritive to the intellect, something that one can return to in order to learn lessons about life, abstracting some kind of deeper meaning from the rules, mechanisms, and dread mathematics that put players into conflict with each other and themselves?

A good game is overwhelming and all-consuming. It requires a person to focus on it exclusively, inviting one to weaponize one's intellect and personality completely. It requires you to be logical and to execute strategy, but also to be flexible and to learn from momentary setbacks, changing your plans in the face of new information. It requires you to be social and to make alliances, or else to go it alone in the face of unified opposition for the thrill of being a game-steering villain. A good game becomes its own world, colonizing your mind and invading your dreams. It leaves you no space to worry about your mundane problems. A good game is totalitarian, using every part of you.

This is what business has become for me. Running the Nylo Corporation is a very good game.

I have a bedroom right off my office. It's actually much nicer than the bedroom in my Townhouse in Carroll Gardens. I think this is because it gets cleaned once a day (sometimes twice) instead of once a week. There is absolutely no evidence of me here. I get obliterated every morning after I wake up and I leave. The room is always fresh and clean.

My bedroom has a massive bed with black silk sheets. Nearby is a custom-built gaming table and an extensive gaming library. Caravaggio prints adorn all four walls and an original Jeff Koons balloon dog stands on a pedestal by the door to the bathroom. The bathroom is how I like it: prison style. A drain sits in the floor beneath a massive waterfall shower, with water that runs hot and forceful. There are two marble sinks.

I sleep here more often than I do at home. When I sleep here, I am always the first one at my desk and the last one to leave.

Never leaving work is one way I have managed to stay in charge of Nylo, despite nearly constant threats from inside and outside the company. Have you ever seen how a runty cat is able to dominate a much bigger cat? It climbs to the highest possible point in a room and watches the bigger cat constantly, making sure it can't relax. The runty cat strikes whenever the bigger cat tries to eat or rest. Eventually, the bigger cat succumbs to a state of exhaustion and crippling feline anxiety.

There is a fully stocked kitchen on the same floor as the office. Executives have access to the personal chef, but I sometimes like to make elaborate sandwiches and pasta dishes late at night, just for myself. I leave the leftovers for the assistants, and sometimes they even eat them, effusively praising my cooking with bootlicking adulation.

My ex-husband never liked the food I made—never even lied about liking it.

"Why cook?" Ben would ask. "We can eat anywhere we want in this whole city every night of the week. We can get Central Park hot dogs delivered to us at four a.m. Why bother cooking? Why go through the psychodrama of cooking and doing dishes?"

"Because I like it," I would say. "Because something from my hands goes into your body."

"I can cook," he'd counter. "I used to cook for a living. Is doing laundry going to be your next hobby?"

"'How much sharper than a serpent's tooth it is to have a thankless child,' etcetera, etcetera," I would mumble.

"King Lear said all that because he was going crazy."

One of the other attributes of a good game is that there isn't much luck involved. Variance is the technical term. The more variance there is, the less true skill is required and the less one's strategies need to focus on trying to beat the other players at the table and instead just involve trying to cope with the whims of destabilizing existential uncertainty.

Like your mom blowing her brains out in the White Room on Scavenger Hunt Day.

Just because there isn't any luck involved doesn't mean a game is inherently good. Take chess, for instance. Along one vector, chess is considered a perfect game. With the exception of who goes first, there is basically no variance involved in chess. Each move that one makes is unique, creating an entirely different situation from game to game that creates new challenges and the opportunity for creative solutions.

However, even very simple computers are better than the most elite chess masters, mainly because chess is a game of math and variables, and human beings can't hold as many variables in their heads as machines. We can't possibly be cold enough to beat an algorithm whose only goal is to win, an algorithm that can't even take pleasure from victory or feel despair from a loss.

A truly good game requires you to draw on your humanity, on your skill at manipulation and reading people, on your logic and reasoning and estimation skills (at least insofar as you know what may be calculated), and above all on your fortitude and dignity. It draws on the essence of being human, of conflict in a crucible, of performing your most noble and decent qualities in the face of danger and catastrophe.

It doesn't feel amazing to be a better computer than somebody else. But it does feel good to be better at being a human. Running a massive corporation gives you endless opportunities to feel human. I am addicted to the performance of my own humanity.

It is actually rare that a private, family-owned corporation is entirely run and operated by the family itself. Why bother, when you could just count and spend your money?

But Alistair and my father and I love running Nylo. There is no better game. It's a totalizing competitive experience. It's always there for you. And unlike most games, the rules are only limited by the laws governing your country's financial sector.

For instance, it feels like I have been trying to buy Playqueen—the hip new feminist toy company making STEM toys for nerdy girls that is trying to eat our market share in the under tens—all year, but I have constantly been thwarted. Dad is always noncommittal when we talk about it and whenever I try to set up a meeting with the execs, someone cancels at the last minute. Just this afternoon, I resolved that my next go will be successful. Deciding this so demonstratively makes me feel slightly dizzy.

I have sent my assistant, Peter, home for the day. I know he is headed upstate with his boyfriend for the weekend, but I also know he will worry and fret over me, no matter how hard he tries to relax. I have to remember to check in with him at least once a day while he's gone, to let him know I am hydrating.

I look at the schedule he printed out for me for the next few days on thick, cream-colored paper. It is embossed like a restaurant menu, with the Nylo logo at the top. "Caitlyn Nylo," it says. "Agenda for June 7–9."

I get these agendas first thing in the morning, along with a perfect popover, a warm pat of salted French butter in its own ramekin, a single soft-boiled farm egg slathered in hot sauce in a separate dish, and a steaming mug of black coffee.

My Friday is unusually empty. There are only two meetings this afternoon: first, a strategy session for what to do about Playqueen, and then a simple marketing meeting about our fall line of video games that I insist on attending—even though I know I will mess up the flow and rattle everyone just by being there because I don't know enough about video games. I need to stay on top of everything, especially the stuff that doesn't innately interest me.

Saturday morning Ben is bringing over the girls, and then there is the birthday party that afternoon. Sunday we'll recover and do whatever the girls want, like always.

Since my day is so clean, I take the elevator up to the very top floor, where my father has his office. There's nothing else up there except a giant conference room bounded by four walls of soundproof glass. The conference room is empty right now, aside from several bottles of water chilling in an ice bucket, perpetually ready for spontaneous meetings.

My father's assistant, Devi, has her kitten heels dangling from her pedicured toes and is chewing on the end of a straw while typing insanely fast into the razor-thin laptop on her glass desk. She closes the laptop as soon as she sees me and smiles.

"He's in there," she says. "Just go right in."

I don't need her permission, but I smile sympathetically just the same and scoot down the hall to my father's office. The door is open. He isn't sitting at his desk or staring out the window with a glass of gin in his hand, which would actually be normal morning behavior for him. Somehow what he is doing is even sadder. He's sitting on the couch with his hands on his knees and his head down. The top two buttons of his shirt are undone, and he wears a blazer and no tie and no socks. He looks deflated—defeated. He looks unfun.

"Hey, hey," I say, knocking on the open door. He raises his head like someone is yanking his bangs up and manages a small smile.

"Player number one," he says.

"So are we going to buy Playqueen or not?" I ask. "I want to buy and gut it, clean it, and crush it. Do I have your blessing? I'm tired of dicking around."

"Always working," he says. "You used to take breaks. You used to get really excited about vacations."

"Did I?" I ask. "I used to like vacations because they reminded me how much I love work. Now I don't need any reminders."

"How are the kids? Are they excited about their cousin's party?"

"I'm sure they are," I say. "I'm not involved with any of it. It's at Bernard's and I'm sure Phoebe is taking care of everything. I'm just going to show up with the girls and do my bit, just like you."

"You work too hard," he says, sighing. He hangs his head again, and I'm not sure what I'm supposed to do. *Are we done talking? Is that it?*

Sorry, Dad. You can tune me out all you want, but I won't give up on Playqueen that easily. I will not be swerved. I will not be ignored.

3

wander down to R&D, which stretches from the fifth floor to the basement. This is the guts of the Nylo empire. Whatever Alistair requests, he gets. I deny him no expenses and greenlight every new budget that he tentatively slides across my desk, no matter how insane. I know exactly how valuable he is as an innovator and specialist, and we have provided him with the best team in the business.

This investment is worth every penny. I can't even remember all the times one of his projects or inventions has saved us. I've learned by now that even product lines that seem to be failing or not reaching their market will eventually become beloved as a result of wistful reminiscence if they are made with love and care. It doesn't take very long for something that inspires joy to begin inspiring fierce nostalgia.

I desperately need Alistair's support with the other executives if we are seriously going to buy Playqueen. The best way to seduce him is merely to visit him—to pay him some attention for a while.

Alistair's empire is as whimsical and chaotic as mine is manicured and muted. Spiral staircases corkscrew down through the translucent floors, tinted in bright primary colors.

The walls are covered in concept art and schematics. Engineers and designers run amok, grinning, wearing tight-fitting T-shirts and khakis. There are kitchen islands overstuffed with donuts, pizza, and breakfast cereal, as well as nap pods and soundproof "yell chambers" where people can have private conversations or just scream alone.

Most of the furniture down here is giant, overstuffed, and plush. You can take a catnap on the fluffy stomach of a reclining Catsnake (the ever-present loyal familiar of *Action Sam*, one of Nylo's longest-running hit animated shows) or you can use a puffy toadstool from *Alice in Wonderland* as your ottoman.

Alistair's lab is surrounded by life-size "Helping Hands" cutouts. Helping Hands are last year's big hit, which made a lot of money for us. The posable hand-shaped action figures have distinct personalities and come from an alternate dimension where all the creatures are animated body parts: feet, brains, elbows, tongues, etc. The hands are the heroes: Grip, Pointer, Knuckles, and Snap.

Snap is the witty, urbane intellectual of the group. She is my favorite and I actually have a Snap figurine on my desk upstairs. Alistair says he based the design on a posable hand he bought from an art supply store to help him draw hands better.

As I walk through R&D, everyone turns to look at me, getting vaguely nervous at my presence. I smile and nod, trying to be reassuring. I don't know why they are so freaked out. I would never intrude on Alistair's dominion by making some kind of personnel decision down here in the bowels, where fun and frolic is the point. I know what artists are like. Just because I'm not one of them doesn't mean I don't appreciate their temperaments—their oppositional defiance, their moodiness, their fragility.

I do find myself noting which employees are actually taking advantage of the nap pods. I can't help myself. I feel a minor unease at my own hypocrisy. I have a bed here, too—but that's because I never leave. I wonder how many of these twenty-year-olds stay out all night in Greenpoint, drinking and Tindering, and then use their jobs as an opportunity to catch up on sleep.

I shake away my crankiness. The rules for R&D are different than the rules for the rest of the company.

"Is Alistair here somewhere?" I ask two young women eventually, becoming tired of hunting for him. The women are both looking at something on their phones. They grin at me as I look over their shoulders, but I can't tell if what they are doing is personal or work related.

One of the girls points and I see Alistair across the room, looking a bit like a jug-eared English royal with his unruly auburn hair and wearing a half-untucked and rather rumpled white button-down, mesmerized by something on his phone. He's holding it up to the wall as if it is a magnifying glass.

"What are you people cooking up down here?" I ask as I approach him. "Some kind of new phone game?"

"Sister!" he says. "You don't come down here often enough. It's great to see you. I was just about to knock off for the day. Gonna try to hit the beach and enjoy this sunshine. Is there anything better than New York City on a Friday in late spring? Want to come?"

"To the beach?"

"Yeah, why not?"

"I have meetings all day," I lie. "Wall-to-wall meetings, trying to make all this fun profitable. So, what is this? What are you working on?"

"Well, it's augmented reality," says Alistair. "We're trying to make it useful, to turn it into something we can sell. Most augmented reality products are gimcrack and sloppy, but we think we can make something that will catch on. Take a look!"

He holds up his phone and I gaze at the wall through it. In real life, I can see it is pink and solid, but the screen shows a swirling purple vortex.

"Reach into it!" he says. "Go ahead!"

Still looking at his phone, I stick my hand out and see it disappear into the vortex. Then all of a sudden the vortex dissipates, becoming a golden scroll that hovers in midair.

"The scroll is a job opportunity," says Alistair. "Now you can use the phone to interact with the scroll, accepting the job or not. Right now, the only jobs available are from Sydney Polytechnic, where we have a small research partnership. They are trying to do facial recognition research, so all the jobs are just tagging whether all the faces in a series of three are the same or not."

"And this is fun to people?" I ask him. "What do you mean by a job? How is a job a game?"

"It's charity," Alistair explains. "Every time you do one of these tiny little jobs that you stumble upon, you not only gain levels that give you access to extra powers and bonuses in the game, you make money for the charity of your choice, money donated by one of our partners. By doing these mindless, rote activities that we've gamified for these researchers and corporations, you're working toward improving the world."

"Interesting," I say. "But I hope you aren't spending too much time on this concept. We aren't running a charity here."

"On the contrary," says Alistair. "We've done the market research. People want their games and diversions to matter more, to feel like they are having an impact on the real world. Imagine if every time you played *Candy Crush* or *Tetris* a small amount of money was donated to Planned Parenthood or the World Wildlife Federation. Imagine if playing Pandemic went to AIDS research. We're trying to do something similar. There's an ancillary concept that we're developing: a browser extension that takes all of your marketing data and pays a small amount to charity every time you play a game using any platform on your computer. But I'm most fascinated by the possibilities of augmented reality. Actually, it was Dad who, hmmm, well. Never mind. It isn't very interesting."

I sink down into a giant chair that looks like a stuffed piece of strawberry-frosted cake. Alistair frowns, sensing my despair.

"Maxim's birthday party is tomorrow," I say. "Ben is dropping the twins off in the morning."

"Bernard always throws a nice party," says Alistair gently. "The whole family will be there. Henley, even."

"I think the twins are starting to hate me a little," I say. "I think maybe I'm starting to hate them a little, too. Like Mom hated us. They are more Ben's children than mine at this point. I don't even really feel like I know them. Is it weird to be scared of your own children?"

"Well, you don't see them very much," says Alistair. "I mean, you could see them more."

"There's no time," I say. "I dread seeing them. No shit. I think they can tell I dread them. Are all children little sociopaths?"

"Children are mostly wonderful," Alistair says. "They just need more from you than adults do."

"Maybe," I say. "Or maybe they are doomed to be spoiled little shitheads who will never be worth a damn, like Henley. Being useless runs in our family just as much as loving toys does."

"Anyway, I'm looking forward to seeing them," Alistair says. "Are you doing okay? You don't seem particularly well."

I lean forward and take the phone out of his hand. I use it to scan the walls for more portals filled with more scrolls that might hold more games that will help me make more money for Planned Parenthood and more abortions. The wall behind him is filled with portals.

"I want to buy Playqueen," I tell him. "Dad won't even talk to me about it. There is a ticking clock here: we don't have much time to acquire them, steal everything they make, and put them out of business before the next shareholder meeting. Are you going to back me on this?"

"They do good work," says Alistair. "I like their physics kits and detective playsets. I think they have a very inventive point of view, and obviously they have a real insight into the preoccupations of under-ten girls, which has always been a weakness of ours."

"It won't work unless you are behind me all the way," I tell him.

"You know I'll support you," he says.

"I can't even remember being under ten anymore," I say. I reach into one of the portals and pull out another scroll. I click the button on the phone, which lets me interact with it. Three faces show up. Three middle-aged black guys are scowling while walking down the street. Two of them are the same person and one of them is different. I click on the one who is different and am rewarded by another set of faces. All three are teenage girls with black hair, sitting in a diner booth. I frown. Actually, all three images are of the same girl. There is a button to click if that's the case. I click it. In one corner of the screen, a counter shows me how much money I am making for Amnesty International.

"Look at me," I say. "I'm saving the world. Actually, it does feel kind of good. I can see this catching on. The games need to be a little more complex, perhaps."

"We don't really have control over what the jobs might be," says Alistair. "Those will all be set by our partners."

An idea hits me. "Of course, we'll also have access to whatever data gets harvested through these games," I say.

"Yes, I suppose we would. But what would we do with it?"

I look around the R&D department. All these fun, creative people making fun, creative products. They are brilliant engineers and artists, but they aren't playing the same big-picture game that I am. They don't have a twenty-billion-dollar business to protect.

"You know CAPTCHA?" I ask. "Those little tests that websites do to see if you are human?"

"Yes," he says. "Of course."

"Well, the data from all those CAPTCHA tests is being used to help train AI. Did you know that? Very efficient. Use every part of the buffalo, right?"

"What are you suggesting?"

"Well, we could work the same hustle," I say. "We're getting people to do the same kind of work as CAPTCHA by playing a fun game for charity. That's all up-front and aboveboard. But we could then use all that data for our own purposes, creating a massive database of all the 'good people' of planet Earth that we could then exploit, while at the same time using the aggregate of all this data to train our own

AI, which we would be able to train much faster than any individual client." I pause, noting the sardonic look on Alistair's face, and add, "I use the term 'exploit' here in the technical sense."

"That's very sinister," says Alistair.

"You are so sweet, little brother. So dedicated."

"Are you sure you're okay?" he asks me again. "Seriously, is something wrong?"

"I can count on you, right? All the way? We're on the same team here?"

"All the way," he says. "I am Knuckles and you are Snap."

4

Eventually, I have no choice but to go home for the night. I have to get things ready and prepare emotionally to see my little angels in the morning.

My Townhouse is actually rather modest, considering. But it is just me living here and I don't need much.

Like my office, it is immaculate. The housekeeper comes once a week and cleans the place from top to bottom. She does an inventory of my refrigerator, getting rid of anything past its prime and replacing it, to ensure that my food is always fresh.

My refrigerator is packed with bottles of Corona, slices of capicola and cave-aged Gruyère (what I've always called "cave cheese"), sirloin and ribeye, Fresca, plastic clamshells full of prepared salads from Whole Foods, and many, many containers of Greek yogurt, one of every flavor available. In my freezer, there are bottles of pepper-infused vodka, three different kinds of ice cream (I am more interested in variety than I am loyal to any particular flavor), and frozen tater tots. I don't often end up eating any of this food, I must admit, but it doesn't always get wasted. When things are on the bubble, I encourage my housekeeper or gardener to take what they want for their own families.

I like my house to be empty of people when I arrive, but I also like the lights to be on and some soft music playing: old indie rock, ideally. Arcade Fire or the Strokes or the Killers or Franz Ferdinand or Tom Waits or something.

Tonight, I come home and head straight for my study on the top floor, which is in a gabled attic full of natural light. I pour myself a bourbon, filling to the brim the glass kept chilled in a little freezer up here. I sip it slowly at first, then more greedily until the warmth and sweetness spreads into my brain and my belly and I start to feel more solid, more sensible, freer.

I drink Fresca because LBJ drank Fresca. He remains my favorite executive and a model as a power player with respect to winning games by any means necessary. But Fresca doesn't go very well with bourbon, so I have a supply of specially ordered "White Coke" up here in my study. I have several cases that I purchased illegally from North Korea, where the product is still manufactured. What else are you supposed to do with money? I don't do normal snortable coke anymore. This is as close as I get.

During World War II, General Eisenhower once gave Marshal Zhukov of the Soviet Union a Coca-Cola. The two famous generals were keen admirers of each other, but even so, General Zhukov was flummoxed and frustrated with how much he enjoyed the rust-colored imperialist beverage. He asked for more. Much more. He drank as much as he could in secret while fighting the Nazis and guzzled it by the chilled bucketload afterward at the Potsdam conference. Yet he still couldn't get enough.

After the war was over, Zhukov had to go back to Stalin's Russia. It was a major drag for him. As a gift to Zhukov, when Eisenhower became president, he ordered the Coca-Cola corporation to find a way to remove the coloring from Coke and put the clear liquid in white bottles with straight sides, like vodka. The corporation even added a red star. Eisenhower then ordered Coca-Cola to begin shipping this White Coke directly to Zhukov via its Marshall Plan–era factories and distribution centers in Eastern Europe.

Zhukov returned the favor on his end, helping Coca-Cola move its products more easily through jointly controlled Austria. And Zhukov was able to enjoy drinking Coca-Cola directly in front of Stalin and his own troops, who assumed it was just vodka. Rust-colored Coke became White Coke, which eventually became a staple for the high command of many communist countries after the formula for Coke was outright stolen during the Brezhnev era. North Korea, my current supplier, was one of the first countries to begin manufacturing it in bulk.

I consider my supply a delicate luxury, and I hope it lasts me the rest of my life. It tastes the same as regular Coke, though one time there was a giant beetle in one of the bottles, which somehow only added to the authenticity and mystique.

I finish my first straight glass of Four Roses and then crack open a bottle of White Coke. I pour a little into the glass and mix it with more bourbon, then I stare out my attic window at the neighborhood below me. Young people are starting to come out to mingle at the bars across the street. I consider going out. But to do what? To meet someone new?

No. I finish my bourbon and White Coke, and by this time I'm a little hungry and a little sleepy. I make myself a full pan of tater tots, but I only end up eating a few. I eat a cup of blueberry yogurt and snuggle into my giant bed in my room, which is exactly the same as my giant bed at work. I fall into a deep, dreamless sleep that seems to yawn on forever, like a warm throat swallowing me for infinity. I only wake up once in the middle of the night, which is unusual for me. I typically wake up four or five times when I'm sleeping at home all alone. I get up to use the bathroom and while I'm sitting there on the toilet, staring through the open door at my empty bed, I suddenly realize that my children are older than I was when my mother killed herself.

"That means that I am a better mother than she was, by default," I say out loud. I throw myself back into bed, and the next thing I know,

I've been awoken by the doorbell, which someone is basically leaning on, ringing it over and over again.

I hit the buzzer that opens the door and then fumble around until I find a clean sweatshirt, which I slip on over the Arcade Fire T-shirt that doubles as my pajama top. Somehow I managed to fall back asleep with my pajama bottoms still attached to one of my ankles, like a snakeskin I couldn't quite shed, and now I pull them all the way up and hop into the elevator and take it down to the bottom floor.

It's morning. *How did it get to be morning?*

My girls are in the kitchen, looking annoyed, wearing their bright pink backpacks. They seem slightly happy to see me at first, but then catch themselves and revert to haughty preteen aloofness. Though they are twins and look exactly alike (except for the fact that Olivia currently has blue hair), they really aren't very much alike as far as their personalities go, though they do share a history and a certain measure of divorce-inflected trauma. Olivia is the creative, outgoing one, and her grades suffer for it, but she is far better company, albeit rather lazy. She is so charming, though, that it doesn't matter. Not to me. I expect that she will bring me an incredible amount of trouble in years to come, but I am hoping that most of it falls on her father. I'll probably have to worry more about Jane, who is the cerebral one, the one who most takes after me. She even wears her hair like I do, blond and straight and cut at her shoulder, which must make her father uncomfortable. Not that he would ever say anything about it.

"You guys ready to party?" I say to them.

"Mom, not yet," says Jane. "Maxim's party isn't until this afternoon."

"Your father just dropped you off here and left you? All alone?"

"Well, he's coming back, now," says Olivia, sheepishly. "We called him, since you weren't answering the door."

A united front. It was most likely Jane who called him, but Olivia is backing her, which is a bad sign. Usually, my only way to deal with them in an effective manner is to divide them up.

"It's my weekend," I say fiercely. "I don't want to see him. He isn't

allowed to come here. Text him and tell him that you're fine now—
that I let you in, that everything is okay."

"We called him, though," she says. "So now he's worried. He just
wants to make sure."

There is a knock at the door and then Ben just opens it right up,
which is fucking ridiculous.

"Oh, go ahead and just come in, then!" I yell. My ex-husband is
definitely not the first human adult I want to see this morning, or
really any morning.

"Girls?" he asks. "Is everything okay?"

"Yes, we're all fine," I say. "You can go ahead and leave now."

Ben Fotopolous divorced me, so I'm not sure why he's always trying to edge his way back into my life. He's a beautiful man in a way
that I have always found annoying, except when I am fucking him or
trying to make other people jealous. He is kind and solicitous. He is
my same height, and he is strong, and slender, and pale. He has one
Greek grandfather, one Chilean grandmother, and the rest of him is
Anglo, but certainly not WASP. Flawless skin with dark hair. Warm
eyes. Nice dick. He's funny and a good listener, and he has always been
an attentive father, which is one of the reasons I picked him out to
fill me up with kids. He's a high school history teacher with a Bolshe-
vik streak. Even after marrying me, he never stopped teaching in the
Brooklyn public school where he first interned with AmeriCorps and
then later took a job.

His job is the one that Jane and Olivia respect right now, since they
are still in the world of school, where teachers are the ultimate author-
ity and where grades are the ultimate currency. Teaching "big kids" is
super-impressive to them, and my outright bribes aren't. Plus, Ben has
custody, so he's the one who makes sure they get fed and get to school,
and he deals with all of their tawdry little emotional problems.

Like how he used to deal with all of my tawdry little emotional
problems. Only they are grateful in a way that I never was. And they

can still grow and change and learn, whereas I am done growing up and definitely done changing, and I guess he finally figured that out.

"Big birthday party today, right?" he asks me, smiling.

"Yeah, the whole family is coming. Even Henley, for some reason. He's flying in from China. I guess he needs money."

"What's he doing in China?"

"Embarrassing himself. Probably embarrassing the country. I think he likes the attention. I think he hopes that someday he'll be kidnapped as one of the heirs to the Nylo fortune and held for leverage. That's when he'll finally truly find out how much he's worth to us. Boy, will he be surprised."

"How are you doing, Caitlyn? Are you feeling okay?"

"Why does everyone keep asking me that? Look, the girls are fine. You are fine. I am fine. You can go now. You are the good parent and I am the shitty one. Are you girls ready to have fun?"

Olivia and Jane ignore my whining. They finally set down their backpacks.

"Yay," says Olivia pathetically.

"Have a good time, girls," Ben says, and turns to leave.

"Bye, Ben," I say.

5

let my children walk all over me, as usual. They are civilized about it. We order food from wherever they want, like every time. For lunch, that means we get Chinese dumplings delivered from Ginger House in Flushing, Queens. The dumplings are only about eight dollars an order. Getting them delivered to my Townhouse costs fifty dollars. I am not one of those world-disdaining elites who doesn't know how much things cost. I am one of those tight-fisted penny pinchers who loves the steady jangling increase of coins in my coffers.

We also get lemon chess pie from Two Little Red Hens, which I am more excited about. I eat a few dumplings with the girls in solidarity. We talk about games, about school, about boys, about movies. Olivia is going through some kind of crisis with one of their friends, who is evidently "fake." Jane seems to think this crisis will blow over, and perhaps it is only me who catches Jane's insinuation that it is Olivia who is truly not being the genuine one.

"Do we really have to go to Maxim's party?" Jane asks.

"I mean, no," I say. "We can tell the family to go piss up a rope. But your Uncle Henley has flown in from China. You haven't seen him in forever. Also, Grandpa will be there. Also, your cousins."

"Maxim is creepy," says Olivia.

"I don't like leaving the city," says Jane.

"Yeah, me neither," I say. "Why live in New York if everybody isn't going to just come here, where all the stuff already is? But Bernard likes to show off his big dumb house, and there is nature and whatever. Remember trees? I promise we won't stay long."

We have a couple hours to kill, so we watch some horror movie that Olivia chooses, which Jane avoids by focusing instead on her phone. The movie is something about the ghost of a murdered child returning to haunt a family, and the whole thing is done through security cameras that pan and shake. The movie is in black and white and there are often subtitles when the people are whispering to each other. *Did the ghosts add the subtitles in later?* The metaphysics of the film are very silly, barely even internally consistent.

Promptly at 3 p.m., a car arrives with a driver that I often use who knows to never even try to talk to us, and he drives us out to Bernard's compound on Long Island. Bernard lives in the terrible part where all the people are rich and boring and for some reason can't handle living in a proper city and instead need lots of space for things like horses and extra cars and drones and dumb shit that represent the suburban trappings of wealth, and not real wealth. Real wealth is having all the city shit that matters, like the ability to pay people to do exactly what you to tell them to do, who then live in total quaking fear that you might someday stop paying them. Who wants freedom when you can have power?

At Bernard's, there are no balloons or streamers or other evidence outside to suggest it's a child's birthday party, and aside from us Nylos, the guests are all Bernard's friends and their kids. The catering is nearly invisible, which gives the event a cul-de-sac vibe that I find nauseating, since I know where this aesthetic comes from: some unspoken craving on Bernard's part for the remnants of our idyllic childhood. *Sorry, little brother, Mom kind of ruined that when she offed herself in our living room.* It is so transparent and sad.

When we arrive, Bernard says hello and then disappears. His wife,

Phoebe, grins and grabs us and gives us big hugs as if we're all one big, happy family. She is wearing about thirty different bracelets and has limpid blue shark eyes that don't seem to dilate. They have two children together: Maxim, who has just turned ten, and Julian, who is eight. We are all fairly certain that Maxim is a budding serial killer who will one day bankrupt his father in legal bills, but for now he satisfies himself just being surly and spoiled. Julian, on the other hand, is adorable.

"Helloooooo," says Phoebe. "Thank you for coming all this way!"

"It's good to see you, Aunt Phoebe," says Jane, ever the proper diplomat. Olivia doesn't even bother, not willing to pretend that we have any kind of relationship with "Aunt Phoebe."

"Looking fit, Feebs," I say, cruelly. She and I both know that my brother will never, ever, ever be faithful to her, no matter how nice or in shape she is. Her smile falters, but not actually that much, which is impressive.

"What's up, Nylo bitches!" shouts someone from the upper deck of the foyer balcony. My little sister, Gabriella, is wearing a sparkly silver caftan and almost hanging from the skylight, her curly brown locks flying every which way. I can tell she arrived much too early and now is extremely bored and no doubt ecstatic that I am finally here.

Olivia and Jane run up the stairs to greet their Aunt Gabriella. They are excited to see a familiar, friendly face among all of these dull Long Island ghouls who smile with pained expressions and move out of the way deferentially in the presence of us honest-to-god Nylos. They all know who I am, so I don't bother saying hello to any of them. Why am I even here? I wonder. Just so Henley can borrow money from me? In fact, where is Henley?

"Where's Henley?" I ask Phoebe. "And where did Bernard go?"

"Oh, Henley is here… somewhere," she says. "And Bernard went to go check on… something?"

"Well, it's been nice catching up, Feebs," I say. "There are so many people here! How do you guys know so many people?"

"Sands Point is a very tightly knit community," she says. "Bernard and I are very active in the local church and in the PTA. Bernard and the other moms—"

"Yeah, I'll bet," I say. "Bernard and the other moms all day."

Now she turns away, red-faced, but I can tell she is suitably afraid of me again and will leave me alone for the rest of the party. I feel slightly bad, but not bad enough to apologize or worry about it longer than it takes for Gabriella and my girls to work their way through the crowd back down to me.

"What's up, boss?" says Gabriella.

"What are you wearing?" I ask. "I am totally willing to give you money for real clothes. You don't have to make dresses out of the curtains."

"It breathes!" says Gabriella. "I like to feel the cool wind on my budding nethers."

"Are you here by yourself? You usually shove some rock star in my face first thing."

"I broke up with the black metal guy I was dating and now I am between artists," she says. "Dane Wizard was very good at making brutal shapes of solid metal with his fuzzed-out bass, but he was less good at being vulnerable enough to accept my love."

"You prefer drug addicts. You like it when they need you."

"At least I'm not married," Gabriella says, shooting a sidelong glance to Phoebe, who is arbitrating some pointless conflict between preteens.

"You look good," I say. "Good tan. You don't look too broken up about the sudden ending of your very important love affair with Dane Wizard."

I vaguely remember the man: skeletal to the point of looking unwell. Black eyes that were like shiny bugs about to fly away.

"I went to Thailand for a while and I reconnected with the real Gabriella," she says.

"Which Gabriella is that?" I say with raised eyebrows.

"You mock me because you just have the one self," she says. "I've got hundreds. Masks and personas. It's hard to say who I would even be if it weren't for the centering power of dance. Maybe you get the same thing out of your job?"

"Maybe," I say. "Have you seen Henley? He is supposed to be here somewhere, right?"

"He came in last night," says Gabriella. "I think he got into some kind of trouble in China. He's very on edge. He was hitting on Phoebe as much as possible, which I think she enjoyed, but which was making Bernard rather irritated at him."

"You and Henley have always been close," I tell her. "Which is good because I can barely stand him anymore. I feel like he's always about to confide in me, which would be tragic, because I don't care."

"You just have to breathe, and center yourself, and find the deep well of patience inside," she says.

"To breathe, like your caftan," I say.

"Yes!" she replies, pleased.

"Are you still making your soaps?" I ask.

"Helping people cleanse themselves—body and soul—is still my life's work, yes."

Gabriella has tried to start many businesses, but she has had the most success as an Instagram entrepreneur, selling soaps with earthy smells that she invents herself, sending the recipes to a facility for production in New Jersey. Pine and peat, cedar and rose, lime and grass. She has some marketing savvy, but she lacks what you might call a killer instinct. I check up on her more than she knows. Actually, this soap business is almost breaking even. I'm proud of her, but I know that I need to be a little withholding if I want her to keep striving for my respect.

"I have your pine and peat bar in my guest bathroom," I say. "Everybody loves it."

"That's so sweet," she says. "Do you know where I got the idea for that one?"

"No," I say.

"This drummer I used to see," she says. "For some reason, the floor-board of his van was always covered in pine needles."

I nod to her, maintaining my poker face. So my guest bathroom smells like Gabriella fucking some homeless drummer in his van. Great.

"I'm gonna go look for Henley," I say.

I wander through the many rooms and alcoves of Bernard's osten-tatious mansion. There are expensive paintings on all the walls and ornate vases in the corners. The décor is frat-boy brothel. I feel for Phoebe. She must have little say in how the money gets spent, seeing as how it's all Nylo money. I pass through a library full of leather-bound tomes of history and law, all of which have surely never been read. I hope that at least Julian accidentally grows up to be a reader. Reading books is one route away from the loneliness of money.

I wind my way upstairs, dodging children and their harried parents, getting nervous looks from the peasants. *That's right: it's me, fuckers.* I peek in a few of the guest bedrooms, enjoying the stillness. There are seemingly endless empty rooms full of perfectly made beds and giant mirrors above empty dressers. Who sleeps here?

I hear voices in one of the adjoining bathrooms, so I creep into the bedroom and crane my head around the cracked door to see.

There is Bernard with his pants down around his ankles. A young-looking mom in a sleeveless dress and YouTube-makeup-tuto-rial-bright-red lipstick is jamming her ass onto his cock, watching her-self in the bathroom mirror. Bernard catches my eye and then gently closes the bathroom door all the way.

Back in the hallway, I decide I could really use a smoke.

I root around in my purse, hoping I have a hidden pack that I didn't purge from my latest attempt at quitting, while I look for an open balcony. I glance into a billiards room as I pass by, then retrace my steps, hopping backward.

A shadowy figure is leaning against one wall, blowing jets of vapor at the ceiling, scrolling furiously on his phone, and joggling one leg.

"There you are," I say.

Henley starts at my words, but quickly collects himself and smirks, throwing his arms open wide. He spins the vape pen dexterously around his thumb and it disappears out of sight.

6

"You look very adult and serious and stressed-out," he tells me.

"In fact, I am trying to smoke a cigarette," I say.

"I bet you can light up in here," he says. "This house is so big, what does it matter? Ashing on some of these rugs will give them character. They're all so dreadfully new."

"I don't want to set off any smoke detectors. Does that window behind you open?"

He shrugs. I push past him and undo the latch. There is a mesh screen behind the window and a gleaming tripwire that must be part of the security system, but at least I can blow my smoke outside.

Henley doesn't look bad. He is still as impish and wiry as ever, lacking Bernard's solidness but also his middle-aged paunch and jowls. He also lacks the clean good looks and fitness of Gabriella, but he has always been attractive, albeit in a less obvious, more devilish way. He knows too much about other human beings. Of my four siblings, he has always been the one who has unsettled me the most. He doesn't have Bernard's coldness, or Alistair's genius, or Gabriella's good nature. He has some kind of dissipated wisdom, something beyond me. It has always been intimidating, even though I know that on some level he admires my own comparative advantages: my ambition and drive.

"You should really switch to a vape," Henley says. "They're better for you and you can vape anywhere."

"It's very psychologically important for me to control a flaming piece of paper," I say.

"Where are Alistair and the father figure?" Henley asks me.

Actually, I have no idea where they are. It is a little strange that they aren't here yet. I see them both so often at work. Maybe I am a little happy they aren't here. I do get tired of them.

"They must be around somewhere," I say.

All of a sudden I get a whole bunch of texts at once. The cell phone coverage out here is terrible. I look down at my phone (Henley has not yet put his away) and see that they are all about the Playqueen acquisition. Our lawyers are finding some obvious anomalies, but I am actually glad. I like knowing exactly how something is fucked-up.

I look at the headlines and then save all the messages, feeling the itch to work. I need to respond to them, but I haven't seen my baby brother in... two years?

"Has it really been two years?" I ask him.

"You've been busy with Nylo and your kids. Last time I saw you, you were just coming off that ugly divorce from... Ben?"

"That's right," I say. "That's his name."

"Anyway, how does it feel to be free?"

"Terrible," I say. "I don't like freedom. Not for me, not for anybody. I am a natural-born authoritarian. People only truly thrive under iron laws that take away their dread."

"Yes, well, you haven't been to China."

"Haven't you been thriving over there?"

"Not exactly," says Henley. "In fact, I might not be able to go back for a while. I may or may not have done something that may or may not mean that my very important and delicate life of ease is at risk in the glorious Middle Kingdom."

"What did you do? Fuck some Party leader's daughter?"

"Ha, definitely, many of them. But that doesn't make anybody mad.

Wiggling out of a marriage can be tricky, but luckily I am quite wiggly. No, I didn't get into trouble with the state at all. It was more with what you might call a private organization."

"Tell me what happened," I say. "Gabriella is certain you need money. Do you need money?"

"Did she say that? I don't know how she got that idea. No, what I need is a job. Someplace to hide out for a while. Something to hold my attention and chill me out."

"Do you even speak Chinese?"

"Sure," says Henley. "It's not so hard to pick up, if you're motivated by colossal loneliness. Plus, there are those Party leaders' daughters, as you mentioned. Expats bum me out, so I've spent a lot of time in giant dim sum restaurants, listening to endless drunk conversations. Anyway, I'm safe now. How are you?"

"What do you mean you're 'safe now'?"

"Not in peril? Unmurdered? Not being threatened and blackmailed by bloodthirsty men in bad suits, certain that I have wronged them?"

I sigh, rolling my eyes.

"And if I give you a job this will help you somehow?"

"It won't hurt," says Henley. "Remember how we all used to work doing playtesting for Dad's games during the summers? I always enjoyed that."

"You never took it very seriously."

"But I was always good at it," he counters.

"Last time we spoke, you wouldn't shut up about how the future was China."

"The future is still China," says Henley. "Do you have any idea how starved they are over there for diversions and games?"

"Anyway, I'm glad you're back. And I'm sure the father figure will also be glad to see you."

"Phoebe looks good," says Henley with a wry grin. "Don't you think? Better than when I last saw her. She certainly takes care of herself."

"Stop," I say. "Just stop."

I stub out my cigarette and give Henley a long and lingering hug, until we are interrupted by shouts from downstairs. Alistair is here with presents for everyone. I always forget to bring bribes for children, but he always remembers. I guess because he doesn't have any children himself and so he doesn't quite hate them all yet.

Henley and I make our way back to the front entrance of Bernard's house, where all of the kids are gathered. I even see Bernard finally pop his head in from a back room. He smiles at his wife. I look around for the mom who was just grinding on his dick and see her joggling some two-year-old who is entranced by the skinny man with the knapsack full of drones, board games, stuffed bears, Helping Hands action figures, and video game consoles.

"A lot of the children here are underprivileged," Henley whispers in my ear. "Veritable urchins, lifted right from the streets of Long Island. Poor unfortunates. Phoebe told me that they are all going to one of those Evangelical churches now. They are learning how to be true Christians."

"Yikes," I say.

"It makes Phoebe happy, and I think Bernard likes making new friends," says Henley. "Don't you think?"

"Henley!" shrieks Alistair, running to hug our little brother. "Look at you!"

I take the opportunity to step outside and check my messages. I light up another cigarette, unconcerned now if anybody sees me. I am a little shocked that there aren't any messages from our father. He seems to have disappeared completely. It's at times like this that I almost wish he had remarried, just so we would have someone else to call in order to keep tabs on him.

Swiping from message to message, I learn it isn't just the lawyers who are freaking out about Playqueen. Now some of the vice presidents are weighing in, convinced that acquiring the company will be a huge mistake on account of how "narrow" Playqueen's focus is. I grit my teeth, refusing to take the bait. Why is it my job to remind these executives that there are more women on planet Earth than men? How many shaky companies have we bought for way too much money over the years, just to stay in the market, just to keep our plan of attack diverse?

"Look out!" someone yells at me. I dodge sideways just in time. A drone the size of a basketball whizzes by my head. Maxim is standing on the front porch piloting it, and I see Olivia and Jane beside their cousin, looking glum and embarrassed. I take a long drag of my cigarette and then tromp up the front porch stairs.

"Are we ready to go?" I ask my daughters, not bothering to wish Maxim a happy birthday. Jane nods vigorously and Olivia shrugs. We say our goodbyes. I tell both Gabriella and Henley to come visit me in Brooklyn this week. I don't say goodbye to Bernard, who seems relieved that I am leaving. Alistair is busy showing some children how to make the Helping Hands action figures spin around on one finger.

"Has anybody heard anything from Dad?" I ask my useless siblings. They all look at each other blankly and shake their heads.

"Well, when he shows up, tell him to call me," I say.

On the drive back home, Olivia and Jane spend the whole time complaining about their evil little cousin and his creepy hobbies, including the mutilated, pinioned, and dissected bodies of small animals that he collects: squirrels, opossums, raccoons, birds, and even something he said was a fox but looked "just like a little terrier," according to Jane.

"He calls it his taxidermy," says Olivia.

"He kept coming up behind me and like leaning against me," says Jane. "Just, like, wrapping himself all over my shoulders and legs. He wouldn't stop. I think he was getting something out of it. He would get all red in the face and giggle."

"If he makes you uncomfortable, you totally have my permission to bop him right in the face," I say. "I don't like him either, but the little one is nice, isn't he?"

"Yeah, Julian's sweet," says Olivia.

When we get home, I keep the girls up eating ice cream and gossiping about their aunts and uncles. When I start to see them fading, I ask if they want to watch some TV or a movie. I'm trying to squeeze in as much face time as possible this weekend, before I have to be alone again for another two weeks.

When Ben half-heartedly asked for full custody, I think he was surprised I agreed. Everyone was surprised. I loved how monstrous it made me feel. But he is a better nanny than any I could ever hire. And the idea of him living alone as a swinging bachelor made me sick. So now I am the swinging bachelor. I am the fun one. I am the one they will run to when they are old, when they want the truth about life.

"We're bushed, Mom," says Olivia. Jane doesn't even say goodnight. She just goes up to her room and falls asleep facedown in her bed.

"Your family is so much more fun than Dad's family," says Olivia, giving me a hug before taking off for her own room. "Except for Maxim."

"My family?" I say. "It's your family, too!"

"Ha, yeah, right," says Olivia.

I take the elevator up to my room, checking again to see if my father ever arrived. But there are no messages from him. I'm just about to text Bernard when my phone rings. It's Alistair, who has never quite learned the etiquette of texting first.

"You're up," he says, short of breath. "Oh god, none of us know what to do. I'm so sorry to call you like this, but we are all freaking out over here. Bernard just took off at top speed. I guess he's going to swing by your place to pick you up?"

"What's wrong?" I say. "What's the matter? You have to slow down and explain yourself."

"It's Dad," he sputters. "One of his maids found him in the shower. He fell down or something. Anyway, it doesn't matter. They're saying he's dead. But that can't be true, can it?"

I crumple to the floor, my hands shaking. I scramble for the phone, which has fallen through my fingers. When I pick it back up, I accidentally hang up on Alistair. I frantically tap at the screen but can't seem to remember the code to unlock the phone, or maybe it won't unlock because of my sweaty fingers. I keep pressing the buttons but nothing happens.

7

In the pew at St. Patrick's, the girls are bookended by me and Ben. They seem to be handling everything okay, which is more than I can say for myself. This is a full Catholic funeral service, and the bleachers are packed.

There are reporters here from *New York Times, Wall Street Journal, Washington Post, The New Yorker, New York Magazine,* and even from *The Guardian.* They all want to interview me, and I am too shell-shocked to fend them off very well. They are blending in with work acquaintances and Dad's old board game buddies and low-level executives he was mentoring, and honestly the entire funeral is just a giant fucking unplanned mess. Luckily, almost everything I have said so far to these vultures has been garbled and unusable for any stories they might be trying to file.

I should have been better at bringing everyone together and making sure this goes smoothly, but I just don't have it in me, and so everything has fallen on Angelo Marino, my father's personal lawyer and best friend. Angelo Marino has done his best, but the past two days have been a whirlwind of shock and grief and funeral arrangements, and until we got here, we didn't even know whether it would be me or Alistair speaking at the vigil.

I don't have anything prepared, and Alistair is terrified of public speaking. I am the oldest, but Alistair had a closer relationship with Dad. In the end, we decided to both say something short.

When it is time, Alistair walks up to the altar first and immediately freezes. He clutches the lectern while the priest looks on encouragingly. Alistair has actually been holding up better than I would have expected, but now it seems like the public speaking is fucking him up more than the tragedy of our father's accidental death.

"Prescott Nylo was a legend in business, a legend in game design, and a legendary competitor and friend," he finally manages to choke out. "But for me, he was just a dad. A very good dad."

He shuffles his notes. He looks around. He coughs.

"Jesus, he looks like he's about to throw up," whispers Henley, leaning forward from the pew behind me. "You'd better get up there and save him."

I stand up discreetly and approach the altar. The aging Irish priest has gunk-covered spectacles, a sunburned scalp, and food crumbs in his luscious beard.

"We always knew our dad was proud of us," Alistair eventually continues. "How many people can say that? We always knew that he loved us, and I hope that wherever he is now, he knows that we love him and that we are proud of him."

Polite applause breaks out. Alistair stumbles down from the podium and gives me a long hug as he makes his way back to his seat. His eyes are dry. Only Gabriella has broken down in tears so far this morning, and even this seemed forced to me.

I glumly ascend the podium myself. I reach into my pocket and pull out some hurriedly scribbled notes, but when I smooth them out on the lectern, they don't seem to make any sense.

I look out over the congregation. Henley—that demon—is grinning at me. Bernard and Phoebe look exhausted. Maxim is in fact totally asleep, and Julian is trying to stay awake but keeps nodding off.

I don't blame them. Is there anything more boring and soul-crushing than a full-length Catholic funeral?

Olivia and Jane look up at me expectantly, and I remember that I am supposed to be representing the strength of the family. I am supposed to be representing the permanent, unshakable power of the Nylo Corporation. I am supposed to be a living symbol of our family's excellence, cunning, and creativity.

"I don't care who you are," I begin, my clear voice filling the room. "It doesn't matter if you are a good person or a bad one, a rich person or a poor one. Prescott Nylo wanted to make you happy, or at least take away your cares for a few minutes on the long, unswerving road to oblivion. We all loved him passionately, those of us who knew him. But he was more fun than any saint. He was better at cards, at *Sea Farmers*, at *Twilight Struggle*, at jacks, and at *Tetris* than Satan. There is that old trope of challenging death to a game in exchange for your immortal soul. Well, Prescott Nylo didn't just win games against death and the void and meaninglessness of existence and all that: he invented new games."

I look over at the priest, who seems to be both encouraging and confused in equal measure. I don't believe in God, but I know that our dad did somewhat and that he went to mass every Sunday, as well as on the extra holy days of obligation. *What a fucking waste of time.*

I sigh and glance up at the ceiling before continuing.

"The world is a shittier place now that our dad is dead. That is just a fact. We have all been robbed of so many new games and toys, and those of us here who were actually his sons and daughters and grandchildren and friends have all been robbed of future good times, of future demented laughter, of future immeasurable joy. We are all going to have to work very hard from now on to give back everything that he gave to us. But he taught us well. Thanks to him, all of us here celebrating his life know how to kick back, to slack off, to play hooky, to procrastinate, to dawdle, and to fritter away a lazy hour in the company of the ones we love. Now we get to give it all back. He had his turn, and he spun the wheel and he made his move. And now it is our turn. Thank you all for coming. We will miss him so much."

I sit back down to thunderous applause, but I hardly hear it. Giving a good speech makes everyone grateful because we all feel so terrible and embarrassed when somebody gives a bad one. Olivia and Jane lean against me, snuggling, and even Ben gives me an appreciative nod. We settle in for the long Catholic mass that follows.

When it's finally time to go to the cemetery, Bernard refuses to ride with us. He doesn't trust Phoebe to drive his champagne-colored convertible—a hideous antique testament to dwindling testosterone, and about as energy-efficient as a coal-burning steamboat—so he says he will follow us.

"The point of not driving yourself is that you might be too broken up with grief to drive safely," says Henley. Bernard gives him a withering look.

"I'm sad," says Bernard. "Same as you."

"Of course, you have your sweet family to take care of," adds Henley. "You have to be strong for them and not show any emotion. We get it."

Henley, Gabriella, Alistair, and I pile into a limousine that takes us to Calvary Cemetery, to the family plot where Mom already lies buried. Olivia and Jane ride with Ben. All three of my siblings look nervously at me as soon as I sit down and get situated, as if expecting me to rip off my own face and then spray them with acid saliva from a set of razor jaws extending from my neck hole. They know my moods better than me, sometimes.

"Good speech, sis," says Henley after I grow bored and start looking out the window. He begins rooting around inside the door of the limo, in search of snacks.

"Hey look," he says. "Free animal crackers."

He opens the box and bites the head off each animal, then puts the half-eaten cookies back in the box.

"Why are you being gross?" Gabriella asks.

"I just want the heads," Henley says. "You know, at Chinese funerals, everybody gives the family money. And then the family is supposed to burn joss paper to give the dead person ghost money that they can spend in the afterlife."

"I could burn some incense," says Gabriella.

"Please don't," I say.

"So what's going to happen now?" Henley asks.

"Well, we are going to put him in a box in the fucking ground," I say.

"No," he says. "I mean with Nylo."

Alistair and I look at each other.

"Dad has talked to us already about what will happen at Nylo when he dies," says Alistair. "As far as the company is concerned, Caitlyn will just keep running it and nothing will change."

"Nothing will change," I agree. Although my statement comes out sounding more despondent than firm.

We arrive at the cemetery and the limo driver parks in the gravel lot. All around us, other mourners that I vaguely recognize but don't feel like acknowledging are slamming doors and finishing hushed cell phone conversations.

"Look at all those grackles," says Gabriella, pointing at the sky over the tombstones. "They're coming this way."

We watch the birds swoop and swarm for a moment. I see a glint in Henley's eye.

Bernard has parked his convertible so that it takes up a whole row of spaces. I suppose this is an effort to keep it from getting scratched. It looks like some kind of Roman chariot. I'm certain that Bernard's will decrees he is to be buried with his car, and I think for a moment how satisfying it will be to lower him into the ground with his moldering priapic corpse sprawled against the Italian leather.

Henley walks over to the convertible as if mesmerized, staring at the oncoming birds. The path to the gravesite is in the other direction and we all wait for him.

"Henley!" I finally yell, as he stands there with his back to us, leaning over the car as if in a trance. He jogs back and we all begin walking to the big finale of the day's entertainment. Olivia and Jane and Ben catch up, and we form a nucleus of family. I notice Henley wiping cookie crumbs from his hands and slacks, and he gives me a malevolent grin that I don't quite understand.

During the ceremony, I keep looking at Henley, who keeps looking at Bernard. Every once in a while, his eyes dart up and he stares again at the swarming birds, which seem to be covering the sky like a Biblical plague.

As the oldest child, it falls on me to toss the first shovelful of dirt onto the mahogany coffin. I do so dutifully, just wanting to be done with this horrible day. I can easily imagine Dad making a lame joke from down there. "Hey, knock it off! I'm trying to sleep!"

We all throw some dirt on him and then file back to our cars. Olivia and Jane seem relieved that it is all over. They lean against me as we walk. Ben hangs back, giving us space. As we near the cars, Henley grabs my arm, cackling with glee.

"Oh, goddammit," we hear Bernard shout. He begins running. We see birds leap out of his car and disappear into the sky, covering the smooth leather and glossy paint with ropy streams of gritty feces. They must have been feasting on Henley's scattered crumbs.

Henley jumps up and down. He is so proud of himself. Honestly, I am astonished. I bark out one small laugh and then catch myself, not wanting to sanction Henley's sociopathic behavior.

8

That night I sleep at the office, which means I am awake at 5 a.m. Wednesday morning. I wait around in the conference room kitchen, wearing a bright pink dress, hovering over a carafe of civet coffee with my head low until an assistant arrives with a plate of muffins and bagels at 6. Her eyes widen when she sees me sitting there already, but she recovers quickly and gently sets down the platter. I chow down on a carrot muffin that's more like a piece of cake while finishing the pot of coffee.

I take the elevator up to Dad's floor. In his empty office, I feel his absence acutely. I lie down on his couch and let myself cry a little. His smell lingers, haunting the place: the smoky sandalwood of his aftershave and the sweet lime coconut of his hair oil, the secret cigarettes that have soaked into the wallpaper and wood paneling. Sneaky smoking is a habit we share, but neither of us ever managed to acknowledge it in the other.

Then it hits me: I never got to smoke a cigarette with Dad and now I never will.

Why didn't I ever just stick a Dunhill in the corner of my mouth and ask him for a light? Why did we have to be so close to each other but so far apart? What good is that kind of dignity of distance now?

I wipe my eyes and stand up. I guess this is all mine now. I go through his drawers, looking for any messages or sealed envelopes with my name on them. I'm not sure what I expect to find. I lie back down on his sofa, curling into fetal misery. No mom, no dad. I am an orphan.

When Devi arrives, bleary-eyed and puffy, we give each other space. I ask her to bring up more breakfast food: plates of bacon and poached eggs, pitchers of orange juice, cookies-and-cream donut holes from the bakery on the corner. She is glad for the distraction, glad for my exacting demands. I am happy to have someone to order around so early in the morning who seems to like it. We make common cause.

At 8 a.m., Angelo Marino comes in. He seems startled to see me. He should know better. He knows my habits. He immediately becomes even more clandestine and circumspect than usual. His long jaw clamps shut, and his wiry limbs become springy and coiled like a rangy leopard.

Angelo Marino has always been here—a handsome cadaverous presence who knows all of our secrets and seems indifferent to them—and I've always enjoyed the way his name rolls around in my mouth, the words frothing out like waves on the Sicilian shore: Angelo Marino. He and my father went to college together. My father was the engineer and Angelo Marino was the lawyer. Surprisingly, Angelo Marino never wanted any points in Nylo, but he has been at my father's elbow ever since they first opened up shop.

He is seventy years old, but so olive-skinned and oleaginous that he has aged with the same tenderness as an expensive wallet. He still has a full head of iron-gray hair, and he has stern, vulpine features that I'm sure have been dropping Ivy League panties all over the Upper West Side for decades. He has never married, but I know from the unrestrained lust with which he looks at every comely assistant or intern (yet he never acts on these impulses—he is a passionate man, but a disciplined one) that he is not gay, as Henley has always insisted. "Prostitutes—very mean ones" is my rejoinder to Henley.

After saying hello to each other, we sit in silence for an uncomfortably long time.

It is Angelo Marino who finally speaks.

"It wasn't painful, just so you know."

"Oh?"

"I looked at the coroner's report," says Angelo Marino. "It happened very quickly, in the shower. Just turned his head to the side and that was that. The fall didn't kill him, like we originally thought. I've actually never heard of anyone dying so peacefully. Usually, people stagger around, clutching their hearts and shrieking. Or else they fight to the end, eyeballs twitching as they relieve themselves on hospital beds in front of their children. He had a perfect death. A giant stroke. The H-bomb of strokes. I think he would have liked for you to know that. That his death was a good one."

"I guess that does make me feel a little better," I lie.

We sit across from each other in my father's office for another hour. I answer emails about the Playqueen acquisition while Angelo Marino shuffles papers, getting documents in order.

Finally, at 9 a.m., Bernard arrives. He seems bored and slightly irritated.

"I'm the first one here?" he says.

"Uh, second one," I reply with a mild snort of exasperation.

"I don't know why we all have to be here," says Bernard, oblivious. "Seems strange, right?"

"Don't worry," I say. "Nothing is going to change. You're going to be just fine for the rest of your damn life."

"There is ten billion in tangible assets," says Angelo Marino. "That does not include the investments, property, or company, of course. We are talking about ludicrous sums of money, and almost none of it is going to be taxed in a confiscatory fashion, on account of the various trusts and holding companies that we established together before his passing."

"His passing," snorts Bernard. "Where did he pass to? Where is he now?"

Gabriella and Henley arrive together. They are both a little drunk and I can tell that they have been up all night. Gabriella is bowlegged in her short cocktail dress and Henley is wearing a purple velvet suit with a giant purple ribbon around his neck that is tied like shoelaces.

"We are here for the formalities!" says Henley. "We are here for the ceremony of apportionment!"

"Can we please just get this over with?" asks Gabriella.

"I have an announcement to make," says Henley, drunkenly. "I have decided to produce films. From now on, you must think of me as a film producer. I intend to be public-spirited about the whole thing. We will be adapting modern American classics for the screen, just like Merchant Ivory Productions in the UK. This will be an attempt to fight back against the intrusions into culture of godless China, which seeks to threaten democracy itself with its new cultural imperialism."

"Is Bernard really going to get an equal share?" Gabriella asks Angelo Marino. "You know he will just gamble it away. Or spend it on mistresses. Or give it to his dumb church. What?" She gives Bernard a withering look. "We're all thinking it."

Bernard scoffs.

"I'll call Alistair up from the basement," says Angelo Marino, "to let him know everyone else is here."

While we wait for Alistair, Henley tells us more about his plans for a new movie studio. He will first hire a team of readers to visit every respectable and ancient small publisher in the city and inquire about their forgotten classics, their most obscure masterpieces.

"The more unfilmable the better!" he says. "I want to produce works that mystify and bemuse foreigners. I want to show the real America, the one that exists outside of marketing departments and sales meetings."

"What the fuck do you know about the real America?" Bernard

says. "What the fuck do ancient small publishers know about the real America?"

Thankfully, Alistair arrives at that moment and the conversation halts. He sits down next to me on our dad's sofa and pats my leg.

"So, you are all here now," says Angelo Marino. "That means we can officially begin the reading of the will."

He sends a text and a team of assistants pours in from where they have been waiting in the next room. They set up a projector and bring in five giant steel briefcases, which they stack by the door. One of the assistants shows Angelo Marino how to work the projector. Angelo Marino slots a flash drive into the USB port, queuing up a video that he has preloaded.

"Your father recorded a video message to be played in the event of his death," says Angelo Marino. "He was very worried about all of you, if you must know the truth. He was more worried about you individually, as people, than he was about his legacy or about the fortunes of his company. Anyway, I'll let him tell you in his own words."

Angelo Marino sends the assistants out and locks the door to our father's office. He presses a button on the wall and the giant windows dim. The room is dark except for the glow from our phones and the blue holding pattern that the projector throws on the wall.

All of a sudden, our father's face fills the screen. Gabriella gasps.

"Yes, yes, I am dead," he says, chuckling. "I know this must be a little awkward for all of you, but the simple fact is that now you are all going to have to fend for yourselves without me to settle your disputes or keep you from being damned fools. Henley, I am mostly talking to you here."

Henley shifts in his seat, crossing and then uncrossing his legs.

"But I'm not *only* talking to Henley, although it is now all of your jobs to keep him out of trouble. All that you have now is each other. As I'm sure you all know by now, you can't really trust anyone else in this awful old world. You can't even trust Angelo. I'm dead now, so I can say it: he's more snake than man."

Dad chuckles and Angelo Marino looks at the ceiling, cracking his neck.

"Gabriella, you are the baby. But that doesn't mean you have to act like it. I know you have a good head for business, but you are easily distracted. I want you to learn to focus, and to reap the fruits of your diligence and goal-directed efforts. I want you to feel the thrill of personal achievement. I know that the Nylo Corporation doesn't hold much interest for you. I know that you do not like the competitive challenge of games. However, that doesn't mean that the Nylo Corporation couldn't benefit from your insights and natural wisdom.

"Bernard! Are you there? I have always admired you, my cold and analytical child, for your fine mind and your skeptical nature. You have to keep your siblings down to earth. You must keep them from getting a big head or losing sight of the bottom line. I know that you have your own strange urges and inclinations, and I know that you have always had a very… shall we say… romantic spirit. I know you are lonely. I know you don't always understand other people. But you are part of this family, and you need to know that no one in the world will ever understand you better than your own brothers and sisters, not to mention your own wife and your own children.

"Alistair, my boy. I don't have much to say to you now that I haven't already told you a million times in person. It has been such a gift and a joy and a luxury that I have been able spend so much time with you and to see you grow so much as a creator. Some of the best work I have ever done has been at your side and I have always been so inspired by you. I have marveled at your restless, relentless, inventive mind. I'm sure you will continue to make great things for us. We are very alike, you and I. For that reason, I don't really know what advice to give you. Certainly, I was often my own worst enemy. Don't be yours.

"Henley, did you really outlive me? I find that hard to believe. Sober up and do the right thing. And if you can't do that, at least make sure to share the fun. It's no good to keep all the pleasures of the world to yourself. I do believe that eventually you will discover that the best feeling in the world is doing things for other people and I do believe that eventually it is the feeling of service that will overtake you as your final addiction. In the interim, please do everything that your older and wiser siblings tell you to do. They know better than you. You are a delightful and charming idiot.

"Which brings me to Caitlyn, my oldest. I guess you expect that you are going to inherit everything that matters, don't you, Caitlyn? I guess you expect that the Nylo Corporation is now going to fall frictionlessly into your capable hands? Well, I am here to tell you that this is indeed very far from the case. I am here to tell you that if you expect to take over the company, you are going to have to earn it. And I am here to tell you that your sister and your brothers have just as much of a chance to take over control of the Nylo Corporation as you do. Yes, gather round, children. Because you are about to go on an adventure. I have a game for you to play. One last game. And the winner gets everything."

9

With Dad's shocking words echoing in our heads, we all sit stunned. Sensing the mood, Angelo Marino walks over to the projector and pauses the feed. Our father's affable face still fills the screen, but his eyes are slitted, mid-blink.

"What the hell is going on?" I say. "A game? Like in a bad sitcom?"

Henley walks over to our father's sideboard and takes down two glasses. He fills them each with the Japanese bourbon that our father liked so much. He takes a big sip and then brings me the other glass. Bernard, scowling at him, retrieves the bottle for himself.

"This is some kind of joke, right?" I say.

"I'm afraid not," says Angelo Marino. "He went to elaborate lengths to set everything up before he died. I've been working nonstop since the body went cold to get everything in place. This is really what he wanted."

"Then he was obviously crazy," says Bernard. "And we don't have to accept the will of someone obviously mentally incompetent."

"What do you care?" says Gabriella. "It's not like you were getting anything anyway. Maybe this way you have a shot."

"He wasn't crazy," Alistair says. "I saw him every day, practically. He wasn't any crazier at the end than he ever was. I mean, maybe he was always crazy. But if that were the case, then the reason we are all rich is because he was crazy, which I guess also means that he can dispose of his riches any crazy way that he sees fit, logically speaking."

"Well, this is beyond crazy," says Bernard. "This is malicious. We are all supposed to just play some game against each other for the family wealth? I think if we all just decide that we won't do it, no court in the United States will force us to. We might have to pay higher taxes on account of ignoring his will and its network of holding companies and trusts, but I think it will be worth it."

"He had himself checked out by four separate psychologists before making this will," says Angelo Marino. "They all signed affidavits certifying his sanity. Those will be hard to challenge in court. Additionally, there is a corollary to the will that says that anyone who refuses to play the game will get nothing." He pauses, letting that statement sink in. "You don't even know what the game is yet. Do you all truly refuse to play? If that's the case, the money will be put into a trust and eventually used for charitable endowments in African universities."

"Gasp," says Henley.

"Well, we can't just give all the money away," says Bernard. "That's stupid and naive. Most of those countries are run by dictators."

"What if it is something that favors one of us?" asks Gabriella. "Like poker or something. Bernard does nothing but play poker. Or it could be one of those stupid strategy games that Caitlyn loves."

"Or what if the game is soap-making," says Henley. "Then you would win!"

"Shut up, Henley," says Gabriella.

"Look, we should just watch the rest of his will," I say. "We don't know enough to make a decision yet."

"I think I know what the game is," says Alistair. "Dad was making me work on something for him privately. That augmented reality stuff I showed you. I think it must be related to that."

"There you go," says Bernard. "So Alistair has a clear advantage."

"No, it's not like that," says Alistair. "I just know some of the tech. But not any of the details."

"Just press play, okay?" I say to Angelo Marino, exasperated.

"Of course," he replies.

"The game will be very simple," our father booms from the screen. "Remember how you used to love the scavenger hunt every year? Well, you will be hunting for these black boxes."

He holds up a box about the size of an old answering machine. There is a blinking red light in one corner, but otherwise it is completely sealed without wires or ports. The ominous nature of this box that does not seem to have a function gives me goosebumps.

"You will each get three lives, as in any rudimentary video game. You will need to find a box every day, or you will lose a life. If you all manage to find the box, the last person to do so will lose a life. The winner will be the person who stays alive, plain and simple. They will get my entire fortune. The way I see it, the rest of you have been helped enough in life. I have always been there for you and you have never wanted for anything. I'm sure that you will thrive, no matter what direction you choose to take, whether that is professional gambling, professional dissipation, or professional scents and sundries. Angelo will explain any questions you might have, and as always, the real fun is in the details." A wistful grin spreads across his face.

"As you all know, the first game I ever made was *Sea Farmers*, the family-friendly resource-management game of undersea farming for ages ten to infinity. What made it work was the novelty of a game where people did not compete against each other directly, through combat or by scoring points, but where people competed by being able to cultivate their coral reef the most shrewdly in order to feed all the other fish in the kingdom. Was *Sea Farmers* a great game? Probably not. Nylo made many better games, in my opinion. But families could play without hating each other. It was fun even if you lost. I hope this game will be similar. I hope it will bring out the best in you and not the worst."

He looks down briefly, then brings his eyes back up to meet ours and continues in a rueful tone.

"I know that I have not always been there for you. So many children without a mother! I know that I have possibly been better at designing fun things than I have actually been at experiencing them with you. But those scavenger hunts I used to create were one of the highlights of my life. I always cherished those special days with my family, hunting around the neighborhood for clues. The tragedy that killed your mother ended all that. We never did a scavenger hunt again. But since you are now dealing with yet another tragedy, what does it matter now how gruesome my final request may be? Have fun, my children. Play honorably. But do try to win."

Dad smiles one last time, then reaches up and switches off the camera. The screen goes black and then blue.

"Well, that's basically it," says Angelo Marino. "The game begins today. Every day, you have to find one of these boxes. The last person to find the box each day will lose a life. The last person left alive wins the fortune."

"What if none of us find any of these boxes?" asks Alistair. "What if we all lose at the same time?"

"There isn't any stipulation for such an occurrence," says Angelo Marino. "I suspect that your father does not feel that it is possible that every single one of his children is a loser."

It is ironic that our dad invoked *Sea Farmers*, a game that has possibly ruined more relationships than politics or meth. He was always a fan of those passive games where you build your little world "at" another player, competing against them indirectly but no less brutally. It is a good metaphor for business itself, but I can't remember a time that we ever played *Sea Farmers* as a family that didn't end in tears, where Gabriella or Bernard didn't get pissed that the game itself "cheated." Alistair or I usually won, as our corals thrived and fed the multitudes. Only Henley ever seemed to truly not care about winning or losing.

Angelo Marino reaches for the stack of briefcases by the door and hands them out one by one, checking the name engraved in the top before giving it to its new owner. We open our cases and see that inside each is a phone with our name on the back, and also a T-shirt with our father's face on it that says "Nylo Family Scavenger Hunt 2020."

"We're supposed to wear these?" I say in disbelief.

"At least they're each in our size," says Gabriella, holding hers up against her torso.

"I'm not wearing a damn T-shirt, like this is some kind of charity fun-run," says Bernard.

"I'm definitely wearing mine," says Henley, stripping off his velvet jacket and pulling on the red shirt over his purple ribbon bowtie.

"Your father hired a game master to administer the game," says Angelo Marino. "He will get in touch with you at noon every day to give you that day's clue, and then you will be off to go find the box. All the game rules apply as long as you are hunting for the box, but once you find it, the rules are off for you until the next day. When you find the box, all you have to do is hold your game phone up to the box and it should click something inside that will register that you have found it."

"This was some of the technology that he was having me develop," Alistair notes.

"That's not all," continues Angelo Marino. "You get three lives, but you can trade in your lives for extra powers if you so desire. One option is to spend a life to buy transportation."

"What do you mean by transportation?" asks Bernard.

"The usual kind: trains, planes, automobiles, etcetera. Otherwise, in the course of the game, you must walk or hitchhike everywhere. And if you hitchhike, you can't pay for it. Nor might there be any future expectation of remuneration implied to anyone you convince to transport you."

"How will you know whether we bribe anybody or not?" asks Bernard haughtily.

"Your phone will be recording everything you do or say," says

Angelo Marino. "It will also record everywhere you go. It is all in the rule book. You should each have one in your briefcase."

I see that Alistair is already reading the rule book, a thin pamphlet printed on gold-embossed paper.

"I am definitely not walking anywhere," says Henley. "I wish to spend a life on transportation, yes indeed I do. Who do I see to perform this dark magic? Is there some necrophagous clerk? Some devilish ombudsman or diabolical concierge?"

"Everyone just turn on your game phones," Angelo Marino replies. "The first screen should guide you through the process of getting started."

I drain my glass of bourbon and pour myself another one. I turn my phone on and am immediately greeted with a bright and cheery welcome screen. There is a short video of all of us together as children and then an eagle swoops down and rips the picture in half and eats it.

"Scavenger Hunt," reads the title card. There is a flashing button that says "Play." I press it and look around at my siblings as they do the same.

Now we move to a character-creation screen. My character is just me, wearing a glowing purple pantsuit. I am slightly offended by this corporate representation of who I am, but I guess we are all probably cartoons of ourselves in this game. At the top, the game shows that I have three lives left. There is a slot for my transportation and also a slot for something that says it is my "superpower."

"What are the superpowers?" Bernard asks.

"Don't worry about that yet," says Angelo Marino. "Once you all click yes or no, the transportation will be randomly assigned and we can move on to the superpowers."

I don't want to walk everywhere. Not in this city, not in this sticky June weather. I click "yes" to transportation and then move to a loading screen, which shows me that four out of five of us have all made a decision.

"Who hasn't decided yet?" says Henley. "Hurry up!"

Gabriella sighs dramatically. The loading screen suddenly says that all five people have made a decision, and then the app moves back to the character-selection screen. My character now says that I have the transportation "train pass."

"Look," I say, suddenly overwhelmed at how stupid all of this is. "Let's agree to do this scavenger hunt but let's also agree that whoever wins will just divide up the fortune equitably. We can have a good time playing, but let's all agree that the victory won't mean anything. I'm sure we can create a quick contract right here that will be legally binding. Angelo Marino? Will you draft something up like that?"

"There is no provision in the will that precludes me from drafting such a document," says Angelo Marino. "Is that what you all want me to do?"

Nobody says anything.

"Do it," I demand. My siblings nod in silent assent.

"I got a Lamborghini as my transportation," says Henley with a wide grin. "Does that come with a driver?"

"I got a helicopter," gloats Bernard.

"You better hope it comes with a pilot," Henley says, then bursts into gleeful laughter.

10

"Wait, you mean these boxes could be hidden anywhere in the entire USA?" says Gabriella, her face falling. "Why didn't you say that before?"

We are all slightly embarrassed for her. She is the only one of us who didn't opt for transportation. She'll have to walk or hitchhike.

"Listen, you and I are basically in the same boat," says Alistair. "I got a motorcycle. I don't know how to ride a motorcycle. In fact, you're in better shape than me. You still have a life, whereas I wasted one of mine on this motorcycle I can't ride. Do any of you know how to ride a motorcycle? Can we trade?"

Bernard snorts.

"Certainly not," I say.

"So there you go," says Alistair.

We all stare at Angelo Marino as he finishes writing out the contract, hunched over our father's desk. He calls in an assistant and asks him to type up the contract and print out eighteen copies, three for everyone.

"Tell us about the superpowers now," I say, once the assistant is gone.

"I don't know much about them," acknowledges Angelo Marino. "All I know is that you must spend another life to get them."

"No way," says Bernard. "Then I'll only have one life left."

"I might as well," says Gabriella. "Since all the rest of you are down to two lives already."

"Me too," says Alistair. "The motorcycle certainly isn't helping me."

"I love throwing lives away," says Henley. "Sign me up."

The assistant returns quickly with the stack of contracts. He hands one to each of us and then leaves, shutting the door behind him. We take seats around the conference table and read over the contract, which simply says that whoever wins agrees to share the fortune five ways.

"Five equal ways?" says Alistair dubiously.

"It's only fair," says Henley, grinning.

"Works for me," says Gabriella.

"Look, if I win, I will make sure everybody is taken care of," says Alistair. "But I won't split things equally. I will split things in a way that makes sure that we stay in business. We'll all be compensated according to how valuable we are to the company."

At this point, all of my siblings turn to look at me. I take a long sip of bourbon and stare at my hands.

"I'm not signing this as is," says Alistair. "But that doesn't mean I won't split the fortune. I just want to do it on my terms."

"I agree," says Bernard, his eyes flashing. "I'm not signing either. For the same reason."

"Oh, bullshit," says Henley. "I trust Alistair to do the right thing, but not you. If you win, you'll just keep all the money. Or else you'll take it all to Macau and burn it all at the craps table."

"Craps isn't my game," says Bernard. "I play poker, as you well know. And I don't lose money."

"Yeah, right," says Henley.

"If I win, I will split it between the three of us who are worth a damn," retorts Bernard. "You can get a small stipend, Henley. But the real money will go to me, Alistair, and Caitlyn."

"Oh, fuck off," says Henley.

"Listen," I chime in. "The point of money in the first place is control. That is what we are really arguing about here. Control. I don't care who gets the fortune, as long as you all agree to leave me in charge of Nylo. Do any of you seriously think you would do a better job running the company than me?"

Only Bernard seems to twitch at my question. Gabriella looks down at the table and Henley looks up at the ceiling.

"The contract benefits some of us more than it does others," I say. "Some of us are better at games than others here and that's what this is: a game."

"I'm not signing," says Bernard.

"Well, me neither," says Alistair. "But for different reasons."

Bernard and Alistair are my real competition, and so if they aren't signing, the contract is essentially meaningless. We all know this, even though none of us explicitly wants to say it out loud. Henley sighs loudly and makes a big show of taking the contract and signing it with a flourish. He passes it to Gabriella, who signs right under him. They begin working their way through all eighteen copies as Angelo Marino smiles sympathetically at me. The contracts pile up in front of me and I sit there with my pen in my hand, unsure. The contract was my idea. But now?

"Look," I say, capping the pen. "I am not signing, but I am as good as my word. If I win, Alistair and I will make sure that all of you are well compensated and that you will never have to come crawling to us for money ever again in your lives. But we will also make sure that the company is not damaged by bad publicity as a result of the insane parameters of Dad's will leaking out to the press. The shareholders would shit themselves if we suddenly revealed that we were giving Henley four billion dollars. No offense, Henley."

"None taken," he says.

"So I'm not signing either," I say. "But that doesn't mean this contest has to be some brutal family blood sport, like a game of *Sea Farmers*."

"I think Dad would want us to take care of each other," says Gabriella. "He never wanted us to stop being a family, especially because of money."

"Very true," says Henley.

Angelo Marino collects the unsigned contracts.

"Shall we move on to superpowers?" he asks.

We all look down at our character-creation screens. I know that this is a trick. Our father always used to tell us that we didn't need superpowers, that our superpower was the family itself. He hated comic books and adolescent power fantasies that relied on brute strength. I wonder if anybody else remembers how often he said this. I open my mouth to remind them all, but something bad in me makes me shut it again. I click "no" on the character screen and watch as the others make their decisions.

"I got 'invisibility,'" says Henley.

"I got 'the ability to open any lock,'" says Alistair.

"I got 'impervious to bullets,'" says Gabriella, looking worried. "There won't be bullets, will there?" She looks at me for reassurance and I shrug my shoulders.

Bernard leans back in his seat, smiling.

"No superpower for me, thanks," he says.

"I passed too," I pipe up.

"Dad always said we didn't need superpowers," says Bernard.

"Right," I say, giving him a cold look.

"What does invisibility even mean?" asks Gabriella.

"I guess we'll find out," says Alistair.

We all shift around in our seats, pouring ourselves more drinks and looking over the rule book. There isn't much that Angelo Marino hasn't explained already.

"We are ahead of schedule," says Angelo Marino. "But we can go ahead and get started if you like. I don't see any reason why you shouldn't have some extra time to complete today's hunt, since you are all here together already."

"Sure," says Bernard.

"I have a meeting this afternoon," I say. "So yeah, we might as well get started."

Angelo Marino sends out a text and all of our phones light up, vibrating and ringing at the same time. The song the phones play is the Nylo Corporation theme, a bright, trilling chime that we have used for decades in commercials to create a unified sonic brand, ideally meant to brainwash generations of children into associating Nylo with the sound of "fun" and "adventure."

I suppose that is what is about to happen to us now. Fun. And adventure.

This whole game feels a little silly. Thrown together. It doesn't have the polished obsessive professionalism of one of Dad's signature amusements. But he didn't plan on dying, after all. I'm sure he was going to refine this game over the years. The augmented reality technology is new and untested. We are breaking ground as gamers. It is not surprising that one of Dad's final acts would be to use us yet again as free play testers for one of his half-good ideas.

We all stare at our phones. After a few moments of fuzz, the screen clears, revealing a Chatroulette-style video feed. A person in a Guy Fawkes mask is leering at us in front of a green screen showing a cascade of falling cartoon gold coins.

"Fucking seriously?" I mutter.

"This is quite embarrassing," says Henley.

"Hello, gamers!" The voice has been digitally altered to make it deep and sludgy, with vaguely electronic undertones. The person behind the mask could be a man; it could be a woman. I discover very quickly that I don't really care who it is. I am already bored by this contest and want it to be over. I try to focus on the money, on winning, on power, on control.

"You are about to embark on an epic quest," says the Game Master. "You will learn about yourselves and you will learn about each other. Has there ever been a game of skill and chance with higher stakes in the history of human events? Probably not, unless you *consider war itself* a game! Ha ha!"

"I hate this so much already," says Gabriella.

"And now for your first clue, the location of your first box. Remember, the last person to find the box will lose a life and you only have until the end of the day. Are you ready? Here we go: 'Your empire awaits atop cage 1.' Good luck to you all! Bernard: on the roof of this building, you will find your helicopter gassed up and ready to go with a pilot hired from American Helicopters who knows nothing else and cannot help you. Henley: in the parking garage on level 1, there is a Lamborghini waiting for you. Alistair: on level 2, there is a motorbike. Caitlyn: your phone itself is now a transit pass good for any train or subway in the country. Gabriella: the day is very fine outside! I hope you enjoy walking."

"I can't even take the subway?" Gabriella asks, her brows raised in shock.

The Game Master in the Guy Fawkes mask disappears. Our phones all display the clue, hovering in pink over the image of cascading coins: "Your empire awaits atop cage 1."

I look around to see if anyone else has figured it out yet. I already know exactly what the answer is and where we are supposed to go. Bernard seems to be lost in thought. Henley is rubbing his temples. Gabriella looks frustrated. She is furiously scrolling on her other phone. What is she looking up? A map of the city, perhaps? Alistair is biting his lower lip, making the same expression as when he is coding.

There is nothing in the rules that says I can't just blurt out the answer and then we can all head out together. But I keep silent.

"Well?" says Angelo Marino. "Any questions?"

Nobody says anything.

"This is so stupid," sighs Bernard.

"I have to go to the bathroom," says Alistair. "Excuse me."

We all watch him get up, cross the room, and leave. Bernard stands up and then sits back down.

"He's not coming back," says Henley. "I hope you all know that."

Now Bernard bolts for the door. Gabriella and Henley look at each other. They both stand up at the same time.

"I have some work to do," I lie. "I'll be in my office if anybody needs me."

11

stuff the T-shirt and rule book in the briefcase and take the briefcase down to my office. I then take the elevator to the first floor and go out into the street. It is a nice afternoon in Dumbo and the breeze hits my face and dries the tears that have mysteriously started leaking out of my eyes. I wipe them away and almost hail a taxi before remembering the rules.

How long has it been since I've taken the subway in this town? Years, certainly. I know Olivia and Jane take the subway all the time. Their father is always trying to make them into peasants. But now I must venture underground myself, like a dirty pill bug.

I am briefly confused by how the game phone works as a subway card, but it turns out that all I have to do is move the phone close to the turnstile. It clicks and beeps, letting me know that I have successfully paid for a ride. The bars click around as I step through effortlessly. An old woman carrying a giant tote bag full of Polish-language magazines looks at me suspiciously, but she doesn't say anything.

I take the F train into Manhattan. The train is practically empty, on account of it being the middle of the day. I sit down and put on my best "fuck off" expression, but no one even tries to bother me. Actually, the train is much nicer than I remember. There are station clocks and everything, letting me know when the next train will arrive. I guess this is where all my taxes have been going.

I get out of the F train at Herald Square. The station here is also almost empty, but aboveground there are swarms of people, and I am reminded exactly why we moved Nylo headquarters down to Brooklyn. I'm extremely relieved I don't have to come here every day.

I walk over to the Empire State Building. Empire was even in the damn clue, as if "cage 1" hadn't given it away. "Your empire awaits... "

We must have all heard the story of our father's first date with our mother a million times.

Our mother wasn't from New York City, unlike our father. Misty Lynn MacAteer was a Southerner from Alabama, and when they met she was working at a disco called Scorpio's as a coat check girl. Our father was trying to meet someone in the feverish early seventies singles scene, and he was having a hard time in the clubs. But the coat check girl at Scorpio's had no choice but to talk to him and laugh at his awkward flirtations.

After several weekends of clumsy overtures, Dad finally asked Mom out, and for some reason she said yes. She must have been feeling lonely. Anyway, something about his persistence appealed to her. I have often found that people who don't know what they want are too depressed to fight off those who do.

Dad quickly figured out that Mom hadn't yet done any of the dumb tourist stuff, like visiting the Statue of Liberty or seeing the Empire State Building. She had been too busy trying to make money to pay rent. In a bombastic gesture of nerdy glee, he booked a reservation at the restaurant in the Empire State Building and invited her to join him there for their first date. He wasn't a famous game designer yet, but he wanted to show off that he wasn't just some penniless hustler. He had family money to spend and he wanted to spend it on her.

They met at a grim Irish bar around the corner (Doolan's? O'Hanahan's? Fluterty's? Rafafafaf's?—it doesn't matter, all these Midtown bars are exactly the same in a way that is actually a little eerie). They had a quick drink and made awkward conversation, and then they went to the Empire State Building on 34th Street.

This is where things became mythopoeic instead of just quotidian. This is where our family history starts, since none of us would exist without that evening at the Empire State Building. When she got drunk, Mom used to say that she was having second thoughts about even going on a date with our father right up until the moment that he kissed her.

What happened was that on their way up to the restaurant, the elevator came to a crashing halt and then actually jerked downward a few feet, sending both of them tumbling. It was everyone's worst nightmare: being in a falling elevator in an NYC skyscraper.

The elevator didn't drop far, but it was enough for our mom to scream and clutch our father. They were only trapped for fifteen minutes (they were rescued by the Empire State Building security team), but this was long enough for Dad to become a fearless protector in her eyes merely by staying calm. He took advantage of her dewy dependence. He kissed her.

She never forgave him for that. In a cute way, sometimes. But often in a very non-cute, real, vengeful way.

In exchange for signing release forms that said they wouldn't sue, they were treated to a free five-course meal and open bar. They were given an exclusive tour of the building, including the underground rooms where the closed-circuit security cameras showed the video feed from them falling: our mother clutching our father, our father grinning and remaining totally calm, the kiss that he stole.

Do the rest of them remember that the elevator was called "cage 1"? That our mother remembered the fact vividly and always included it as an addendum in her retelling of the story? The first cage in their life together but definitely not the last, she would say. And Dad would laugh but she wouldn't be joking.

This is a stretch of the city that I know well, mainly because the best board game store in town is right on this block, the Compleat

Strategist. I used to compete in Magic: The Gathering tournaments there as a teenager (I exclusively played a blue control deck, obviously). It wasn't quite fair: I was able to buy every single card I wanted. But I was honorable about my dominance. As I got older, I switched over to competing in Diplomacy and Cosmic Encounter tournaments, also playing a lot of the board game version of Dune with very old men who leered at me as they lost.

Now, back on the same block, I walk right up to the front desk of the Empire State Building, where ten bored security guards all compete against each other to ignore me.

"Hello," I say. "I am Caitlyn Nylo, CEO of the Nylo Corporation. Could I see the head of security here?"

I give one of the security guards my card. He squints at it. He is a portly man with a walrus mustache and stubble all the way down his neck to his shoulders.

"Yep, alright," he says, looking me over. Soon, we are joined by a man in a cheap suit and a headset microphone.

"Hi there," I say. "My name is Caitlyn Nylo and I need to know which elevator is cage 1. I am only asking for sentimental reasons. My mother and father came here on their first date. They are both dead now, and I just wanted to ride in the same elevator where they first fell in love."

"Cage 1?" asks the security guard. He stares at the guy at the help desk, giving him a "why did you call me over for this?" stare.

"It's the first one," he says. "The one closest to the ticket counter. But you gotta buy a ticket like everyone else." He points to the line of tourists weaving through a maze of velvet rope barriers and stanchions. Thankfully it's not too long.

"Okay, awesome," I say. They are definitely going to watch me now on the security cameras. I have to be smart if I don't want them to stop me and question me on my way out.

"I'm going to take a million selfies in there," I say flirtatiously. "Gotta get a picture from every angle for the Insta."

"Okay," he says, shaking his head and walking away.

I join the queue behind a family speaking French and am soon sandwiched between them and a large group wearing matching T-shirts and name tags on lanyards around their necks. We move quickly and when I reach the ticket counter, I again explain how I want to ride up in "cage 1" for sentimental reasons. The ticket seller raises her eyebrows but doesn't skip a beat.

"Sure, no problem. Just stay in line and tell Frank over there which elevator you want to be in, and he'll take care of you." She gestures toward a tall, thin man in a maroon jacket and slacks, one of many identically clad workers who guide the masses through the building.

I take my ticket and soon find myself at the front of the line.

"Frank?" I ask, putting on my sweetest smile. "The woman at the ticket counter said you could help a girl out. My parents had their first date here back in the seventies and got trapped in an elevator—cage 1—on their way to the restaurant. My dad just passed away over the weekend and I want to remember their love by riding in the same elevator they did all those years ago. Can you put me in cage 1 for the ride up?"

Frank's face opens into a wide grin. "Of course, ma'am. I love me a good love story. You wouldn't believe how many people come here with stories like yours and we always try to honor them. You just stand over here with me until cage 1 opens up." He gently grabs my arm and pulls me to the side, letting part of the big tour group fill the next elevator. It only takes two more rounds before the doors to cage 1 slide open and Frank holds out his arm with a flourish to guide me in.

I step inside, along with another tour group and a woman with a baby strapped to her back and a toddler clinging to her leg.

"All the way to the top!" jokes one of the tourists, a man in a Michigan Wolverines T-shirt. I laugh too loudly.

"My parents met in this elevator!" I tell the group. "Do you mind if I take some pictures?"

"Go right ahead," says the doughy, red-faced wife of the Michigander.

The mom is too busy pulling their tickets out of her toddler's mouth to respond.

I take out the game phone and start moving it all over the elevator. I hold it to each side, pretending to take a picture of myself. Nothing happens. I glance again at the clue on the screen: "Your empire awaits atop cage 1." Of course, the box must be on top of the elevator.

I hold the phone up as high as I can. Standing on my tiptoes, I scrape the ceiling. I hear a click and a whir and my phone starts playing the Nylo Corporation theme.

"*Sea Farmers!*" says the Michigander.

"Totally," I say. I put the game phone back in my purse. Eventually, the Nylo music stops playing. We ride the rest of the way up in silence. At the top, I immediately hop in the next open elevator going down.

I take out the game phone again and look at it. The clue has disappeared and has been replaced with a gold medal that says "First Place." My name is above the medal. It also shows me four other slots for medals, but they are currently empty.

Outside, I stand by the doors and light up a cigarette, checking my real phone now, seeing if there are any more messages about Playqueen. There aren't. Instead, there are about fifty messages of condolence from other CEOs, from "friends" at my Ladies in Business Women's Roundtable, even from some old boyfriends and acquaintances from college. I don't feel like answering any of them.

Actually, maybe it's the game, but I suddenly don't feel like our father is actually dead anymore. It doesn't seem real. He is still sending us messages and we are still fighting each other for his approval, each of us trying to be the best at some arbitrary set of rules and tasks.

I can't tell if this whole thing is going to be therapeutic or traumatic. Funeral plans and last requests are often about helping the living feel some sense of closure—of giving them something arbitrary to do while they are reeling from grief, while they are still talking to their dead loved one in their head. We make up for the fact that we can no longer love them or hate them in person by doing their bidding in an effort to banish them.

But this is an extremely complicated wake and possibly not a healthy one, since none of us can really rest until the game is over and we have either been defeated by or beaten our siblings.

I finish my cigarette, feeling pretty sanguine. I will win this thing easily and I will dole out Dad's fortune fairly and wisely.

There's no need to be bitter that he hasn't just given me control over the company's assets outright. I can prove that I deserve them. Maybe that will be better.

12

I can't resist stopping into the Compleat Strategist on my way back to the subway.

It is the middle of the day, so the store is empty. I look over the new releases at the front, then make a circle of the shop, lingering on the bookcase of war games, the fussy hex-based tank cavalry games where you are invited to win World War I for the Germans, World War II for the Soviets, or the Civil War for the Confederacy.

I do like the new trend in card-based games, where you draw cards and deploy them in order to gain influence in sectors across a massive world. There are versions of this kind of game set during the Cold War, providential American elections, Vietnam, even the War on Terror. The trick to these games is being able to absorb pain. Every decision you make will cause you harm, but you have to know how to make the least bad decision, how to take blows only when you are ready for them, how to manage your pain in a way that doesn't cripple your broader strategy. They are good metaphors for business itself. There is variance in the deal of the cards, but there is something very satisfying in playing a poor hand well.

On my way out, the woman at the register catches my eye, nodding to me. "Sorry to hear about your old man," she says, not getting up off her stool. "Read about it in the *Post*."

"Thank you. Yes, it has been devastating."

"*Sea Farmers, Sea Farmers: Pirate Cove,* and *Sea Farmers: The Krak-en* are still huge sellers for us. Not to mention all the other games you guys make. The diehards like that new one, where you play as ghosts trying to get out of hell? With the psychic jewels and how you can possess people? The combat wheel on that one is really innovative."

"You mean Soul Break," I say. "Yes, board games are my favorite division. Though we do so much else now. Augmented reality, even."

She nods at this as if she knows what I am talking about. I exit the store and head off to the train.

Back at Nylo, I peek into Dad's office. Everyone is gone, including Angelo Marino. All the evidence of our morning spent dealing with the will has vanished.

I go back down to my own office. I can barely open the door, the room is crammed so completely with flowers and gift baskets and stuffed animals. The head of Twitter's New York office has sent me a giant lasagna from Pio's, which is still warm in its aluminum casserole, along with a single black balloon. It is morbid as hell, but the lasagna actually looks pretty good.

"Would you mind getting rid of all this stuff?" I tell Peter, who runs in to greet me as soon as I set down my things. He knows better than to give me a hug, but he can't hide the sympathy in his eyes, which I of course ignore. "Or could you at least spread it around to everyone else on the executive team? Actually, I want to keep the lasagna, and also all the cookies. But yeah, put these flowers on people's desks. And you can just go ahead and burn all of these stuffed animals. Thank you notes all around, obviously."

"Already done," he says.

I carry the casserole into my bedroom and take off the plastic lid. The lasagna is still piping hot. It must have just been delivered. It's a ton of food, but I don't feel like sharing. I don't want to eat with everyone else around me not knowing what to say, sharing stories of how great my dad was, telling me how I will definitely be able to fill his shoes.

I get myself a Corona from the refrigerator and I pry open a garlic and onion bagel and toast it in my little kitchen, melting some butter on top.

I am lifting a forkful of steaming pork ragu layered in spinach, ricotta, and truffles to my mouth when my game phone buzzes. I look down and see that Gabriella has solved the clue and activated the box. Her name fills in the second slot above a silver medal. She had to walk across the bridge and all the way into Midtown in this heat. Of course, out of all of us, she would also be the one most willing to hitchhike and also the one most likely to be picked up by a passing stranger.

Surely the rest of them will be able to figure out this clue, or maybe Alistair has already died in a motorcycle accident? Maybe Bernard can't get clearance to land his helicopter anywhere near 34th Street?

I have a big Playqueen meeting at 3 p.m. and it's only 1, which gives me some time to kill. I don't like the fact that there is so much surrounding this game that I don't know. I search my private emails for "Pescare and Associates." I can't remember when I last gave Pez a call and put him to work on something. Was it to find out if Dane Wizard was abusing my sister? Or when I had him look up Bernard's new church and make sure it wasn't some kind of cult?

Pez's phone number is listed in his email signature beneath a quote attributed to Columbo: "I don't think the world is full of criminals and full of murderers, because it isn't. It's full of nice people just like you. And if it wasn't for my job I wouldn't be getting to meet you like this. And I'll tell you something else. Even with some of the murderers that I meet, I even like them too. Sometimes like them and even respect them. Not for what they did, certainly not for that. But for that part of them which is intelligent or funny or just nice. Because there's niceness in everyone. A little bit anyhow."

I shut the door to my office and ring up Pez.

"Pescare and Associates, please hold," says the man who answers.

"Wait—it's me! I know you don't have a receptionist. Don't—"

Too late. My call goes to music. But after only an instant, Pez comes back on the line.

"Caitlyn, is that you?"

"You put people on hold now?"

"It makes it seem like my time is important and I'm completely swamped with clients. Actually, I'm doing the crossword, and I was just about to take a nap. I'm sorry about your father, by the way. I sent you some candied pecans."

"The New York head of Twitter sent me a lasagna from Pio's. It's incredible. Come over and help me eat it. I have work for you."

"Right now?"

"How soon can you get here?"

"I'm on my way," he says.

Vic "Pez" Pescare is a weird little man, but he has always been extremely effective at finding things out for both me and my father. We've been retaining him for years, ever since we got into a corporate espionage war with the game company Rascal Tinies back in the nineties. They made handheld electronic games for preteens. They were mainly lame sports games where pixels very slowly moved around on puke-colored screens to mimic baseball, tennis, hockey, and so on. You can tell a game is bad when it is impossible to be good at it. If everybody has the same experience playing a game, it is likely that the game is shit.

I get another plate from the kitchen and make space on my desk.

Pez arrives in fifteen minutes. He is slightly winded as he sits down at my desk and I pour him a tall glass of water from the pitcher next to a leather-bound photo array of Olivia and Jane.

"It's so humid," he says, taking the glass gratefully. "The air is like a single fibrous mass, like a jungle canopy. I am chewing the air. But then also I have these allergies. Hold on—" He sneezes. "You see?"

He takes a long sip of water.

"Your father was a great man," he says finally. "I was at the funeral. You gave a very good speech. What a tragedy. I loved him like a brother."

Pez is about five feet tall, and he is thick all over, but there isn't an ounce of fat on him. He moves like a knuckleball, dipping and dodging, always looking at everything askance. His eyes are shiny and always a little wet and he often has a sensual leer on his face that people mistake for lust, though he's actually quite reserved, almost priest-like. He is about fifty years old, but he has a full head of black hair and no wedding ring. I have never asked him very much about his personal life.

His slightly dopy demeanor isn't any kind of act, but he makes you reevaluate your definition of what a smart person is like. I always get the impression that his ability to read people and to find things out about them is a result of having a perfectly clean conscience. It is a rare conversation in which he doesn't declare his absolute love for the human race in a way that seems out of step with the time and place, possibly out of step with every time and place.

"Pez, something very strange is going on and I need your help," I say. "I'll just get right to the point. It is Dad's last will and testament that all of his children play a game against each other for his fortune. We are in the middle of it right now."

"Strange, but oddly symmetrical and appropriate," says Pez. "Tell me more. I am awestruck by the beauty of the future of the Nylo Corporation being decided by Prescott Nylo's very last game."

"Yes, well, I find it slightly less appropriate," I say. I heap an oozing square of lasagna on the plate in front of him and scoop myself a second serving. I give him half of the buttered, toasted bagel and take a long swig of my beer. While we eat, I tell him everything I know. He takes it all in, listening with a smile on his face, pausing every now and then to let me know exactly how good the lasagna is.

When I am finished, he frowns for the first time and leans back in his seat.

"Aren't you cheating by calling me in here to help you?"

"There's nothing in the rule book that says I can't bring in outside help," I say. "And anyway, I don't need any help with the clues. I want to know about the game itself. I want to know who the Game Master is, where these phones come from, what the deal is with these stupid T-shirts. I want to know how much Angelo Marino knows. I want to know how involved Alistair was in the creation of this augmented reality system."

"You want an edge," he says, rubbing his knees.

"Name your price, obviously," I say. He frowns, looking down at his hands, sort of disappointed.

"I have some questions," says Pez after a long time, his face resuming its sad smile. I can see he doesn't want to talk costs and expenses. I pick up a basket full of lavender macarons and bite into one. It's heaven. *Whatever. I am going to run like ten miles tonight. It's fine. I'm grieving.*

"First of all," he says. "How long did you say it has been since Henley was in town?"

I think about it.

"Years. Two years."

"That's what I thought," says Pez. "I have known your family for a long time and I don't think I have ever seen all of you in the same room together. I am just a little bit amazed that your father managed to die with all of his children in town."

"Isn't this the time of year when old people die off? Isn't heat the great culling for people with heart conditions and undiagnosed clots and all that?"

"Old people die all year round," says Pez. "What did you say was the reason why Henley came back? He wants a job from you? Something to do with being in trouble in China?"

"Yeah, he didn't give any specifics," I say.

"I will find out the specifics," he says sadly.

"What are you saying? Are you saying that Henley had something to do with our father's death?"

"I am just asking questions," says Pez. "Now, you also said that

Alistair was the one responsible for developing the technology that makes the game work?"

"Yeah, although so far I'm fairly underwhelmed," I say. "Maybe there's more to it than I'm seeing."

"Does this give him an unfair advantage with respect to this game?"

"Maybe, but there's not much we can do about it. I'm sure Bernard will find a way to cheat to even things out. And Gabriella has one of those faces you just want to help, like a little lost teacup pig."

"And here you are, talking to me."

"We all have our angles," I say. "And liabilities. I do intend to win, however."

Pez stands up.

"What a thing to do when you should be mourning your father," he says. "I'll get back to you if I find anything out. No promises, though. Your father was very good at keeping secrets."

I press some macarons on him for the road. He is just about to leave when Peter runs into the room, his face white and his eyes wide.

"There's been an accident," he blurts. "Olivia's been hurt. Coming home from school. Ben's with her now."

"What are you talking about?" I say, taking my phone out. I have a bunch of missed messages. I frantically scroll down to find the earliest one. *MOM, ARE YOU THERE????* it says, from Jane.

"She's alive," says Peter. "She ran into a car door while riding her bike home from school. It flipped her over the handlebars and she landed on her shoulder."

"And?"

"She's not dead or in a coma or anything. But they're all at the hospital still waiting for results about her arm."

I am already up and headed for the door.

"I'll push the Playqueen meeting back to tomorrow," Peter says as I reach the door.

"Yes, do that," I call back as I walk out.

Behind me, I almost don't hear Pez mutter thoughtfully, "Another tragedy. So sudden. So unexpected."

13

By the time I get to the hospital, Olivia has already been seen by the doctor and she and Jane and their father are sitting around waiting to sign the discharge papers. None of them seem particularly freaked out, but my heart is jackhammering and I'm sweating like a bottle of champagne on a hot summer day.

"Oh, my baby," I say. "Are you okay?"

Olivia's forehead is all scratched up and she has a bandage over the bridge of her nose. Her arm is in a sling but not in a cast. She has cuts across her collarbone and big scrapes on both her palms that are covered in iodine.

"She's going to be fine," says Ben, coldly. "She wasn't wearing her helmet and she wasn't looking where she was going and she was going too fast, but she didn't break anything, thank god. It's just a sprain."

Olivia smiles at me painfully.

"Are they giving you the good drugs? Dilaudid? Oxy?"

"Tylenol," says Ben.

"I'm not even going to miss any school," complains Olivia.

"Nope," says Ben. "Though you won't be riding your bike again for a while."

"When does summer vacation start, anyway?" I ask Ben, perplexed.

"Not until the end of June," he says.

"Jeez," I say. "When I was a kid, we got out in May. So, is somebody going to tell me what happened?"

"It wasn't actually my fault," says Olivia.

"Oh yeah?" I say, sensing an opportunity to get on her good side and to sow division against Ben by being the cooler one here. This seems like a moment of trauma. A moment that will be remembered forever.

"Yeah, I was, like… obeying the law. It's true I wasn't wearing a helmet, but did you know that people who wear helmets actually get hit more often? They don't have good balance and they can't see as well. Also, drivers are way more likely to be careful around people not wearing helmets. They seem more human. If they can see your face, they, like… they don't want to hurt you and they will swerve around you."

"You have to wear your helmet," says Ben. "If I catch you riding your bike without your helmet again, I'm taking your bike away."

He looks at me meaningfully. United front.

"Totally," I say weakly. "But okay, what actually happened?"

"I was on one of those side streets that run perpendicular to the Eastern Parkway," she says. "I don't even remember which one. Anyway, it's the same route I always take coming home from school. Nothing has ever happened there before. Mom, it is, like, a really quiet street."

"That is exactly what makes it dangerous," says Ben.

"Okay, but like, it was so weird," says Olivia. "Honestly, I wasn't even going that fast! I was in the middle of the street, in the bike lane, when this person, like, opens their door just a crack, looks over their shoulder, and then opens the door all the way. I braked, right, and that's when I flew over my bars. I caught myself, but then the person shut their door and drove away. Like, why were they even opening their door if they weren't getting out? And I was hurt and stuff! But that wasn't even the weirdest part."

"What was the weirdest part?" I ask.

"The weirdest part is that they were wearing a mask, like a full-on Halloween mask. So I'm saying that I think they did it on purpose."

"That is just so hard to believe," says Ben.

But as soon as she says "mask," I feel the bottom drop out of my stomach. What the hell is going on?

"Was it a Guy Fawkes mask?" I ask.

"I don't know," says Olivia. "What's that?"

"You know, like Anonymous, from the internet."

I pull up a picture on my phone and show it to her. Ben cranes his head to look as well. I hate it when he gets close to me. I can smell his aftershave and his post-teaching sweat smell, which reminds me of sex. I hate him for it. I hate how much I like it.

"No, it wasn't a mask like that," says Olivia. I'm surprised at how relieved I am, even though what she is telling me is still objectively horrible. "It was hairier and with teeth, like a werewolf. It scared me, which was good, otherwise I might have run right into the door!"

"Maybe you interrupted a robbery in progress," says Jane. "Maybe he was the getaway driver and you spooked him, and so he drove off, leaving his partners behind."

"You're right," says Olivia, getting excited. "I'm probably a hero. But, like, you're being sexist to assume it was a man."

The doctor, who turns out to just be some tired girl in her twenties, shows up then with a stack of papers to be signed.

"Which one of you is the parent?" she asks. I snatch the papers out of her hands and search my purse for a pen. Ben doesn't say anything. I sign and then we all make our way out of the emergency room. The contrast between the chilliness of the ER air conditioning and the hot day outside makes me shiver a little, but it feels good.

"I'm calling us a car," says Ben. "Actually, can I ask you for a favor?"

"Yeah, you can ask," I say.

"Would you mind picking Olivia and Jane up from school tomorrow?" he says. "Olivia can't bike home now, and she probably shouldn't be walking home, and it's the end of the year, so for me that means the Quiz Bowl. We've got after-school practice tomorrow for the big tournament this weekend."

Ordinarily, I would relish the opportunity to steal them for an afternoon. But I can't swing it.

"Actually, I hate to say it, but tomorrow is terrible for me," I say. "Can't they just take Ubers home?"

"That's what I said," agrees Olivia.

"I just don't feel comfortable with them taking cars like that," says Ben. "They really aren't old enough."

"Fine, well, I can send a car from Nylo around for them," I offer.

"You really can't just swing by?" says Ben.

"I really can't," I say. "Not tomorrow. I'm busy as well, and what I'm doing is way more important than your Quiz Bowl."

"Oh yeah, sure, okay, I'm sure it is."

"I just mean in the greater scheme of things," I say. "Obviously this Quiz Bowl is very important to you."

"And to all the children I teach," he says. He looks stubborn and pained. Whatever amorous stirrings were being provoked by his scent and by his attention to our daughters simmers away, cooked off by his weird inferiority complex energy. The sex was always good between us, but I guess he was the first one to realize that it was only good because we hated each other. Maybe I just didn't mind the hate as much. Our hate did eventually lead to the creation of human life.

The worst part is that I can tell that Olivia and Jane are both a little disappointed that I won't be picking them up. I can't fathom why. All they do lately is "merely tolerate" me. I feel like I'm blowing a chance to make a connection, to scoop up a trick that Ben is leaving on the table. But I can't make any promises, not with this game going on.

"So what, then? Two weekends from now?" says Ben.

"Yeah, that should work," I say.

The Uber rolls up and Ben opens the door for the girls. We help Olivia duck inside, but she honestly doesn't seem that hurt by what has happened. She's way tougher than I would be. I am such a baby when it comes to pain and sickness and injury and all that. Jane gets in next to her and Ben slips into the front seat.

I find myself leaning forward as if by habit to give him a kiss on the cheek, to wish them all safe travels, but I'm not allowed to do that anymore. I am still allowed to be overwhelmed by silent rage and resentment, though, so I do this instead as they drive away and leave me alone on the sidewalk.

14

I drink more White Coke and bourbon alone up in my study at my Townhouse while thinking about the events of the day, just like General Zhukov would have done.

Zhukov is an underrated general, but he isn't my favorite. My favorite is Grant. He was legitimately strategically interesting and always dependable, not particularly prone to dramatic flights of romantic fancy. He wasn't as skittish or paranoid as many men of his era, or many men after. I admire his strategic acumen and also his ability to keep cool while his own country was "torn asunder."

It's hard to kill a foreign enemy. It's almost impossible to kill rebels in your own country, inspiring your troops to be merciless against their former friends and family.

Grant was a short, sad, stoic drunk whose best quality was his loyalty to his men and officers. He wasn't put in charge because of connections or because he looked good in uniform. He achieved command of the Union forces as a result of being one of the only generals who was not afraid to take risks, to execute bold plans, to follow up and chase retreating rebels in order to capture men and materiel. He successfully split the Confederacy in half, and then in half again, doing the hard work in a long war. He was elevated to his command as a result of what he proved that he stood for, not what he said. He was unconflicted and uncompromising.

I log on to the proprietary Nylo online board game platform, Kingmaker. I open one of my many anonymous accounts and start up a new game of Paperclip, which is a strategy game where you compete with the Soviets in order to abduct-slash-rescue Nazi scientists in a collapsing WWII-era Germany.

It's a fun game. There are two separate games, actually: a card-based dynamic where you work as the OSS versus the KGB trying to bribe and kidnap scientists inside Berlin, and then a war-game dynamic where you try to beat the Nazis faster than the Soviets in order to get a better position for the postwar. Also, some scientists are worth more points than others. Mengele doesn't help you much, but Wernher von Braun basically wins the game for whoever manages to capture him.

I drink my White Coke and bourbon and play Paperclip for hours, trying not to think about Ben or my kids or my father or any of my rotten siblings. I play a game against someone from Minnesota with the handle VikingLightning. I randomly draw the Soviets.

VikingLightning is pretty good, but he focuses a little too much on the card game part. He keeps trying to make big plays, ignoring the late game positioning and troop-movement dynamic. It becomes clear that I am going to get to Berlin first. VikingLightning starts to make bigger mistakes, playing prissily out of frustration rather than trying to win, even when he snakes some big plays away from me.

I can't help but start getting maudlin as the evening wears on. I think about how Ben and I first met and what we were like back then. First of all, I didn't give a shit about things like history or generals. That was all his fault. Back then, he didn't like rich people. Hated them, in fact. It was a wonder and a majesty that we even survived our first date.

I asked him out after he came in last at a Magic: The Gathering tournament, which he seemed to have entered as a joke. Everyone knew me there already, and while I wasn't one of the top contenders, I was certainly holding my own. I enjoyed the competition, even though, like I said, Magic is mostly a game where you can buy your way to victory.

We were in some smelly food court in Koreatown where everything was too bright and where the whole place smelled like sesame oil and cheap meat. It was mostly empty, but people were still tending the food court booths, texting on their phones and serving the occasional customer coming in to get a plate of hot cheap buns between lunch and dinner on a Sunday.

The entire back section of the food court seating area was filled with Magic players, taking advantage of the long cafeteria-style tables to run the tournament. Ben was there with a group of his teacher friends.

He was obviously the most attractive guy in the place, and I was obviously the most attractive woman. It felt like we were the last two people on Earth, surrounded by shambling hordes of the bungled and botched. Everybody in the tournament was making fun of him, but he didn't seem to care. He didn't even quite know the rules, but he did seem to be learning a little more each time he played a game.

We were never paired up against each other. In fact, he didn't make it past the first bracket, which meant that he became part of the audience, leaning over the shoulders of his friends as they played. There is no more hated interloper than a cool person in a den of nerds, and so he was basically shunned. I felt for him. At the time, I was trying to reverse-engineer what worked about collectible card games in order to begin the process of developing our own knockoff version for mobile devices at Nylo. Even so, I had managed to actually place in a few tournaments and I was in the process of getting enough points to qualify for nationals.

These nerds knew I wasn't one of them, but I respected what they loved, so they didn't give me any shit. They were merciless to Ben, however, especially when I started openly flirting with him.

I was enjoying the dynamic. It was erotic, especially since Ben had no interest in the game at all. These nerds hated the way he revealed that the dominance ritual of the game was purely second-order symbolism. Being fuckable in a sea of the unfuckable can be quite an aphrodisiac.

"Come on then, I know you're bored," I said to him, grabbing his hand and leading him away while his friends "ooooooooohed." I took him into the food court men's room.

People from the tournament awkwardly peed and then left without saying a word while we made out in the bathroom. I got him hard but didn't finish him off. I just wanted him as conquest, as tribute.

The erotic pitch of the afternoon brought us to the boiling point. We both knew where we stood. I made him ditch his friends and take me out for gogi-gui and he told me all about teaching the poor unfortunates, referring to them by name as if they were his own children. At the time, I found this noble or something.

For the first three months, I let him pay at bars and restaurants and then I put an end to that. It stopped being fun to watch him spend his teeny government paycheck on me.

However, unlike a lot of guys I have dated, he didn't seem to mind me picking up the tab. He was completely cool about it. Grateful even. He let me take him to the nicest restaurants in the city and then he let me take him away for weekends upstate and then down to Miami. We widened our orbit as we began to trust each other. Before long I wasn't even leaving him behind when I went away on business for the weekend in Hong Kong and Prague and Tel Aviv.

I finish beating VikingLightning from Minnesota and then I log off of Kingmaker. I think about watching some television, but then I remember the Playqueen meeting tomorrow. I panic, wondering how I'm going to sell this acquisition to Dad, and then I remember that I don't have to explain anything to Dad ever again.

If I want Playqueen, I can have it. All I have to do is write up a report that addresses the concerns of the lawyers. I want Playqueen's niche and I don't want to reinvent their business. By tomorrow evening, Playqueen will be a signed and sealed asset of Nylo. A new prize for the same old humiliation of having to play dumb games against sweaty nerds.

On the player rank screen, VikingLightning goes down a point and my rank remains unchanged. One of the beauties of having a moderator account is that I don't have to deal with the addictive neurosis of worrying about where I stand. I can simply enjoy playing.

I draw myself a bath in my big claw-foot tub. I have just taken my clothes off when I hear the Nylo Corporation theme song play from my purse. I walk to the big easy chair beside my bed and fish out the game phone, wondering if this means that somebody has lost a life. Who will it be, Henley or Bernard?

I see that I am still in first place, followed by Gabriella, and then Alistair, and then Bernard after all. I guess it will be Henley who comes in last.

Suddenly, the screen changes to a "loading" icon, which is our father's grinning face spinning in a circle. I guess he thought this would be funny when he was developing it, but now it just seems gruesome.

The spinning beach ball of my father's severed head is replaced by a closed-circuit video feed. What am I watching here?

I realize after a few moments that I am looking at security camera footage at the Empire State Building. The elevator bay is empty of people, but a janitor strolls into view, half-heartedly pushing a mop bucket. I recognize the way the janitor moves. I recognize his insouciant stroll. It's Henley. He's dressed in a janitor uniform and sporting a weird fake handlebar mustache. The black mustache doesn't match his russet-colored hair.

He waits for cage 1 to open up. He gets inside.

The camera footage cuts to a view from the top of cage 1. Henley gets inside and the doors close. He pushes a button. The elevator starts to rise, and Henley stands there for a while, unmoving, clutching the mop handle. Eventually, he takes out his big game phone and stares into it. He holds it up to the ceiling, raising his hand above his head as far as he can reach.

I know he must be interfacing with the box in the ceiling. He brings the phone back down and looks into it.

All of a sudden, Henley flies into the air. His head cracks against the ceiling and water from the mop bucket flies everywhere, soaking him, soaking the camera. The elevator is falling.

Henley's neck is bent at an impossible angle and his arms are flailing as he is suspended in the air. The elevator seems to fall for an impossibly long time, and then the feed goes black. The phone returns to the player rank screen. Henley is in last place. Above his rank, a little tombstone appears, and flowers sprout up in front of it.

I am staring at the phone in my hand, unsure of what I am seeing. My other phone, my real phone, starts to ring.

15

t's Alistair. He is giddy, horrified, confused.

"Was that Henley?" I ask.

"It had to be," says Alistair.

"We've got to call the Empire State Building," I say.

"And the cops."

"You call the police and I'll call the Empire State Building."

I hate talking to cops. I hang up just as a call comes in from Gabriella. I don't have time for Gabriella. I don't bother answering.

I realize that I am not exactly sure how to call the Empire State Building. I run back to my computer and Google it. There are a lot of phone numbers, but none of the ones for security or the front desk are listed.

"Fuck it," I say. It's just after midnight. I order myself a car, throw on some clothes, and head downstairs.

The Uber picks me up and we get over the bridge and then snake up the east side into Midtown. I call Gabriella back.

"What the hell was that?" she says dramatically. "Was that Henley?"

"It was probably just some kind of hoax," I say. "Just part of the game or something."

"It didn't look like a hoax," she says. "It looked like it was really him. It looked like he broke his fucking neck."

"I'm on my way to the Empire State Building," I say. "Do you want to meet me there?"

I consider calling Bernard, but I assume he is asleep. Should I wake him up? I don't really want to deal with him, and we also don't know anything yet.

"I'm actually at a friend's place," says Gabriella.

"You should call Bernard," I tell her, passing on the duty and knowing that there's a good chance she won't bother.

I take out the game phone, flipping it over, staring long and hard at my name on the back. The name is in my father's handwriting. The screen now just shows the character-creation page. I don't have a superpower. My travel method is "train pass." I realize that I can't turn the phone on or off. How does it even stay charged? I try to press buttons, to make something happen, but nothing I try does anything. The game phone is definitely a one-way device. Eventually, it goes black again.

The car drops me off on 34th Street. Parked in front of the Empire State Building are an ambulance and two police cars, but no officers are in sight. I run to the front doors of the building, but they are locked and it's dark inside. I bang on them and then run over to a service entrance and bang on that door, too. I don't quite know what to do. After a few minutes, a tired-looking man in his late twenties walks out of the service entrance. He has a cigarette in his mouth, but he hasn't lit it yet.

"Hi, hello, excuse me," I tell him. "Was there an accident in there? Did an elevator just crash? Was there a person in the elevator?"

The man stands there stupidly, looking at me. He seems like a waiter or an out-of-work actor. He has light brown skin—Middle Eastern, maybe?—and is almost attractive. He's covered in a sheen of sweat.

"I'm a police detective," he says. "There's a police substation underground, connecting all the buildings. How do you know about the elevator crash?"

"You are a detective?" I ask dubiously.

"Lieutenant Pete Jay," he says.

"Well, Detective Jay, did an elevator just crash?"

"How do you know that?" he asks. "It just happened thirty minutes ago. Are you a reporter?"

"No," I say, cringing. "I'm his sister. The sister of the man in the elevator. Is he okay?"

"You are the janitor's sister?" he says.

"He isn't really a janitor," I explain. "He's my brother. We were playing this game… my father is making us play it. I don't know, but I think it's all some kind of a hoax."

The detective lights his cigarette. He sucks in and then blows a bunch of smoke out through his clenched teeth.

"You're going to have to slow down," he says. "There was an elevator crash and there is one fatality. But you say you are a relative? Not a reporter?"

"Fatality," I say, feeling faint. I sit down on the curb.

Another man comes out through the service entrance. He is roughly the same age as Detective Jay, but more intense and smoldering. He has a jumpy, frenetic energy, like a street preacher or a smartphone salesman at a kiosk.

"She knows about the crash," says Detective Jay. The other man shakes his head.

"Craziest damn thing, huh?" he says. "I'm Detective Carter Rutledge."

"Listen," says Detective Jay. "You can't go anywhere, ma'am. We need to ask you some questions about why your brother was in the building. We are so sorry and we understand if you are upset, but we are still trying to figure out what happened. We're having a hard time getting the body out of the wreckage, if I may be perfectly blunt."

I sigh, shuddering. I put my head in my hands.

"You seem like a lady who can handle blunt," says Detective Jay. "Now could you please tell us the name of the man?"

"Henley Nylo," I say flatly. "Of the Nylo Corporation. I am Caitlyn Nylo, his sister."

Jay and Rutledge look at each other.

"Of the Nylo Corporation?" asks Jay.

"So damn strange," says Rutledge.

"What's open around here?" asks Jay, looking up and down the street.

"There's a pizza parlor," says Rutledge, pointing.

"Outstanding," says Jay.

Just at that moment, a long black limousine pulls up to the curb. The doors open and Alistair and Angelo Marino get out, looking haunted.

"What happened?" asks Alistair. "Is it real? Is it some kind of prank?"

"These are two detectives," I say. "They're telling me that Henley is dead."

"What precinct are you?" asks Angelo Marino.

"This precinct," says Detective Rutledge.

"We service the tunnels beneath Midtown," adds Detective Jay.

"Can I see your badges?" asks Angelo Marino. "I am the personal lawyer of the Nylo family."

The detectives look at each other and then one of them shows Angelo Marino a badge on a chain from under his shirt.

"We are still investigating what happened," says Detective Rutledge. "Let's all go to Joe's Famous over there on the corner and talk."

"If I may speak for my partner," Detective Jay adds, "first of all, we must say that we are a little confused about how you are all here. Did you get some kind of fucking Google alert?"

"We saw it," I say. "We saw a video of it. He lost all his lives in this game we are playing. And then he lost his life for real."

Angelo Marino steps in front of me.

"Gentlemen, she is distraught and exhausted," he says. "Her father died a few days ago, and now her brother has been killed in a gruesome accident. We would love to answer your questions and also to be as helpful as possible. But you must tell us what is going on here."

"I need food," says Detective Jay. "Come on."

Detective Jay leads the way as Rutledge goes back inside, presumably to check up on what is happening with the wreckage in the elevator. As we walk over to the pizza place, a paramedic strolls out the front doors of the Empire State Building, walks over to the ambulance, and kills the lights. No more emergency, I guess. There's nothing that can be done.

I do a quick count. I have two lives left, Bernard has two lives left, Gabriella has two lives left. Alistair only has the one. But what does any of that mean? Could Henley's death just be some kind of horrible coincidence? Or did someone just murder my brother? And if so, is it possible my father's death wasn't an accident? Was he murdered too, by the same person?

Joe's Famous Pizza is completely empty, except for a man with forehead and neck rolls who is wiping down the tables and looks glum to see us walk in. I sit down at one of the booths in the back. Angelo Marino and my brother join me. The entire restaurant is lit in fluorescents and neon. There are mirrors on all the walls. I stare at myself in the mirror right beside my shoulder. I look haggard and frightened.

Detective Jay is more eager to order food than to talk to us. He gets four slices, picking them out from where they sit cold on the counter behind glass. As he joins us, Detective Rutledge also comes in and orders four slices. He grabs an extra chair from where it is pushed up against a wall and sits at the head of the table.

"So that's your brother in there," says Detective Rutledge. "We are so sorry for your loss."

"Could you please just tell us what happened to him?" asks Alistair.

Jay and Rutledge look at each other.

"The internal Empire State Building security aren't sure if it was an accident or not," says Jay. "But your brother fell forty stories and snapped his neck on the ceiling of one of the elevators."

"Cage 1," I blurt out.

"Yes, that's right," says Jay. "They are afraid you are going to sue the fuck out of them, frankly."

"We probably will," I say.

Angelo Marino looks at me sternly, but I can't help myself. His gaze then shifts to the detectives and I can see him studying Rutledge and Jay, trying to size them up.

I do the same, wondering what they might want in life and how they might be persuaded to help us to the maximum of their abilities instead of resenting us for our wealth and power. Police detectives have the same chip on their shoulder as other cops about the elite, about their social betters, about people who have chosen any kind of life other than one that brings them into daily contact with criminals and victims. Police detectives are insecure about their intelligence, which is what draws them to the job. They get to feast on the power of knowing things other people don't know, much like doctors. They get to sadistically withhold and draw out information in order to destabilize the people that they target. They get to be in charge of people who would otherwise despise and ignore them.

In fiction and in media, they are often portrayed as heroic, as above the anodyne concerns that torture the rest of us venal sinners. In real life, they control the chaos of their own lives by controlling other people. Like doctors, they deal with finalities. And like doctors, they are the last people on Earth who should be given this dread responsibility. But by the time you discover this for yourself, it is usually too late. You find yourself up against some dead-eyed detective or surgeon who looks at you like a bug, and you squirm as a reflex, hoping they don't crush you.

Something odd about these two detectives is that they are both conventionally attractive and they both seem rather easygoing. I'm having a hard time figuring out which of them is more intelligent. I decide to address myself to Detective Jay, merely because he was the first one I encountered. I do this also because his gaze has fallen on me the hardest, and I wonder if he might be feeling some kind of hormonal stirrings that I can bend to my advantage.

"It was my father's will that all of his children—there are five of us—play a game against each other for his fortune," I say, getting a subtle nod of approval from Angelo Marino. "In the game, we each get three lives. At the very moment that Henley lost all of his lives, he was killed by this falling elevator. Then the rest of us were sent a video of his death. It can't be a coincidence. He was murdered. I'm sure of it. I hate to say it, but the likeliest suspect is our own father, which can't be true because our father died on Sunday."

The detectives stare blankly at me for a long time. A bell dings at the front of the restaurant and Detective Jay hops up and retrieves his four slices of pizza: two cheese and two chicken bacon ranch. Detective Rutledge cranes his neck to the counter, searching for his own food.

"Did you hear what I just said?" I ask.

"Yeah, we heard you," says Detective Jay.

"We hear crazy shit all the time," says Detective Rutledge.

I pull out my game phone and put it on the table. Alistair looks at me and then, reluctantly, pulls out his game phone, too.

"These phones are how the Game Master is supposed to get in touch with us," I say. "Whoever our father hired as the Game Master is some kind of fucking maniac. None of us are safe."

"Okay," says Detective Jay, staring at me blankly.

Detective Rutledge picks up the two game phones and they both turn on, showing our respective character-creation screens. He turns them over and sees our names on the back. He plays with them a little bit, but soon he sees that there isn't much that can be done with them.

"Pretty neat," says Detective Rutledge. He hands my phone back to me and then gives Alistair's phone back to him.

"You aren't taking this seriously," I say. "How else do you explain how we knew our brother was dead before you did?"

"Who knows?" says Detective Rutledge. "Maybe you killed him. We don't even know why he was in the elevator in the first place."

"Check the footage," I say. "He was there because we were all supposed to hold these phones up to a box in the ceiling. The box will still
be there. Maybe there are fingerprints or something. At the very least,
if you check the footage, you will see me and my brothers and sister all
getting in the same elevator throughout the day. He was the last one,
and I guess he had to sneak in because the building was closed, which
is why he was dressed as a janitor."

"We'll check the tapes," says Detective Jay. "But look, honestly, I
don't know what you want us to do here. It looks like an accident. The
Empire State Building execs are freaking out, just so you know. Like
we said, they're terrified you're going to sue them. Now here you are
telling us that you think he was murdered by your father. We don't
really know what to say."

"It wasn't our father," I say. "It was this Game Master, whoever that
might be."

Detectives Jay and Rutledge share a long, exasperated look at
each other.

"We have some questions for you," says Detective Jay. "But we want
to interview you separately, if you don't mind."

"I'm afraid I can't allow that," says Angelo Marino, again stepping
in. "I'm afraid that won't be happening."

I want to tell Angelo Marino to leave us alone, to stand down and
let the detectives work. But it isn't just us he is protecting. It's the entire
Nylo Corporation. He knows better than we do.

Detective Jay sighs.

"Right, figured as much," says Detective Rutledge. "Look, we'll investigate all the angles here on our own. Thank you for your help, but
if we need to talk with you, we'll be in touch."

The bell dings as he finishes speaking, and Rutledge gets up to retrieve his own haul of pizza: two pepperoni slices and two large squares
of deep-dish Sicilian.

"You want a slice?" Detective Jay asks me, noticing me staring at
their pizza.

I stand up and so does Alistair, following my lead.

"Look, go home and get some sleep," says Detective Jay. "We'll be in touch if we have any news to tell you. Thank you for all of your interesting leads. We are so sorry for your tragic loss."

"So that's it?" I demand.

"Unless you want any of this pizza," says Detective Jay, grinning as he takes another bite.

Disgusted, I storm out of Joe's Famous. The three of us walk back to the limo. We get inside and start driving, headed for the office, unsure of where else to go.

"I could try and trace the calls," says Alistair. "Try and figure out where this Game Master is."

"If the police don't care, what can we even do?" I ask Angelo Marino. He stares out the window a long time, weighing my words, watching the bright lights and drunken revelers of early morning Manhattan speed by.

"I guess you keep playing," he says.

16

The office is dark and silent. The security guard on the ground floor is surprised to see all three of us. He gives me a cool nod. We ride the elevator in silence to the top floor, to my father's office. It's clear from the tension that all three of us are thinking about Henley's last moments, of the terror he must have felt as the elevator plummeted forty stories and killed him.

The abrupt cut to black as the camera was destroyed in the fall was chilling. It is the blackness that consumes us all in the end.

"Gabriella and Bernard are on their way," says Angelo Marino, after we enter the office.

I pace back and forth, helping myself to my father's bourbon while Alistair mumbles something again about trying to trace the game phones. He leaves. I excuse myself and go into one of the conference rooms and call Pez.

"Oh my god, Caitlyn, it's so late at night!" he says after a few rings.

"Pez, I want to know if you've learned anything yet about why Henley had to come back so soon to the United States. I want to know what happened to him in China."

"I have learned a little," he says. "Mostly just rumors and tidbits. I don't have anything concrete yet, though I am meeting with one of his many exes tomorrow to see what she can tell me."

"I am specifically wondering if you know any reason why anybody might want him dead," I ask, my voice trembling. I am trying to stay calm, but it isn't quite working. I slowly pace around the conference room in a tight circle, like a tiny dog in a bathtub.

"I'll know more when I talk to Sheila tomorrow," says Pez. "She and Henley were evidently in touch these past few weeks and he went to see her as soon as he got back into town."

Should I tell him or not? If I tell him, will he tell Sheila? Will that spook her and keep Pez from learning anything concrete from her? Or will telling her that Henley is dead let her know that the stakes are very high and there is no sense protecting any of Henley's secrets anymore?

"Henley is dead," I finally say. "He was killed in an elevator crash at the Empire State Building a few hours ago."

"What?" says Pez. "I don't understand."

"We saw the video," I explain. "It has to be related to the game."

Pez doesn't know what to say. He is stammering, searching for words.

"I think somebody is trying to kill us all," I whisper.

"You think it's related to this game?"

"Maybe," I say. "Yes. I don't know. Anyway, whatever we initially agreed upon as pay, I'm tripling your fee. But I need information and I need it fast. Anything you can find out about Henley, my father, the game—anything. I need it as soon as possible."

"Okay," says Pez. "I'll keep pushing."

"Call me every few hours," I say. "Even if you don't have anything new to report, I just want to know what you are doing and what leads you are working. I don't really feel like I can trust anybody else here, you know? I don't want to feel all alone in this."

"You can trust me," says Pez. "I loved your father and I love all of you kids."

"You love everyone," I say generously.

"I do. And I'm going back to sleep now," he says. "So I can get right on it in the morning."

I hang up and head back to the office, where Angelo Marino is sitting at a laptop, typing furiously. Alistair is nowhere to be seen.

"Alistair went down to R&D," says Angelo Marino, answering my unspoken question. "I'm emailing the police. I'm typing up statements for all of you. I will need you to look over them just so there aren't any surprises if they bring you in for questioning later."

"What are you telling them?" I ask.

"The truth," he says. He blesses me with one of his rare, unnatural smiles. I feel like I am being stared down by a hungry wolf, spittle foaming down its jowls.

Bernard and Gabriella show up right about the same time, and I call Alistair's lab to bring him back up. Even when all of us are gathered together again, we don't speak.

I realize that we are all unconsciously waiting for someone.

Henley. But he isn't coming.

"Okay," I say. "We have to all agree to stop playing this game. Henley was murdered. We have to find out why and who did it."

"Murdered?!" exclaims Bernard.

"The Game Master sent us all the snuff film!" I say. "It was murder. And that means that any one of us could be next."

"Not any one of us," says Bernard. "Strictly speaking. Only whoever loses."

"Right, and Alistair is down to one life, which means he's next on the chopping block."

"It was Dad's game," Bernard points out. "What are you suggesting? That somehow Dad was responsible for killing Henley?"

The notion is preposterous. Dad, a killer? Yet it makes me think back to all the rumors surrounding our mother's death. To all the detectives who interviewed me, all the women they brought in wearing blue gloves who were overly nice to me, but who still asked me to tell them the same story again and again, of walking into the White Room and seeing the bright red sprayed out all over everything.

I think back to the suspicions of my mother's family in Alabama and the ensuing custody battles over who would raise the five of us. My father had pulled my mother's entire family out of poverty, but they weren't even remotely grateful for it. He didn't cut them off. But we didn't really see them anymore after that, either. That was the trade.

We all knew that our father had nothing to do with the death of our mother. Why would a goofy patrician with a love for games and diversions, who found success in business thanks to his creative concepts, murder the mother of his five children in cold blood in the middle of the day when he was supposed to be running a scavenger hunt for all the neighborhood children?

No, it didn't make any sense at all. Plus, we all knew how depressed our mother was. How she seemed to hate life and even seemed to hate us.

I remember when Alistair and I were entering the first grade at Aviators, the private primary school for the richest and most fashionable children in the city.

"Bet you two little shitheads think you're really something special," our mom told us, holding our hands like iron as she walked us down the sidewalk.

I did indeed think I was something special. In fact, I knew it. But I could tell that Alistair was freaking out on account of being forced to be around children who would be a year older than him, and he wasn't taking it well. He was scared and upset that he wouldn't be in the same class as the few friends he had made in kindergarten.

Our mother stopped in front of the school and sat down on the sidewalk, still holding both our hands, hanging her head. She smelled like alcohol and cigarettes and patchouli. She started weeping so hard that her shoulders shook. Her lank hair hung down in front of her face like blond curtains.

"Why did you stop here, Mommy?" asked Alistair, who was

perpetually insensitive to our mother's moods and who never knew
when to just shut up and let her vent. He was always taking her moods
personally, as if her insane rages and catatonic despairs had anything
to do with him. He put his free hand under her arm, trying to drag
her to her feet.

"You're embarrassing us... " Alistair said.

That was when she straight-up cold-cocked him, right in the side
of the head, knocking him to the pavement in front of all the other
mothers. He was more stunned than hurt, but he lay there for a while
with the air knocked out of him. Our mother stood up and looked
around at all the stunned faces of the other mothers. She had just hay-
makered a first grader.

Now, this was the early eighties, so violence against your own children was more tolerated and understood, but still, these were a bunch
of very liberal parents and she had used a fist and it was clearly done
in anger. She was shocked at herself. She knew that what she had done
was unforgivable.

"Oh, sweetie, what happened?" she said, trying to remake reality.
"You scared me, I thought you were someone else!"

It didn't work. Actually, after that, we had to go to a different,
still extremely elite elementary school on the Upper West Side. She
couldn't deal with seeing the other Aviators mothers.

After her suicide, the detective didn't just want to know the details
of what I saw when I stumbled upon her messy corpse. He wanted to
know if my mother had ever had unusual mood swings, or if she had
ever talked about taking her own life, or if she had been fighting with
my father.

Nobody had ever asked me what I thought about my own mother
before. The weird intimacy of it, and the invitation to discuss my feelings, caught me off guard. I gushed to the police detective about my
mother's fits of madness, about her ups and downs, about her neglect
followed by her hyperattentiveness, about her perpetual giddy strange-
ness and her comfort with—almost glee at—violence and cruelty.

Even as young as I was, I knew why a person might want to die. And even as young as I was, I knew that I was helping my father by telling the truth about how crazy my mother had always been. I also knew I was helping my father by leaving out the fact that she sometimes fought with him as well. Because who didn't fight with my mother?

My eyes dart to the anxious faces of my remaining siblings as I come out of my reverie. "Dad has nothing to do with any of this," I say. "We just have to figure out who this Game Master is and then we can turn them in and stop this madness."

"So we should stop playing the game?" asks Gabriella. "Right? That's the vibe I'm getting here?"

We all stare at her.

"Henley was murdered," says Bernard, finally. "Fine. I agree. The game is over."

17

"We should keep playing," urges Bernard an hour later, reversing himself utterly. "Are we really all just going to give up? He would want us to keep going."

We've all had a lot to drink. The rest of my siblings can't really hold their liquor. Not like me, not like Henley. We've been telling stories about our dead dirtbag brother, trying to make some kind of meaning from his death.

"What are you talking about?" says Gabriella. "We already decided. You even said!"

"No, I've been thinking about it," says Bernard, his normal reticence to express himself shaken loose. "How else are we supposed to find whoever did this if we stop now? Nothing would catch the Game Master more off guard than if we didn't even blink—if we just kept right on playing his game."

"You have a helicopter," says Gabriella. "Of course you would say that."

Angelo Marino has been putting the finishing touches on our police reports in the next room. Now he comes in holding a sheaf of color-coded binders.

"Maybe we should take a vote," says Bernard.

"What does voting matter?" I say. "Surely no one would believe that this was our father's last wish, to kill all of his children. Anyway, whoever wins now, the case will get tied up in court unless we agree to a settlement."

"Yes, but none of that is the point," says Bernard. "The point is to play the game. Maybe Dad isn't running the game, but he still set it all up. We are honoring both him and Henley if we keep going."

What Bernard is saying is undeniably true. The scavenger hunt has all the hallmarks of something Dad would make, of one of his notoriously buggy and lame first drafts, before teams of creative professionals have gotten ahold of it and turned it into something polished and ready for the masses. Before it has been playtested.

"I'm going to keep playing," says Bernard. "Fuck it. Who else?"

He raises his hand. Angelo Marino sits down at our father's desk and lines up the colored folders in front of him. There is one for each of us. *How has he managed to type up what we know and what we have seen so quickly?*

"Okay," says Bernard, when no other hands shoot up. "So it's just me then."

"It's just you," I say. "Congratulations, you've won the big prize."

"So you should all give me your game phones, then," says Bernard. "Since you won't need them anymore."

"I assume they are all evidence, actually," I say. "In a murder investigation. We should give them to the police."

"If they even ask for them," says Bernard. "This Jay and Rutledge don't sound very professional. Do you think they've ever had to work a murder before?"

"Surely," I say, though now that he mentions it, I find it extremely hard to believe that these two men have much experience with the actual work of being detectives. What horrible luck for Henley to fall into the jurisdiction of the subway tunnels under Midtown.

"I'm not giving you my phone," I tell Bernard. "We'll all turn them over to the cops together."

"If they ask for them," Bernard repeats, petulantly.

"These are finished," Angelo Marino says, gesturing to our reports. "If you wouldn't mind signing them, I will have them couriered to the precinct and then we can all go home and get some sleep."

We pick up our file folders. I'm the only one who bothers reading my statement before signing it. Actually, I'm a little shocked to find out how much of the statement is simply the truth, as strange and incomplete as the truth is.

I sign my statement and pour myself another glass of bourbon to take downstairs to my room. I say goodnight to everyone, my eyes lingering on Alistair, who looks like he has something he wants to say to me.

"What?" I ask gently, but he just shakes his head.

When I reach my room, I collapse onto my bed. I try to find some kind of soothing ambient music to lull me into a stupor along with the rocking dizziness of all the liquor, but nothing helps. I lie on my back for a long time, trying to force myself to fall asleep, but sleep won't come.

I think about how I will have to tell my daughters that their beloved uncle is now also dead, just like their beloved grandfather. They'll blame me for it on some level. They'll wonder about their own fragile place in the universe. They'll wonder what it means that even though we have nearly infinite money and all the power that money brings, we were not able to avoid such a strange accident.

Unlike the poor unfortunates, my children will not have dreams of aspiration. They will not suffer from the delusion that if they simply work hard enough and acquire more wealth and power they will be able to avoid their own doom, to bargain with the forces of darkness and then come out on top. Yes, their lives will be easier. But there is something devastating about growing up in a world where you know exactly what money can—and cannot—buy.

I am actually more afraid that this double blow will raise Ben's standing in their emotional calculus. He represents a form of achievement and growth that is not material and that seemingly has no clear boundaries. He represents a fake world of flattering ersatz spiritual transcendence, of proletarian renunciation, of self-denial and commitment to dubious higher principles. I can only teach them to be ruthless and to wield power responsibly in a way that benefits the most people without diminishing the paralyzing force of the Nylo name. I can teach them that being "the one who decides" confers the imperiousness of power but that these decisions don't actually matter all that much.

However, I fear the trauma of this double loss will make them into goddamned pious stylites like their smug father. I fear that if I start to represent dissolution and the grave, I will lose them.

I need fresh air. I take my elevator to the ground level and walk around, smoking a cigarette. It is 4 a.m. in Brooklyn, and the only other people on the streets are drunk bros and shark-like hustlers, trying to see if anybody is good for a free cigarette or worth jumping for their cash or phone.

A thick young man wobbles up to me and stops, staring at me, blinking. He is wearing an untucked silk shirt and tight jeans that do not flatter his already poochy belly. *Is it true that women outnumber men almost two to one in this city?* He doesn't seem to feel that he has to work very hard to be a viable male here.

"Hey, whoa, you are really hot," he says.

"Thank you," I say. "Keep moving, man."

"Do you want to, like… come home with me?"

His massive insecurity is palpable. He wants to be the type of person who can command people into having instant sex with him. He wants to be the sort of person who can ask for instant sex without any repercussions.

I turn away from him, still smoking, hoping he'll get the hint.

"Oh," he says, and I can hear his sneer even though my back is turned. "So you're too good to even talk to me. Okay."

It's true, though. I am too good to even talk to him.

"Fine, whatever, I was giving you a compliment," he says, sidling away, already forgetting our interaction, having gotten what he needed from it. I responded to him once. He proved he was not afraid of me.

It is only seconds later that a completely different sort of dirtbag comes shuffling around the corner. He sees me and his eyes light up with shrewd malice.

"Hey," he says, leaning into my field of vision. "Hey, the thing is, I am trying to get twenty dollars so I can buy a bus ticket and I already got ten dollars so maybe you could give me a ten-dollar bill and I can get a ticket back home to my kids?"

"I'm sorry," I say. "I don't have any cash."

This is true. I don't keep any cash in my purse. I move closer to the front of the building where the security guard can see me.

"Okay, god bless," he says. "But could I at least get a few cigarettes, maybe?"

He knows I am going to say yes, and I know I am going to say yes, but I am resentful of this fact. I reach into my tiny purse and pull out the pack of Dunhills. His eyes gleam with glassy excitement.

"Whoa," he says. "The good shit. Remember when these used to be, like, ten bucks a pack and we thought they were expensive, back when we were in high school?"

His familiarity shocks me. Are we the same age? I don't remember the price of Dunhills. I don't think I have ever tried to buy any other brand.

I hand him three cigarettes and shut my purse, heading for the building entrance. The fun of smoking has been squashed.

"Hey, wait, you got a light?"

"No, I'm sorry," I say, slipping through the revolving door. As a percentage of my holdings, with the amount of money that most people give away as spare change, I could change this man's life forever, making him weep right here on the street with permanent gratitude. Fuck him for not knowing that, for not knowing me.

I look back over my shoulder. The man is still there in front of the building, staring inside. He comes up closer and puts his face to the glass. I give a knowing glance to the security guard and the guard reluc-tantly gets up and slowly walks toward the revolving doors. The poor unfortunate gets the idea. He skips away, stuffing the three cigarettes I gave him into the pockets of his low-slung shorts. He gives me one last withering stare of pure contempt before he disappears from view.

Wait, did we literally go to high school together?

No, of course not, I tell myself. I've never seen the man before in my life. And hopefully I will never see him or anyone else like him ever again.

Why is it impossible to shield oneself completely from the ugly, disgusting world that hates you for no reason?

18

finally fall asleep for a few hours but I am awakened at 7:30 by Peter sneaking into my office to deliver yet another batch of flowers, candy, and cards from fellow CEOs. I stumble to the closet and pick out some gray slacks and a summery blouse. I fix myself up in the bathroom and brew a pot of coffee, which I drink in my office while reading the business sections of the *Times*, the *Journal*, and the *Financial Times*, which Peter has separated from the rest of the papers like shelled pistachios or deveined shrimp.

I can't postpone the Playqueen meeting. It has to be this afternoon or never. I can't let a little thing like the murder of my youngest brother put me off.

It is about 9 a.m. when Peter walks in, sheepishly holding his phone in his hands like a hat.

"I am so sorry," he says. "I was just reading the *Post* online."

"Did they break the story?" I ask, sighing.

"Yes," Peter says. "An elevator crash at the Empire State Building? That is so insane. You must be devastated."

"I am not doing great," I admit.

"I can cancel all your meetings again today."

"Nope," I say. "I'm having them."

"Are you sure? I know everyone will understand. The amount your family has suffered lately… It is a little hard to believe." Peter gives me an understanding smile, even though he can't possibly.

"The meetings will continue as planned," I insist.

He reads my mood perfectly and scuttles out. I squeeze my phone for a while like a stress toy, but then I finally do the horrible, right thing and call Ben.

"Hey," I say.

"Hey."

"So, guess what."

"I am right in between classes—" he starts.

"Henley is dead," I cut in. "He was killed in an elevator crash. It snapped his neck. Last night."

"What?" says Ben. "What the fuck?"

"Look, you can read all about it in the *Post*, evidently. Would you mind telling the girls?"

"They really liked Henley," says Ben. "They'll be devastated. So soon after your father? And so sudden? You must be reeling."

"I am reeling," I say. "So be gentle with the girls but tell them the truth. If they have any questions, tell them they can call me, but obviously I am busy putting everything in order. Can you take care of them?"

"I am so sorry," he says. "I can't even believe this. I am so sorry you are all alone with this."

"Anyway, now you know. I'll call the girls tonight. I promise."

"They have seen a lot of death lately," says Ben. "So have you. Jesus."

"I've gotta go, dude," I say. I hang up.

I spend the rest of the morning alone in my office trying to catch up, working on everything I've been putting off. I get my notes in order for the Playqueen meeting and go over the P&Ls for the various divisions in the next quarter. I read a bunch of dumb memos about upcoming parties and company events, which for some reason will still be happening, even though my father will not be able to attend them. For a moment, I wonder who will take his place with respect to making speeches and rousing the troops. I realize that this person will now be me.

Self-deprecation has never been my strong suit. I make a note to read Grant's memoirs again. I must become someone who inspires people. Grant never wanted to be a general. He just wanted to be a math professor. I, too, can become a general if I must.

As I work, I try very hard not to think about Henley. I try very hard not to remember all the trouble he had gotten into over the years, all the random women running after him who I had to chase away with stern conversations, with cash, with NDAs.

I think about the time he was arrested in an East Village McDonald's for public indecency. He had taken so much acid that he had his pants off in order to soothingly masturbate himself into a stupor in one of the booths. After a generous contribution to the Emerald Society, he was let go and his record was expunged. He promised to keep it to ketamine, coke, and DMT after that.

"I'm too fun for acid," he lamented. "Acid is too smooth."

I try very hard not to remember him getting kicked out of boarding school for an elaborate prank gone awry that involved burning an obscene poem into the manicured lawn of the dean using weed killer. Partway through, Henley realized that the weed killer would take too long, so he switched to gasoline. He lit the gas-drenched letters, somehow not knowing that the grass in between would also catch fire.

"It worked in this movie I saw," he lamented.

I try very hard not to remember how he showed up at my house after the divorce with a team of male strippers and a Ziploc bag full of coke. He insisted that the strippers were working for free after seeing naked pictures of me he had stolen from my phone. They actually all stuck to this story, trying to get my number even as I was kicking them out. I wasn't in the mood to get laid, but he did make me laugh—and I hadn't been able to laugh in months.

"You really should have just fucked a few of them to be nice," he said. "At least one."

I'm so lost in memories that I don't notice when noon rolls around. All of a sudden, Alistair and Angelo Marino are in my office, looking at me gravely. I glance up from my desk and frown at them.

"It's time," says Angelo Marino.

"Right," I say. "Have you heard anything from Jay and Rutledge? Shouldn't they be here?"

"They said they would call us if they need anything from us," says Angelo Marino. "They haven't called."

"I don't think they're very good at their jobs," I say.

"Civil servants," says Angelo Marino. "You don't get to pick them."

I take out my game phone and put it on my desk. Alistair does the same and we stare at each other, searching each other's eyes.

Both phones ring in unison, and even though we're expecting it, Alistair and I both jump. I assume that wherever Bernard and Gabriella are, their phones are ringing as well. The Nylo Corporation jingle blares throughout my office in stereo.

We pick up the game phones, and I pull out my regular phone and start recording the game phone for evidence.

At first, all we see is the character-creation menu, but then static fills the screen. When it clears, the background is highly pixelated lapping waves, blood red. In front of the waves, the Game Master appears, this time wearing a hockey mask like Jason from the *Friday the 13th* movies.

"Welcome back!" says the figure. "We are down to four players and now we are entering day two. Your clue for today is: 'All the *sea farmers* know it was her favorite place to stand.'"

I panic because I don't instantly know the answer to this riddle. I look at Alistair, furrowing my brow.

"Hey, wait a second," someone says. It's Gabriella. I can hear her through the phone. We must be able to talk back. The figure in the hockey mask cocks his head to the side.

"We don't want to play anymore," says Gabriella. "We want to forfeit."

"You are certainly welcome to forfeit, which means you will lose all of your lives," says the figure. "You have two lives left. Do you want to quit playing?"

"No," says Gabriella. "I mean—"

"You killed our brother, you asshole," I interrupt. "We know you did it."

"Your brother lost all of his lives and is out of the game," says the Game Master. "I had nothing to do with your brother losing his lives. So is that it? Are you all not playing anymore?"

Bernard chimes in. "I'm still going to play and I know this clue. I know the answer. I still want to play."

"Bernard, you slime," I say. "This guy killed our brother. I'm recording this conversation so I can send it to the police."

"Nobody else has to play if they don't want to play," he says. "But I know this one."

"I know it too," says Gabriella. "If you're playing, I'm playing."

"None of us should play," I say. "It doesn't matter if you figure out the clue or not."

"The last person to find the box will lose a life," says the figure in the hockey mask. "Good luck to you all!"

The screen returns to static.

"Of course Bernard wants to keep playing," says Alistair. "He has a damn helicopter."

"We should make sure the cops know about his helicopter so they can question the pilot," I say.

"I put it in his statement," says Angelo Marino. "It's all in the statement."

"So now what?" asks Alistair.

"I don't know," I say. "Hold on, I'm calling Bernard."

The phone rings but he doesn't pick up. Exasperated, I dial Gabriella's number.

"So are we still playing?" she asks me. "What if we all work together?"

"We have to stop," I say. "I have a huge meeting this afternoon."

"I think I know the answer, though," she says. "All these questions are about Mom, right?"

"It seems that way so far," I agree.

"Listen," she says. "You get a train pass, but I have to walk everywhere. If this box is where I think it is, it's going to take me forever to get there. I have to leave now. But I could tell you the answer if you want."

"We have to stop," I say. She hangs up on me.

I am a little bit annoyed that both Bernard and Gabriella seem to know the answer already while I don't have the foggiest idea. I send Angelo Marino the recording of the game phone call.

"Send that to the cops," I say. "Maybe they'll believe us when they see it for real."

Our game phones now show the clue and nothing else: "All the *sea farmers* know it was her favorite place to stand." We can safely assume that "she" refers to our mother. I am also getting the sense that all of these clues will refer to places inside NYC. But this black box could be anywhere. I don't have time for this.

19

"Do you know the answer to this one?" I ask Alistair point-blank. He shakes his head.

"Well, I have a ton of shit to do today," I tell him. "I have a big meeting and I have to plan Henley's funeral and deal with the press and I am still exhausted from yesterday. Let me know if you figure it out and we can go together."

"I'm worried about you," says Alistair. "You seem like you aren't taking this very well. Not that you should be."

That's when I start sobbing. It is never tragedy that breaks me up. It is sympathy. I can't handle it. I can't handle a nice person sticking up for me.

I put my head down on my desk and gush fucking tears. All of my memories with Henley come rushing back. I wish I could call him and tell him what an asshole he is. I make a vow that I will use all the resources of the Nylo Corporation to get revenge for his death, no matter what.

Alistair knows me too well to try and comfort me. He lets me cry. He is still there when I am done. I feel a little nauseous. I'm bleary and dehydrated. Hungover. Crying is making it worse. I crack open a bottled water and drink almost the whole thing in one draft. The cold water hits my sour stomach and churns it, causing gouts of pain from all the stress acid, but I manage to keep my bile down.

"I can't believe Gabriella and Bernard are going to keep playing," Alistair says.

"We should hire security for them, for all of us. What was that private firm we contracted after 9/11?"

"Ellsworth Marshall," says Alistair. "Are you sure that's a good idea? Private security is such a pain in the ass."

"We don't really have a choice. We would be utterly negligent if we didn't at least try to protect ourselves."

"I'll handle it," says Angelo Marino. "I'll get full security details from Ellsworth Marshall for all four of you by this afternoon."

"I've got to prepare for this meeting," I say. "I'm not going to be swerved from buying Playqueen by some punk in a mask. The execs will be here soon."

"You don't think Playqueen has anything to do with all of this?" asks Alistair thoughtfully. "That's crazy, right?"

I frown, thinking about it. Would a little company like Playqueen resort to murdering all of us to avoid getting acquired? It seems outlandish, but Playqueen actually has a motive, unlike anybody else I can think of.

"Maybe," I say, after a long pause. "I wouldn't blame them. But they won't win. This is all just a temporary blip on our epic family quest to conquer the whole world of games and amusements, becoming the undisputed leader in every category of fun."

"I'll keep working on trying to figure out how to follow these phones back to some kind of source," says Alistair. "They must have been made somewhere. And there aren't a lot of places in the world that could make something like this. Surely I know them all."

Alistair and Angelo Marino leave. I call Pez. He answers immediately.

"I'm coming in this afternoon," says Pez. "I have news for you. It's not much, but it's interesting."

"And I've got something else for you to investigate," I tell him.

"We're trying to acquire a company called Playqueen. We think it's possible they might somehow be involved in Henley's murder. Dad was warning me about them, but I've been stubborn. I was chalking up his hesitation to general sexism about games specifically targeted to women, but maybe he knew something that I don't know."

"I'll look into them," says Pez. "Anything else?"

"Alistair is trying to trace the source of the game phones, which might be an interesting angle. Also, there is a new clue for today: 'All the *sea farmers* know it was her favorite place to stand.' Does that mean anything to you?"

He thinks about it for a while.

"Something about the sea," he says. "And your mother, presumably. The beach, maybe?"

"Our mother hated the beach," I say. "She was too pale and she hated all the sand in her clothes and all the dumb, poor unfortunates arrayed on beach towels and reeking of sunscreen."

Even as I talk, I get an inkling in the back of my brain: some old memory, some wry joke that our mother used to make. But I can't hold on to it. Even as it starts to shimmer into focus, the memory fades into an aggravating phantasm.

I spend the next couple hours dealing with the heads of various departments. People seem nervous around me, given what's happened the past few days, and I guess they should be. I tell Peter to refer all the press to Angelo Marino, and I avoid the internet, which is blowing up with news about the elevator crash that killed Henley. I'm amused to find that we are being painted in the same light as the Kennedys: a noble, aristocratic East Coast family dealing with unimaginable trage-dy. And I'm relieved to discover they are using flattering pictures of me instead of paparazzi trash. America is a visual country.

I have a dark, cynical thought that all of this might even help the Nylo brand. We provide family entertainment and our family is breaking apart.

I call the marketing department. Chloe Taney picks up.

"Would you mind doing some analytics about how we should best spin the fact that we have lost Prescott and Henley?" I ask her. "Should we try and minimize the tragedy or should we lean into it for maximum brand awareness? I can't think of any similar incidents with similar companies, but I have a feeling we can leverage this to our advantage, or at least minimize some of the bad publicity that could give our brand the taint of tragedy."

Chloe sputters her agreement, bowled over by my coldness.

"Of course, of course," she says.

She won't be able to keep my request a secret. Soon everyone at Nylo will hear about how I'm capitalizing on death. Some people will be shocked and horrified, but mostly this will remind people why I am in charge. How I never crumble in the face of a crisis. How I never stop putting the company first.

And secretly they'll be relieved. They'll keep backing me, no matter what happens. You want a monster at the top, to crush all the other potential monsters who mistakenly think they can match the depth of the top monster's creative malice in the service of the corporation.

I work through the afternoon, periodically racking my brain for memories of our mother, of our mother playing *Sea Farmers,* of our mother and the sea. I try to come up with a reason why Bernard and Gabriella might remember something about her that Alistair and I don't. They were so much younger than we were when she died. It doesn't make any sense.

At four o'clock, the department heads roll into my office. Peter lets me know the Playqueen team has arrived, too, and are waiting upstairs. "Keep them sweating," I say.

My call to Chloe Taney has done its work. The department heads are all terrified of me, terrified of the tragedy itself, terrified of my response to it so far. They are terrified of the fact that I am insisting that we still hold the meeting with Playqueen in my dead father's conference room, where we always hold high-level meetings.

After we go over the internal reports and briefs and charts

(everything is ostensibly in order), we ride the elevator up one flight together in silence.

Playqueen has come in force. They've brought a team of ten, many of whom are lawyers and tax people, but it looks like they have way more execs from the company than they need. I wonder if that means they're going to make this difficult for me. Which I actually find to be a relief. If they were literally trying to murder us all, I assume they would be more low-key here in this meeting.

"Listen," I say, as soon as we are all sitting down and everyone has chosen from the cake, pie, pineapple empanadas, and coffee that we often serve at afternoon meetings. "I know you guys don't want Nylo Corporation to buy you, strip you for parts, and remove everything that makes you unique. You think you want control. But I am offering immortality. There is no apotheosis in this business beyond greater distribution and a bigger marketing profile. Our offer represents a commitment to your mission. We see what you are trying to do, we get it, and we want to make your dreams come true, not just for America, but for the whole world. Right?"

The CEO of Playqueen is a giant bearded man named Salmon Chase Capaldi. He measures my words, looking as often at Angelo Marino as at me. I try to stay open-minded.

"We are going to do the deal, obviously, but that doesn't mean we have to like it," he finally says. "I am frankly surprised you still wanted to meet with us today. Frankly, and I hope you don't mind my bluntness, how can anybody here be sure that you are thinking clearly? I remember when my mother died. I almost joined the Marines. Can you believe that? I didn't know what the fuck I was doing. Do you know what the fuck you are doing?"

He has overplayed his hand. I look around at everyone in the room. I look at my vice presidents, I look at my COO and my CFO. I think about Grant's rules for winning at war: find out where your enemy is, hit them with everything you've got, and then keep moving.

"Thank you so much for coming all this way," I say. "You will find that all of our paperwork is in order and that our lawyers have done their due diligence. We know what we are getting and we are pleased that you have been so transparent with respect to some of the catastrophic mistakes you have made along the way that have put your business in the place that it is right now. Welcome to Nylo. I hope you don't mind if I don't stick around for the gory details of the evisceration?"

I excuse myself from the meeting, countering his belligerence with imperiousness. I have sized him up, taken his measure, and defeated him.

I take the stairs back down to my office and am pleasantly surprised to find Pez there waiting for me. He is holding his hat in his hand while talking on the phone to someone in soothing tones. I know the sound of Pez trying to cajole information out of one of his sources. He holds up a finger as I enter and he steps into the corner to finish his conversation in symbolic privacy.

I find myself weeping gently, thinking about Henley, thinking about my father. I wonder when I will ever have the time to process all of this. Part of me hopes that time never comes.

20

"I have news about Henley in China," Pez says, finishing his phone call. "It comes too late, I am aware. But it might explain what we are dealing with. I'm not sure. I don't know much about Playqueen yet, but it may come as no surprise to you that Playqueen is only accidentally successful. It was created as a laundromat for some New Orleans Sicilians, as a present to the daughter of someone quite family oriented. She turned out to be unexpectedly good at designing games. Some say that Playqueen has been intentionally tanking itself for years, despite quality product."

"That does come as a bit of a surprise," I say, glancing up, where on the floor above the acquisition is being finalized. Perhaps it will be possible to get this young Southern-Sicilian games girl genius to work for me after I take over her company.

"Anyway, the big news is about Henley and China," says Pez.

He stops, tentative.

"How are you doing, by the way? You don't look so good. I don't expect you to look good, but you look terrible. Are you eating?"

"No less than usual," I say.

"I want to see you eat something," says Pez. "It will do my heart good."

I call Peter and ask him to go upstairs to get us salmon, bagels, and cream cheese.

"So listen, I was able to get in touch with Henley's latest ex-girlfriend, Sheila," he says. "I was correct that he has been seeing her while he has been back in town. She was devastated when I told her that he was dead and she wouldn't even believe me until she saw the *Post* online. I promised her that she would be compensated for her trouble if she told me what she knows. She needs some cash. Henley has been paying her rent and now she doesn't know where she will go and what she will do."

"I'll make sure that she is taken care of," I say. Just then my phone rings. "Excuse me for a moment."

I take an emergency call about Playqueen. Our bagels and cream cheese arrive while I'm handling a decision about assets. After it's settled, I hang up and stare at my bagel, while Pez stares at me staring at my bagel. Dutifully, I take a big bite, squirting some cream cheese down my chin. I wipe it off, lick my finger, and chew, actually enjoying it. My stomach grumbles and I realize that Pez is right: I do need to eat. Also, my hangover is fading, which means it's probably time to get drunk again. I walk over to the sideboard and pour myself a bourbon on ice.

"None for me, thanks," says Pez.

"So what did she tell you?" I ask. "Is the Chinese government murdering my family because of something Henley did?"

"Henley definitely got in trouble in China, but it wasn't with the Chinese," says Pez. "It was with plain old, boring, basic Americans. Midwesterners, actually, the most brutal and resentful people. He fell in with a bunch of small-time importer/exporters from Michigan who became his drinking and carousing buddies. I guess he was lonely on account of not being able to speak the language. According to his ex, he rarely even left the hotel where he was staying."

"And what went wrong with these importer/exporters?"

"According to his ex, it wasn't Henley's fault. But I only have his

side of the story filtered through her. I'm attempting to get some cor-
roboration, but that will take time. Anyway, according to her, they got
in way over their heads while gambling and they started moving from
the importing/exporting business into the straight-up smuggling business, which in the new militant version of modern China is extremely
forbidden and not at all as fun and easy as it used to be before Xi
Jinping started cracking down on corruption. Once upon a time, you
could bribe a Party official rather easily to help you transship anything
contraband through Russia. Not anymore. However, making smuggling harder has made it way more profitable, as these things go."

"What were these boring, basic Midwesterners trying to smuggle?"

"Pornography, at least according to Henley's ex. The Party allows
a certain amount of latitude, but when it comes to gay or trans porn,
they are severe, you know? Evidently, these boring, basic, affable Midwesterners knew at least one CIA agent who was willing to help them
out on the American end and throw them some cash, but they were
having a hard time finding a distributor on the Chinese side. I'm
talking *any* distributor, no matter how much they were offering. Everyone was too scared to deal with these Americans, even through a
Russian proxy, and the Midwesterners would set up meetings for their
token Russian only to have Chinese buyers fail to show up or even call
the ministry, which led to some narrow escapes."

"It sounds like these boring, basic, affable Midwesterners were involved in a business that they didn't really understand."

"Well, it wasn't entirely their fault. Putin has been cracking down
as well. Being gay is equivalent to being a child molester in both countries, so when you get caught and do time, it isn't pretty. So the con-
ventional methods of smuggling that have worked so well for years are
simply evaporating."

"But obviously there are still gay and trans people in China and
Russia," I point out.

"Obviously," says Pez, finishing his salmon and cream cheese.
"Fucking tyrants, you know? Their first step is always to flagrantly deny

reality in order to pretend that they control it. Dumb people are always overawed, but eventually they fall."

"You are very hopeful."

"Gotta stay positive."

"So how does Henley fit into all of this?" I ask.

"Well, after these affable, boring, basic Midwesterners had yet another shipment seized and destroyed, they were about to give up altogether, and that's when your brother got involved. He was idealistic about it. He wanted them to keep going. He bought them endless drinks and endless meals and told them what good patriotic Americans they were, helping to promote human rights in a totalitarian country. Even though he was using a different last name, they eventually figured out who he really was. And that was when they got greedy."

It all adds up. Henley reaching out to the only people around who made any sense to him. Overpromising. Underdelivering.

"They tried to blackmail him, didn't they?" I ask.

"Precisely," says Pez. "You got it." He stares at me sadly, sizing me up.

"So then what?" I ask.

"Well, you can play it out from there," he says. "They threatened to expose his louche and luxurious lifestyle in China—the women he was sleeping with, the drugs he was doing, the conversations he was having about what comes next in China after communism. They said that they would wait until they were safely back in Michigan and then rat him out to the Party unless he used his connections at Nylo to help them smuggle porn into the country and distribute it."

"And that's why he had to leave," I say.

"I am actually unclear about that," says Pez. "You told me he was asking for a job here in the company? It is possible that he never actually told them no. I don't actually know what happened with that part of it. That's where things get hazy."

"Who would know the truth?" I wonder.

"Henley, of course. I'm trying to get access to his email and phone records. And then these affable, basic, boring Midwesterners would know. I've tracked them down." He pauses for effect. "You won't believe this, but they're actually here in New York. Whether they're here because of Henley or it's just a coincidence, I don't know."

"It seems far-fetched that they would be the ones running this scavenger hunt game," I say. "Smugglers and blackmailers don't usually become serial murderers."

"I agree with you," says Pez.

"So what else have you learned?" I ask him, staring at the wall, not sure how all of these pieces fit together.

"In one day?"

"Yes, what else have you learned in one day?"

"Well, I did do some background work," he says, sighing. "Stuff the cops never would have got around to doing since they were so quick to classify your father's death as an accident."

"Such as?"

"His cardiologist told me that he had come in for an appointment earlier in the year. The cardiologist said that there was nothing irregular in any of his tests and that he was frankly surprised to learn that Prescott had a stroke. Although, he was quick to inform me that these things can sometimes come on fast in a person your dad's age and that Prescott had always been prone to high stress and a poor diet."

"Even as skinny as he was," I say. "He ate nothing but garbage and drank like he was trying to embalm himself."

"So that's something," Pez continues. "It doesn't mean that he was murdered or that there was anything exceptional about the way he died. All it means is that there is a possibility there is more to it than we thought."

"What else?" I say.

"I have done deep dives into the background for all the transportation that has been provided as part of this game," says Pez. "Let me start with the most hopeful and obvious lead: the helicopter. Hiring a helicopter and pilot for an indeterminate amount of time is not cheap. The helicopter company is American Helicopters. Nothing strange there. But I figured out who is paying for it and where the money is coming from. You're not going to like this."

"Where is the money coming from, Pez?"

"According to the receipts, all of the transportation was hired or purchased anonymously using funds from a discretionary account supposedly set up and managed by your father. So the money is coming from you."

"That just seems so insane," I say.

"Of course it is," he says. "Actually, I kinda fell in love with this lady at the bank. She is about my age and she has two grown children who live with her, which is not ideal, but we definitely had chemistry. Anyway, you don't care about that. I looked at the signature on the account and on the checks and they were definitely his signatures, but they were two different versions of his signature. One was a little spikier than the other. I asked her for a description of the person who opened up the accounts and she actually remembered your father rather well, even though she said he came in years ago. She described him down to his pink and black striped socks. So. There we are."

"So this was definitely his plan all along?" I say. "So what? It was hijacked somehow?"

"The bad news is that your father was definitely involved. The good news is that we are crossing things off as far as where his plans started and where this Game Master has taken over. I am assuming that your father was in charge of the budget and possibly procuring the technology, but not necessarily in charge of the execution of his plan. This makes sense, right? Your father would be dead when the game would begin. He would need somebody he trusts to set everything up and make sure that they couldn't be bribed or threatened by one of you. Somebody he trusted but that none of you knew about."

I think about this. Faces of strangers loom up over the years, people hanging out with my father in the booths of dark bars, cronies with whom he gamed, business buddies, short-term and long-term love affairs ended by his short attention span and long memory.

"So where does all of this leave us?" I ask.

"Listen, like I said, we do have one good lead. These affable, basic, boring Midwesterners. I know where they are staying in the city. The best way to be certain that they have nothing to do with the murder of your brother is to confront them."

"So when are you planning on doing that?" I ask.

"Actually," he says. "It won't work unless you do it. But I'll go with you. I am willing to do that for you."

21

I make Pez wait while I call Alistair. I ask him if he has cracked the riddle yet. He hasn't. We talk about it for a little bit, trying to puzzle out our memories of our mother and *Sea Farmers* and the sea, but neither of us have any flashes of insight. I call Bernard but he doesn't pick up. I call Gabriella but she hangs up on me as soon as she hears my voice.

"Would it be possible to have their regular phones traced?" I ask Pez. "I want to know where they are at all times."

"So you can follow them? And cheat?"

"Can you do it or not?" I push. "There aren't any rules to this game, evidently. I might as well try to chisel any advantage that I can."

"If anybody can do it, it's Alistair," says Pez. "Which means he probably already has."

"He's too sweet-natured for that," I say. "He wouldn't even dream of it."

"In my experience, nobody enjoys losing if they don't have to lose," says Pez. "A good and gentle nature is its own kind of moral deformity. It is one of the things I love most about humans. The way we hide ourselves. The way we are constantly flowing to fit our circumstances. We are all terrifying creatures of dark intelligence and twisted imagination. Even your brother. He is a creative man. He will compete creatively."

"I don't think he will cheat," I say.

"You just said it wasn't cheating," Pez counters. "Don't you think he will be capable of the same moral contortions?"

"Are you going to help me trace the phones or not?"

"Of course I will help you," says Pez. "But part of helping you is getting you to realize that your siblings are fully human and will want the same things that you want. They will be keeping their own tabs on you. They have their own access to boffins and detectives."

I chew on this for a while.

"So where are we going then?" I ask. "Where are these Midwesterners holed up?"

"They are in K-Town," says Pez. "Staying in one of those pod hotels. They spend all night getting coked up and doing karaoke and eating Korean barbecue."

"Will they be there now?" I ask.

"Not yet," he says. "Not until the sun goes down."

"You knew my mother," I say. "Any insights into today's clue?"

"Well, there are a lot of places where you can stand and see the ocean in this town," says Pez. "But I think we can rule out Manhattan, since it is technically bounded by rivers. Unless she liked to hang out in Battery Park."

"She hated the beach," I say. "She got seasick on boats."

"What about Coney Island?" asks Pez. "It is technically the beach. Did she like rollercoasters and freak shows and parades and all that?"

"No," I say. "She hated Coney Island. She hated amusement parks of all kinds."

"Did she like seafood?" asks Pez. "Some of these restaurants have fairly spectacular aquariums inside them."

Aquariums! I nearly fall out of my chair, the memory comes on so sudden and bright. I instantly understand why only Gabriella and Bernard have figured out the clue.

Alistair and I weren't there when our mother dragged our two youngest siblings to the Coney Island Aquarium at two in the morning to go see the jellyfish. We only heard about it later, after our father called the cops. It was the incident that got her sent away for a few months to a treatment facility. She returned to us just as listless and moody as before, but more subdued.

The whole episode must have been seared into their minds. Alistair, Henley, and I were already in school. The three of us had gone to bed just as we would on a normal night, exhausted by our studies, but Gabriella and Bernard were notoriously bad sleepers and our mother was often indulgent about their bedtimes. Our father was still at work, which I resented back then but which I understand all too well now.

Our mother was up reading *Twenty Thousand Leagues under the Sea* to the smaller children, surely swilling a gin and tonic, wrapped in her robe, alternating between maudlin and angry in a way that was always captivating and seductive and scary. Bernard and Gabriella were mesmerized by her descriptions of ocean life, and they kept turning to the big *Encyclopedia Britannica* in our library to look up pictures of sharks, whales, squid, shoals of bright ocean fish.

But it was the jellyfish that were the most captivating to Bernard and Gabriella. The jellyfish were brainless and beautiful, more like bedazzled free-floating organs than animals. Yet they were also supremely deadly. Bernard was especially compelled by the pictures of the Portuguese man-of-war. He was fascinated and disgusted by the polyp fins and the colorful tendrils hanging below like red cabbage.

"I love jellyfish," our mom said. "They don't lift a finger and just wait for you to drift into them and then they paralyze you dead. Would you like to see them? I know where to see jellyfish right now."

She was staggeringly drunk. But Gabriella and Bernard took the bait. She called for a car and soon the three of them were on their way to the Coney Island Aquarium. They got there right around 3 a.m. Of course, it was closed. Instead, they went to an after-hours aquarium-themed bar across the street. Our mother continued to drink while Gabriella and Bernard were entertained by a group of merchant Marines on leave.

Eventually, our father got home from work. He panicked, waking us up and asking us where Mom and the other kids were. We didn't know, but we were also less worried than he was. We had known our mother our entire lives and were not particularly impressed by her nighttime departures. Her insanity was normal for us in a way that it wasn't for him.

Our mother fell asleep at the bar and slept there until dawn. When she woke up, the three of them tromped off to the aquarium, which was just opening up for the morning, receiving its first batch of tourists. They marched right up to the tank containing the jellyfish, where our mother plopped down on her ass right on the floor, exhausted, while Gabriella and Bernard wandered around in the shimmering half-light, enthralled.

"I never want to leave here," our mother said. "I never want to leave this place right here. I want to stay right here in front of this jellyfish tank forever."

Eventually, she fell asleep again on a bench in front of the shark tank. Luckily, Bernard remembered our home phone number. The aquarium people called our father and he went and picked them all up.

After that episode, Mom went away for a while to "rest." When she returned, she was thinner and paler and seemed even more haunted. It would only be one more year before she blew her brains out in the White Room.

For Alistair, Henley, and me, the part of the episode that we remembered was our dad freaking out and calling every single person he knew in an effort to locate her. He was convinced that she had left him. But Gabriella and Bernard had more tangible memories of the affair.

"Pez, you are a goddamn genius," I tell him. "The aquarium! Exactly right."

I call Alistair again.

"I know the answer to today's hunt," I say. "The jellyfish tank. Remember the time Mom dragged Bernard and Gabriella to Coney Island in the middle of the night?"

"I don't remember that at all," he says. "When was that?"

"Listen, just come up here," I say, hanging up the phone.

Pez smiles at me.

"Why are you helping him?" he asks.

"He's only got one life left," I say. "Until we know what's going on, I don't want anybody to end up like Henley. I'll take the hit this time."

"That's not the only reason," he says. "You aren't telling me everything."

"We'll have to take the train," I say. "By the time we get there, the aquarium will be closed."

"So what?" he says.

"Alistair has the game superpower to open any door," I say.

Alistair, Pez, and I go down to the F train. As I approach the turnstile, all the electronics shut off for them just like they did for me. All three of us click through and go down to the platform. It seems that I am allowed to hook others up with my train pass without consequences.

On the train, I remind Alistair of the time when our mother went crazy and dragged our youngest siblings to the aquarium to kick off her nervous breakdown. He believes me, but I can tell that he is only pretending to remember. So much of what happened in our childhood has fallen to me to tell the story. I was the oldest and I remember everything the most clearly.

It is dark outside by the time the three of us arrive at Coney Island. We walk down Coney Island Avenue past the Applebee's and the IHOP, to the aquarium. It was washed out to sea during Hurricane Sandy and most of it was utterly destroyed, but it has finally been rebuilt. One of the strangest things about the aquarium is that it is open 365 days a year, even on Christmas.

I have been out here on my own quite a bit, actually, especially since it has reopened. I find the shark tanks soothing. Watching the silent predators prowl around ceaselessly calms me.

A security guard stands in front of the aquarium, smoking, but as we approach, he turns and walks away, doing his rounds in the back where they keep the penguins and otters. We don't look like burglars or terrorists. We look like we are on our way to some charity gala. We approach the front doors and Alistair holds up his phone.

The doors open and the red lights in the windows turn to green. Not only have the doors opened for us, but the security system seems to have been shut down as well.

"Incredible," says Alistair with a small grin.

It's dark, but the aquariums are glowing, beautiful. It feels like we are intruding, but then again, it's not like the fish are doing anything important.

I can't remember exactly where the jellyfish are. We walk through one room and then another. As we approach barred security doors, they open magically and the security systems around us continue to shut down. It is clear how someone else might have used this same technology to sneak in here and plant the box in the first place, or to tinker with the elevator at the Empire State Building in order to engineer the crash that killed Henley.

I wonder how well Alistair knows the security-disarming technology. Is it something he helped create and that he will now be able to track down?

"Didn't you make this thing?" I ask him, pointing at his game phone. "Isn't it your design?"

"In some ways," he says. "But I didn't design it to be used like this. Also, I've never seen it work before outside of my lab."

We walk through the entire first building but we don't see any jellyfish. We push open a door to the expansive outdoor exhibits, with Pez leading the way. Outside, there are rock-bounded pens with otters and penguins, all of whom ignore us as we creep past the motion-sensor lights. I see the giant new building that houses the sharks and suddenly realize why I can't remember where the jellyfish are. The jellyfish building isn't open to the public yet.

"Cnidarians," I say. "That means jellyfish. They're over here."

We sneak over to the building that has a giant box jellyfish painted on the side below the pronouncement that says "Coming Soon." Alistair's phone unlocks the door, like all the others.

Most of the tanks are empty, but one is full of floating, bioluminescent jellyfish, blooming in hypnotic patterns. Alistair looks at me.

"You go first," I tell him. "That's the whole point of coming together. So you don't lose all your lives like Henley."

"I couldn't have done this without you," he says.

He walks up to the tank and holds his game phone up to the glass. The phone bleeps and he looks at the screen. He gives me a thumbs-up. I go next. I hold up my phone and wait for the fateful bleep. I brace myself for whatever might come next. I look at the character screen and see that I am in last place and that I have lost a life.

"That wasn't so bad," I say, letting out the breath I didn't know I was holding.

That's when the tank explodes.

22

The glass is blown inward, not out, which is all that saves us from being sliced into pieces by the blast.

The concussion still knocks us backward and off our feet. Most of the water drains down the back of the aquarium into some hidden channel, a design feature by an architect who must have anticipated the horrible event of the tank bursting. The room is not flooded, though the splash still soaks us and the jellyfish come raining down around us, helplessly carried by the crashing wave.

It is a small miracle that none of us are caught up in the tendrils or stung as the jellyfish fall all around us. Their tendrils gyrate for a moment but quickly go still as the water recedes. The jellyfish are useless without a current to buffet them. They are glistening jewels on the aquarium floor, dangerous and evil looking.

For a long moment, Alistair and I simply stare at each other, completely shocked, unsure of whether to run or hide. We feel our faces, our hair, our arms, making sure we aren't cut or bruised. Slowly, we come to our senses. We pick our way around the dying jellyfish. Other small fish in the tank, meant to clean the sides and keep the miniature ecosystem churning, flop around in the pool of brine. The smell of clean, wet salt is overpowering.

Pez got it the worst. The blast flipped him onto his back and slid him into the hallway on his ass, knocking his hat off his head. He is dazed and blinking when we find him and lift him to his feet.

"Are you okay?" I ask.

"I think so," he says. "But there's no reason that I should be. I might have broken my neck."

"If it was me who got here last, the glass would have blown outward," says Alistair. "I would have been killed. That's the message of this catastrophe. The Game Master doesn't want us to go even one day without knowing that they are in control."

"What do we do?" I ask, turning around and around. "Do we stay or do we go?"

"We go," says Pez. "Quickly, before the security guard comes."

We scuttle out the way we came in. We don't see the guard. No alarms go off. Possibly this is because the jellyfish house is still under construction and cameras and alarms haven't been fully installed in here yet, but it is more likely that any alarms have been disabled by the Game Master who planned this ambush.

Soaked, we hop into a cab. The driver is dubious and doesn't want us to get his seats wet. I pay him a hundred in cash in addition to the fare and he takes us back to the Nylo office with limited grumbling.

"If it was the Midwesterners who did this to us, I want to find out tonight," says Pez. "I'm going to change my clothes and pick glass out of my knees and take a shower, and then I will come back and pick you up and we'll go to K-Town."

While Pez goes home to clean up, I decide to take a shower in my office. Alistair says he's had enough. He appears to be in shock.

"Can you believe it?" he says, his skin looking even paler than usual. "There will be another clue tomorrow. We'll have to do this again."

"We should all stop playing," I say. "The cops should handle this and we should stop playing this stupid game."

"You're right, of course," says Alistair, mumbling to himself as he wanders off.

I hop in and out of the shower and it's a good thing I'm quick, because Pez isn't gone long. He collects me from my office, his lips pursed with determination. I get the feeling he has taken what happened at the aquarium personally. He understands the stakes.

"Come on," he says. "This isn't just about you and your family's money anymore. There's a real killer out there. I get it now."

We take a cab to K-Town, just off Times Square. This isn't the Times Square of my childhood. There is nothing grungy about this Times Square or this Korea Town, at least on the surface. The restaurants and dessert parlors are bright pink and lime green, lit up with neon and festive video menus that showcase barbecue feasts. We walk through the streets filled with drunken but well-behaved revelers as pop music blares from clean arcades and family-friendly record shops.

Pez checks something on his phone and then doubles back to an alley we already passed. We walk down it to a nondescript building entrance and then into a long hallway empty of decoration.

"Is this really the place?" he asks doubtfully, checking his phone again.

We go back outside and Pez looks at the address numbers on the building.

"This is it," he says, shaking his head. We go back in and march to the elevator. He punches the button for a middle floor. When we get out, we find ourselves in the back of a line for a massive Korean restaurant. We can smell thin slivers of beef burning on open flames, and catch glimpses of people hidden away in private booths, occluded from each other by the high seats. It is a cave-like, shimmering room where patrons are getting drunk on small bottles of plum wine and sake.

"The karaoke rooms are in the back," says Pez. "But I've been told they're reservation only."

I catch the eye of the hostess, a young woman with skin so white and glowing that she could be made of pearl slathered in paste, and inconspicuously offer her a rolled-up stack of hundreds. She smiles slightly and nods, taking the bills from my hand casually as she leads us back to the karaoke rooms, glancing over her shoulder to make sure management doesn't see her taking our graft to privilege us over those with reservations.

"It's two fifty for a room for the night," she says when we make it into the back. I let her charge my credit card, rolling my eyes. There are five private rooms, each with a cutout picture of a different Korean pop star on the door. All the rooms are full. The hostess looks at me knowingly and I slip her yet another hundred-dollar bill.

She barges into one of the rooms (full of drunken Russians, not our Midwesterners) and proceeds to have a long, protracted argument with them. Eventually they leave, spitting on the ground, cursing her, cursing us, but also too drunk to actually care very much.

We take over the room and sit there for a minute, unsure what to do next.

Suddenly Pez stands up. "I'll go investigate," he says and wobbles off, feigning drunkenness. I watch from our doorway as he barges into each room in turn, pretending to be so wasted that he has forgotten where he is really going. Three doors down he lingers, then looks knowingly back at me. He shuts the door and skitters back down the hall to our room.

"There are five of them," he says. "They are all beefy men in their early forties, I'd guess, with deep-set blue piggy eyes and greasy beards. Actually, they don't seem so bad."

"You like everyone," I say. "What song were they singing?"

"'Jolene,'" says Pez, raising an eyebrow.

"Fascinating," I say, surprised by the choice. Dolly Parton's not my first pick, but she is classic.

"They were all belting out the lyrics, arms draped over each other's shoulders. One of them was visibly weeping."

"Let me handle this," I say.

We creep over to the private room together. I charge in first, but I don't say anything until Pez closes the door behind us. I can feel him backing me up and this makes me slightly brave.

The men all stare at me, flabbergasted. I can tell immediately that they know who I am. I try to maintain my composure, to give nothing away, to meet them imperiously on the level of elite privilege that surely I must represent to these pudding-filled sad sacks.

"Gentlemen," I begin.

One by one, they stand up. They form a semicircle around me, towering over my small frame as if I am a Union major general and they are my staff officers, ready to take a rebel bullet to protect me.

Then, as a unit, they all lean into me, squeezing me in a devastating group hug that nearly knocks me off my feet. They are overcome with emotion. I try to back away, but they lower their heads, leaning on me and leaning on each other, assaulting me with weepy neediness. It is a good thing they don't seem to mean me any harm because I would be powerless against their coordinated beer-cheese bear hug.

"He was so beautiful," one of them says. "Just a damn angel on Earth."

"He put my youngest through beauty school," another says.

"He got my jaw broke, that son of a bitch," says an especially burly one, pulling a hand free from the hug so he can rub his close-cropped beard. "But then he paid to have it all fixed up and even made them give me a real chin. Then he bought me a goddang Jaguar car."

"We miss him so much," says the clearest-eyed one of the bunch, who also happens to be the shortest and trimmest. "He taught us how to be better men, actually. More humane. More feminist."

"He also taught us how to be worse men!" chimes in the last one.

Everyone laughs. And it dawns on me that they are all talking about Henley.

This is some kind of funeral or wake for him. I can't help but be touched that I am not alone in my misery, even if they were the ones who killed him.

"We have to be honest with you," says one of the beef-eating bruisers. "We came here to the big city to find him and rough him up."

"To scare him," says another.

"To make sure he would keep his word and help us bring trans porn into China. It's our calling in life. Our Don Quixote windmill."

"We should never have doubted him," says the one with the new chin.

"He must have told you everything," says the one who admitted they were here looking for him. "You must already know about our plans."

"What happened to him?" asks the first one. "Was it the Chinese that killed him? The Russians? Was it really an accident? We are all so confused. We don't know what to do now or where to go. Should we stay here? Should we go back to Michigan?"

"I'm never going back to Michigan," says the short man I've pegged as their leader. "My wife is in Michigan."

They all laugh again.

Then there is a long moment of silence. I don't know quite what to say. It is blisteringly apparent to both Pez and me that these men had nothing to do with Henley's death. First of all, none of them are even close to the right body type to be the elusive Game Master. Second, their sweaty and overpowering American good nature is almost palpable. These are not conniving killers; these are dopy bruisers.

"He really was very beautiful," I say. They all hold their breath, wondering why I have chosen to hunt them down and invade their meeting and what other words of wisdom I might impart. "He was also a total asshole. Drinks on me, fellas. Let's celebrate him properly. Let's celebrate all the good that he did and all the lies that he told."

The five huge men cheer so loudly that my heart rattles the bars of its cage.

They all begin singing the chorus to "Don't Look Back in Anger," out of key.

"Wait, wait," says the leader. "Let me find the song in the booklet."

"No, let her pick the next one!" says New Chin, pulling me in for another hug.

23

Pez and I end up staying out all night drinking with these affable brutes, singing every song we know and telling stories about Henley.

The sly and cunning hostess gives away the room I generously bribed her for to a different band of surly and emaciated Russians with gold teeth and Caesar cuts. You just can't trust anyone in the service industry anymore.

Hanging out with these Michiganders is therapeutic. I learn all about Henley's adventures in China, about how he has made friends and enemies in the vast expat community there.

More information only confirms that none of these men had anything to do with Henley's death. They are fun-loving, good-natured doofuses. The only reason they would have come into contact with someone like Henley would be because they were all out of place and feeling homesick at the same time in the same place.

All of these burly men are very passionate about getting gay and transgender porn into China. Eventually we get so drunk that we start brainstorming ways to make this happen using various NGOs and printers that Nylo uses to make games in China. I am just as seduced by them as Henley must have been.

Eventually, Pez excuses himself, saying that he has to sleep if he means to keep investigating in the morning.

I can see why Henley and these men became friends. I can see why he wanted to help them out, even if he oversold his ability to do so. I do wonder if there might have been somebody else involved in all of their plans. Somebody who remains hidden. An agent of China determined to prevent their smuggling operation, perhaps, but unwilling to commit any crimes in China, thereby preventing an international incident. Waiting until Henley came here to make a move against him.

I just don't know enough yet. I finally excuse myself, deflecting their drunken pleas to stay, and get a car back to the office. I take another shower and eat some old pastries that were left in the break room. An entire roast chicken has been delivered as a death gift, along with some fingerling potatoes. I open the plastic clamshell and pull the meat right off the bone, alternating with bites of cold potatoes spiced with rosemary and garlic.

I pass out fully dressed in my bed. I only manage to sleep for two hours or so before Peter gently wakes me up, a concerned look on his face.

"Just let me sleep," I moan. "I'm sick."

"It's the police," he says. "They are in your office waiting. They say they have some questions for you."

"Fine," I say, rubbing the sleep out of my eyes. "Tell them I'm coming."

I rouse myself and grab a carbonated iced coffee from my refrigerator and drink it down. Then I crack open another one to sip more casually.

I wash my face and put on some makeup. Maybe these police will finally have a lead.

My office turns out to be extremely crowded. Two giant bald men with earphones are standing by the door, hands behind their backs. They must be my new security detail. They don't look at me when I enter the room. I can see the bulges in their suit jackets where they're concealing guns or Tasers or cans of Raid or whatever.

Detectives Jay and Rutledge sit across from my desk, lounging in chairs with their legs crossed, sipping giant cups of coffee and eating glistening, gooey Danishes that Peter must have brought them.

I sit down behind my desk. My brain feels soggy and soft. I turn the air conditioning up as high as it will go, hoping that maybe the extreme cold will wake me up.

"Officers," I say. "Did you catch the person who killed my brother and who is trying to kill all the rest of us?"

Rutledge and Jay exchange a look. "We're working on it," says Jay. "It's all part of a process."

"What does that mean?" I ask. "Do you have any leads or not? Were you able to trace these game phones or figure out who this Game Master might be?"

"We are analyzing all the data down at the lab," says Rutledge. "You really have to trust us that we are on top of everything here."

"So what do you want from me?" I say, taking a sip of coffee. "You got my statement, right?"

"Yes," says Jay. "We got your statement. We got your statement and all the other statements."

At that moment, Angelo Marino bursts into the room, making the office just a little more crowded. He seems out of sorts. His eyes are popping out of his head with tension, but he smooths down his suit jacket and slicks back his hair before speaking. "You don't have to answer any of their questions."

The detectives look at him, gritting their teeth, and then look back at me.

"Look," says Jay. "We know you went to the Coney Island Aquarium last night. There was an explosion and a lot of jellyfish were killed. We want to know why you were there and what happened."

"Are you charging me with a crime?" I ask. I look over at Angelo Marino. He shakes his head slightly. *Don't answer them*, he is saying.

"Not exactly," says Jay. "We don't think you had anything to do with the destruction of the property there, which major crimes wants to call a terrorist attack. But you are a witness, and you are certainly guilty of trespassing."

"Someone is trying to kill my whole family," I say. "I was there because I was playing this game, which is what you told me to do. Should I stop playing? Are you willing to put us all under police protection?"

Rutledge snorts, laughing.

"We still aren't sure your brother was murdered," says Jay. "We have no evidence of that. So you just go ahead and slow down a little bit, okay? Slow down and let the professionals handle the crimes."

"And why don't you tell us real slowly how everything went down at the aquarium?" says Rutledge. "We want to help you. We are on your side. But we need to have something to tell the counterterrorism people, or they are going to want us to freeze your accounts and go public with what is happening. Is the Nylo Corporation declaring war on fish?"

"Look," I say, shooting down an anguished look from Angelo Marino. "I was there. I was playing this game. The clue yesterday led us to the aquarium. When we got there and held our phones up to the jellyfish tank, it exploded. I think if one of us had been out of lives, it would have killed us. You need to figure out how the bomb worked. Dust everything for prints. It's an aquarium! Surely there are fingerprints on glass somewhere."

"All the evidence has been sent to the lab," says Rutledge. "We'll let you know if we find anything."

"And so what the hell am I supposed to do in the meantime?" I ask, slamming down my iced coffee in frustration.

Rutledge and Jay look at each other.

"Well, that's one of the reasons we're here," Jay says. "We intend to be with you today when the Game Master calls. We're going to try and get him to talk."

"It could be a her," I point out, sounding like Olivia.

"That is statistically quite unlikely," says Jay. "Anyway, we want you to know that we're taking this whole situation very seriously. We're glad to see that you have hired your own security. We suggest you don't go anywhere without them. The next time you run off to solve one of these clues you should let us know where you're headed so we can stake the place out and make sure you won't be in any danger. Can you do that for us?"

"Certainly," I say, feeling somewhat mollified. "So, you two are just going to hang out here all morning until the Game Master calls?"

"We'd like permission to question some of the people who work here, if they would be willing to cooperate," says Detective Rutledge. "Obviously, they have the right to refuse. But we think it would be helpful if everyone cooperates, as long as we are here."

"I think you'll find everyone at Nylo is very willing to cooperate with your investigation," says Angelo Marino. "As long as I am allowed to be in the room with you and help protect the employees here from any violations of their civil liberties or from accidentally saying something they don't mean. You know how cops can twist words when they don't want to work very hard to crack a case." He offers his most polite sneer.

Detectives Jay and Rutledge both smile back.

"Of course," says Detective Jay. "You have a business to run here, after all."

"Remind me again why the two of you are the ones assigned to this case?" I ask. "Aren't you Midtown tunnel cops?"

"Detectives," says Jay. "Midtown Underground Tunnel Detectives. That's the precinct where the body is at, I'm afraid. Can't be helped. Tunnels and elevators, that's our beat."

"Right," I say. "Tunnels and elevators."

I stand up and motion to the door. The two detectives slink out. Angelo Marino hangs back a moment, looking at me pensively.

"I feel like we should call some different police," I say. "Can't we get a second opinion?"

"I'm afraid it doesn't work like that," he says.

"Isn't this the sort of thing that you elevate to the FBI? We are public figures. Tunnel and elevator cops aren't going to solve this thing."

"I'll see what I can do about elevating the profile of this case," says Angelo Marino. "However, there is also the company to think about. Do we really want to have the federal government and the media involved? They will certainly use this as an opportunity to audit us and check into all of our business dealings. I'm sure the State Department will be interested in Henley's time in China, and the FTC will be interested in your latest acquisition. Are you sure we shouldn't just handle this ourselves if we can?"

I don't really have an answer for him. He leaves, following the detectives, ready to serve as a silent sentinel as they question employees, reminding the workers by his mere presence that the company comes first, that the most important thing is not to incriminate Nylo in any way, even accidentally.

I look at the two security guards. They stand stoically, nearly identical in their navy suits, not moving but briefly making eye contact with me before returning their gaze out the window behind me, as if at any moment armed soldiers of fortune might swing in on grappling hooks and start mowing us down with automatic weapons.

"Have you strapping fellows ever prevented somebody from being killed in a high-stakes augmented reality game with a twenty-billion-dollar family fortune on the line before?"

Neither of them responds. They stare at me and I stare at them.

Eventually, they realize that my question is not rhetorical—that I actually do want to know if they have any experience that might help them prevent me from getting blown up by some mad game master. They exchange a glance and I have their answer before they can utter the words.

"No, ma'am," they say in unison.

24

My new bodyguards are named Ed White and Mel Fuller. They have both been incarcerated, but not at the same time and not in the same prison. One of them comes from a family of cops. The other comes from a family of Marines.

As a result of my feverish interrogation, I learn that they both are the youngest children of big respectable families and that they have both had problems with addiction in the past, but say they've put that behind them.

"You have so much in common," I say, looking first at Ed and then at Mel.

"I guess that's true, ma'am," agrees Ed, not seeming to find my statement terribly interesting.

I realize that I am slightly delirious from lack of sleep. The timid reactions of these bodyguards to my questions makes me assume I am coming off like some kind of manic idiot. *I need to center myself. To recalibrate.*

I wander around the building for a bit, chitchatting with assistants and vice presidents as my bodyguards trail behind me.

"This is Ed and Mel," I tell everyone, introducing them and making them shake hands. I have to get in front of how weird everything is if I don't want to seem like I am retreating into some kind of literal or emotional bunker to deal with the trauma of losing my father and my brother. Ed and Mel are pleasant enough to my staff. People keep offering them food and drinks and they slowly relax, becoming less menacing in general.

The emotional timbre of the space is hard to gauge, mainly because I can tell people are being extra-sensitive around me. There are reporters camped down in the lobby, and I make the decision not to give any interviews: not to the *Times*, not to the *Post*, not to the *Journal*. I don't know what I would even say. Eventually, the story about this game will leak out somewhere, but I haven't yet figured out the best way to manage the fallout. The game makes us look crazy. It makes us look terrible.

But, then again, we are crazy and terrible.

Honestly, I barely know what to do with myself until noon rolls around. When I return to my office, I am a nervous wreck. Alistair is already waiting there for me. He doesn't look any better than me. There are dark circles under his eyes and his hands are shaking.

"Any luck tracing those phones?" I ask him.

"All I can tell you is that this Game Master is somewhere in the United States and probably somewhere in New York," he says. "But that doesn't mean much. They could just be some lackey hired by the real person in charge."

"Finding them would be a good start anyway," I note.

"I'll keep narrowing it down," he says. "I'm running a carnivore program to help triangulate the likely location of the Game Master, since the Game Master must call all four of us at once. Actually, the longer you can keep them talking on the phone, the better chance I'll have at figuring out who it is. It won't help us trace the call, but the more data we collect, the better chance we have of unscrambling the voice modulation."

"You can really do that?" I ask.

"If you can rattle them and make them speak in their most natural cadence possible, we should be able to get more fruitful data," says

Alistair. "People have patterns in how they speak that we can abstract. If we have suspects, for instance, we can match them against any voice profile that we generate. We might not be able to figure out exactly what this person sounds like, but we will be able to possibly eliminate false positives and to narrow down our suspects."

"Okay," I say. "I'll keep them talking."

Detectives Jay and Rutledge return around 11:45, trailed by Angelo Marino. I excuse myself and step into my bedroom, where I call Bernard, who does not answer. I try Gabriella, who does.

"Alistair and I nearly died yesterday," I tell her, then give her a synopsis of our adventure the night before. "The aquarium blew up when I held up my phone to it."

"That's terrifying!" gasps Gabriella. "I'm so glad you're both okay! You must be freaking out about today's call."

"A bit," I admit. "Bernard won't answer any of my calls. Do you know where he is? We need to coordinate here. We need to all be on the same page."

"I'm not sure that he actually believes Henley is dead," she confides. "He thinks his death is some kind of con or joke or hustle, that it's part of your strategy to win. He thinks you two cooked it up together."

"What?" I say, my features freezing with incredulity. "You can't be serious."

"Yeah, he told me not to believe anything you say," she continues. "He says the cops are in on it. He says Angelo is working for you, because he needs you to win so he can keep his job and because he knows none of the rest of us will keep him on. He says you are the only one who wants the company to even keep going. He says the rest of us would just sell it, so this is all a conspiracy so that you can stay in charge. He says your plan is to make us all feel ashamed of ourselves for having lost to you, to make us feel like you earned the right to stay on as CEO. That it will feel fair because you have beaten us. Like this is all part of Dad's natural fascism."

"How does he explain Henley, though?" I say. "Henley is dead, Gabriella. Does he think I killed him?"

"He thinks Henley is faking his own death," says Gabriella. "He says there are about a thousand reasons that Henley would want to fake his own death. To get away from the Chinese, to get out of his debts, to get away from all the girls he's dating."

"That is insane," I say.

"Listen," says Gabriella. "I don't believe him, but his explanation isn't any more insane than any other explanation for what's happening."

I don't know what to say to this. She has a point. They have no reason to trust me, and they certainly have no reason to trust our father. To say that he played favorites is an understatement. Bernard, Henley, and Gabriella were never offered jobs in the company—not even meaningless posts where they couldn't do any harm. Our father never pretended to be interested in training them to know the family business. There was never one moment when he thought their talents might be useful in helping us stay on top.

"It doesn't matter what Bernard says," I finally say. "We have to stick together. Alistair and I are down to our last life. If Bernard isn't going to agree not to play, then we have to at least all make sure that we beat Bernard. He has two lives left. He can stand to lose one today."

Gabriella is silent for a long time.

"He told me you would say that," she says.

"I'm sure he did, but that doesn't make it any less true," I say.

"No, what you're saying makes sense," she agrees, sighing. "Alright, I'm on board. We'll all work together this time."

She hangs up on me. It is 11:55. I return to my office and take out my game phone. Alistair does the same. The police detectives don't appear to have any special equipment or anything. They're just sitting in their chairs, looking slightly bored and skeptical.

Might as well start drinking. I pour myself a bourbon and go around the room, seeing if anyone else is interested. No takers. Just as I am sitting down, the Nylo Corporation theme comes chirping from our game phones.

"Here we go," I say.

When the Game Master appears this time, I nearly drop my drink. Staring up at me is a werewolf face, like the mask worn by the person who was responsible for Olivia's bike crash.

"You son of a bitch," I cry, squeezing the phone as if I might crack it in half. The security guards and cops all stand up, alarmed by my sudden venom. Rage flows through me in a cleansing, overwhelming torrent.

"Temper, temper," reprimands the Game Master from behind the wolf mask. "Looks like young Bernard is in the lead going into day three. Are you Nylos ready for the next clue?"

"How come you tried to kill us at the aquarium?" asks Alistair. "It's a miracle none of us were injured. We could have smashed in our skulls by slipping on water or gotten stung in the neck by a jellyfish."

"I'm sure I don't know what you are talking about," says the Game Master. "If I may make a suggestion? I am not particularly keen on the way you have been working together. There can be only one winner after all, no matter how closely you collaborate. Families help each other. But families have a hierarchy."

This is a threat. If Alistair had actually lost all his lives at the aquarium, I would have died along with him. Alistair looks at me across my desk, narrowing his eyes, shaking his head.

"Here comes the next clue," says the Game Master. "Are you ready?"

"You hurt my daughter, you son of a bitch," I blurt out. I want to tell them I am going to murder them. I want to tell them I am going to rip off their arms and beat them to death with their arm bones. I want to tell them I am going to burn their corpse and dump the ashes in a Taco Bell toilet tank, where they will be mixed with liquid shit and flushed out to sea. But there are lots of witnesses, two of whom are cops.

"You are going to get justice," I say instead, relatively calmly. "Justice is going to come to you."

I look at the cops meaningfully, gesturing to the phone. *Are they just going to sit there?*

"Excuse me, uh, Game Master?" says Detective Jay. "This is the NYPD. We need you to stop whatever is happening here and turn yourself in for questioning. Please take off your mask and identify yourself. Whatever Prescott Nylo paid you to do, the contract is hereby terminated."

"I'm sorry, I can't hear you," says the Game Master. "Are you on speakerphone? Here is the next clue: 'They painted it together, at the top of the boot.' Good luck, Nylos! This game is getting so close!"

"Wait," I say. "Who are you? Where are you?"

There is a long period of silence, the werewolf face unwavering. The detectives finally look interested. Ed and Mel are tense, ready for action. Then the line goes dead and the clue floats to the front of the game phones, shimmering over a background of raining cowboy boots.

I hate myself that the answer to this riddle comes to me almost instantly. I can't help but puzzle it out. That's the way these sorts of things work: you either get the answer fast or not at all. I look at Alistair to see if he has figured it out yet. He stares at his hands. I open my mouth to tell him what I know, and then I shut it again.

He doesn't have kids like I do. Neither does Gabriella. What the hell am I supposed to do? Help them? Like I just promised?

25

My phone rings immediately. It is Gabriella.

"I am freaking out," she says. "I don't know the answer to this one."

"That was me yesterday," I say, looking around the room.

"You said you would help me," she says. "You said we would work together."

"Let me call you back," I say, hanging up.

Alistair finally looks up. He is grinning.

"You know this one," he says.

"Yeah, I know this one," I say. "How can you tell?"

"I've been playing board games against you my entire life," he says. "I know when you're looking at the board struggling to come up with your next move and when you have a good position or an unbeatable strategy."

"The top of the boot," I say. "The boot is Italy. What is at the top of Italy?"

"Switzerland?" he says.

"Monaco," says Ed, unexpectedly. We all turn to look at him.

"That's true," I say. "But I mean within Italy."

"Genoa," he continues. "Also San Marino and Bologna."

"Jesus," says Detective Jay. "That's pretty amazing. Are you some kind of geography savant?"

"Bologna!" says Alistair. "It's a reference to Little Bologna. That little restaurant. We used to go there all the time."

"And why did we used to go there all the time?"

"Because it was right below Dad's old office."

Understanding dawns in his eyes.

"That was the office that he was renting when he and Mom first started dating," he says. "The one she made him repaint like fifty times because she could never settle on a color she liked."

"He always had a perpetual migraine on account of the paint smell," I say. "Not that he ever dared to complain."

"So one of these boxes is in that office?" says Detective Rutledge.

"Yep," I say. "Listen, Alistair, you go ahead and tell Gabriella. Wait for her here and then the two of you can walk over to Hell's Kitchen together. It's going to take you a while."

"Where are you going?" he asks.

"I want to check up on my daughters," I say. I look at Ed and Mel, my two new best friends. "I guess you guys are coming with me, huh? Will you be okay, Alistair? Will you be safe alone?"

"I've got my own guys," says Alistair, gesturing outside where two more security guards are waiting. "And I'm sure Gabriella will have hers."

I make a quick phone call to the security agency, letting them know that Olivia has already been attacked once and that we need tighter security around the twins. I call Ben and tell him to meet me at the school, letting him know that there has been an emergency. I call the school and tell them to have Olivia and Jane waiting when I arrive. I call downstairs to one of the accountants and tell them to get ten thousand in cash and put it in a briefcase. When I leave my office, Jay and Rutledge are discussing where they should get lunch.

It is slightly maddening that Bernard has told Gabriella that I am manipulating everything to put myself in a better position, but I don't know what to do about it. It's typical Bernard. He's always been exceedingly paranoid and cynical, a perverse contradiction to his otherwise extremely analytical mind.

People who are good at narrowing down the world to sets of critical, quantifiable information are always the same people who crave simple, clear answers to the incomprehensible madness of existence. And there is always someone unscrupulous to provide those answers. Look it up: engineers, dentists, and surgeons are the most likely professions to become terrorists. These people are always happy to have a right answer that makes the squirmy horribleness of uncertainty disappear, even if that right answer is utter bullshit or a self-serving justification for violence or selfishness, like Bernard's decision that Henley's death is somehow fake and only meant to help me consolidate my own power. Bernard would have made a great engineer, if he wasn't such a useless gambling addict.

Well, fuck Bernard. Maybe he would feel differently if someone in a wolf mask broke the arm of one of his boys.

I hop on the train and head to Jane and Olivia's school with Ed and Mel in tow. We make quite a conspicuous threesome. It is easy to tell that they are my security detail. The train is empty at this time of day but they refuse to sit. Instead, they stand on either side of me like sentinels, looking suspiciously at every person who gets on or off the train.

What kind of weirdo needs security goons but takes the fucking train?

We get off at the stop nearest the girls' school and I practically run to the front desk. Ben is already waiting for me, his brow furrowed.

"What the hell?" he says. "What is this emergency? Does this have to do with Henley?"

"Dude," I say. "Just shut up and do what I say."

Ed's phone rings and he picks it up. He has a hurried conversation and then he runs outside, returning with two more bodyguards that look exactly like him. We all crowd around the front desk.

"Where are they?" I ask the woman staffing the desk, tapping my fingers impatiently on the counter. "They should be here already."

"I don't know where the girls are," she says, catching on to my panic.

I almost call the cops again when Olivia and Jane both come sauntering down the hall, looking irritated.

"Where the hell were you?" I ask, gathering them into a hug and nearly crying with frustration and anxiety.

"We were in speech class," says Olivia, keeping her sling protected from my squeezing arm.

"We were right in the middle of a debate," adds Jane. "We had to finish or our team would have been super-pissed at us."

"Does this school not understand the word 'emergency'?" I say, seething.

Now there are the three of us and six security guards: two each for Olivia and Jane, plus Ed and Mel.

"Are you going to tell us what is going on or are you going to just let us all be freaked out for no reason?" demands Ben. "I had to get Coach Jackson to cover for me and that means I'm going to owe him. Teaching his remedial history class is like being in a prison riot."

I look at Ed and Mel for support. They smirk at me. What the hell does Ben know about being in a prison riot? He's soft and naive; he hasn't seen the kind of real-life shit Ed and Mel and I have.

"Look," I say. "The three of you are going to get out of town for a while, and these nice men are going to go with you. It's going to be an all-expenses-paid sudden vacation to Nantucket for a week or so, just until I figure out what's going on around here."

"But I've got Quiz Bowl this weekend," complains Ben.

I take a deep breath to swallow my annoyance. "This is life or death," I enunciate slowly. "My dad died Saturday, possibly under suspicious circumstances. Henley was murdered on Wednesday, the same day some lunatic ran down our daughter. So yeah, Quiz Bowl is out." He goes ashen and for once in his life doesn't argue with me.

I bend down in front of Olivia and look her in the eyes, not wanting to freak her out but needing to know more about the person who attacked her before I let her leave. Surely the three of them will be safe on a damn island with four bodyguards watching their every move. Ben is a smug asshole loser who I hate, but he is actually fairly shrewd and careful when appropriately motivated, like any good New Yorker.

"Olivia, can you tell me anything else at all about the person in the werewolf mask who broke your arm?" I ask.

"Mom, it's not broken," she admonishes. "Just sprained." But then my words click and she exclaims, "So you believe me! Finally."

"I definitely believe you," I say. "Do you think you can remember how tall they were or if their nails were painted or not, for instance? Did you get the sense that they were a woman or a man?"

"Mom," says Jane. "Sex isn't real. Only gender is real, and only sorta kinda real."

"Well, did you get the sense that they were trying to present as a woman or a man?" I ask, exasperated.

Olivia thinks about it and then shakes her head.

"They were kinda short," she says. "It seemed like an accident, actually. I think they were trying to just scare me but then they opened the door too late and I ran into them. They got away as fast as they could. I think it was a man, but like, not a big one. Not like one of these security guys. Oh, and they were definitely white. Like, I could see their neck a little bit. Their clothes were baggy, so I guess maybe it was somebody more, like, female-identified or something, but probably not, right? Like, only a dude would be that incompetent and then wouldn't care if I was, like, dying in the street about to get hit by a car, right?"

"Right," I say, unconvinced. I wish she could give us more information, but this is at least something.

Ben pulls me aside.

"I don't really have time to get into all of this," I say, anticipating his questions. "I have to take the train to Hell's Kitchen, and I have to beat Bernard there or I will lose my last life. He has a helicopter and I only have a train pass, so he has a clear advantage."

Ben stares at me and then shakes his head, bewildered.

"I haven't been getting much sleep lately," I say. "Listen, you will all be fine in Nantucket. The girls love it there and it will only be for a week. Their grandfather and uncle just died, for god's sake. I am going to tell the school that this is a family retreat, which is mostly true, okay? You are going to take care of them and help them not freak out, and you are going to make sure that Olivia doesn't break her other arm. I will try to join you in a few days, and hopefully I can tell you more then, but for right now, every single person in this family is in danger, including you. If you absolutely need to do this dumb Quiz Bowl, I guess I can't stop you. It's up to you how important the lives of your daughters are to you."

"Do we really need four bodyguards?" asks Ben. "Won't one be enough? Or three?"

"A square house has four sides," I say. "One bodyguard for each side. When you get up there, find a place to rent in town and pay in cash, okay? Don't use your own phone to find an available Airbnb. Go through the security agency, which knows how to do that kind of thing securely. And keep a low profile, dammit. Don't let the girls go out alone."

Ben nods, taking me seriously, which makes me relax a little.

"I don't know what's going on," he says, "but freaking out for no reason isn't like you. It really must be serious."

"I don't know for sure, but I think it is," I say. "And all the responsibility is falling on me. The cops are useless and my siblings are useless and even Angelo Marino is useless. I feel like I'm all coked-up and having a panic attack, but I'm mostly sober, if you can believe that."

"You look like you need some rest," he says. "But actually, you look good. I haven't seen you so excited about anything in years. You've got some color in your face, finally."

"I guess somebody trying to murder me has brought out the best in me," I joke half-heartedly. "Now get the hell to the airport. I want you to fly commercial instead of taking the Nylo jet. Anything that says Nylo on it is dangerous right now."

I snap my fingers and one of the new security guards brings me the briefcase full of cash.

"There's ten grand in this briefcase," I tell Ben. "You probably won't need all of it. Just keep the rest or whatever."

"You don't really know what things cost anymore, do you? How much do you think an apple costs, for instance?"

"Don't be a jerkwad. If you need more, just call Nylo and ask for it. They'll get it to you through the security agency. Don't use your bank card. Don't use your credit card. Only use your phones in an emergency, okay?"

26

I hop back on the train, accompanied by Ed and Mel. They don't quite seem to know what to say to me.

"You guys can sit down if you want," I suggest. "I don't think there are any assassins about to target me in this train car."

"You never know, ma'am," says Ed.

"You don't think I'm overreacting, do you?" I ask. "I mean, we have had death threats and stalkers in the past at Nylo. Disgruntled employees, overeager fans. But nothing like this. I mean, my brother is dead, right? Somebody tried to break my daughter's arm."

"You are definitely not overreacting," says Mel. "Anyway, we are providing a service. It's not our job to figure out whether or not you need our help. We don't ever think about it like that. If you are using our services, you have a good reason."

"If it were your daughters, you would do the same thing, right?" I say.

"Absolutely," says Mel. "What is money for if it doesn't buy you security and peace of mind?"

"Damn right," I say. "Listen, my brother Bernard is not returning my calls and he won't talk to me. But if this person is targeting my girls, then there is every reason to suspect that he is also targeting Bernard's boys. Is there any way you can get a message to him through the security guards assigned to him? Can you tell him what happened to Olivia and that he should send Phoebe and the boys away for a while? Maybe to her parents' place?"

Ed and Mel furrow their brows and exchange worried looks.

"He has instructed his security detail not to interact with the rest of us," says Mel. "But we'll see what we can do."

"Great," I say. "Yeah, see what you can do."

Incredibly, unaccountably, Little Bologna still exists and is still open. The building is as old as the pyramids and in far worse shape. It is leaning slightly and there are actually giant steel beams at an angle attached to the side and buried in the ground. The beams are holding the building up, keeping it from slumping sideways and crashing down on some lamb-and-rice cart guy. It occurs to me the restaurant should be renamed Little Pisa. It's funny, but I don't laugh.

I look around for Gabriella and Alistair, but I don't see them. I call Alistair.

"Where are you?" I ask when he picks up the phone.

"We're almost there," he says. "It's an extremely long walk. We stopped to get some lunch. I never do this much walking. Actually, stick your hand up in the air."

I stick my hand up in the air. I see somebody down the avenue waving back at me. I hang up. My brother and sister soon jog up to meet me, trailed by four security guards.

"I can't believe we just did that," says Alistair. "My legs are cramping. I don't even own a pair of tennis shoes. I think there are holes in the bottom of my loafers."

"Do you even remember this old office?" I ask Gabriella.

"Not really," she says. "I remember Little Bologna, but not the office."

The building is essentially condemned and so the street entrance to the upper floors is chained and bolted. We have to go in through the restaurant to get upstairs. Our security detail fans out, covering us from every side.

"Let us check the place out first," says Ed.

Little Bologna is your basic bad New York Italian restaurant: white tablecloths and an ancient waiter milling around aimlessly, staring out the window with a towel over his shoulder. There is a giant faded picture of St. Catherine on one wall. When he sees us, the waiter grabs a stack of menus and holds them out begrudgingly, but the security guards trudge past him to the service stairwell through the kitchen.

"You aren't gonna eat?" he asks, astonished to see the six large men disappear behind him.

"We'll eat," I say.

Gabriella, Alistair, and I all take menus and sit down in one of the booths. We order coffee and cannoli.

"Our dad's first office was upstairs," I tell the waiter. "Nylo Games. Do you remember Prescott Nylo?"

"Ah yes, Mr. Nylo!" says the old man, a smile brightening his solemn face. "He hasn't been here in ages. Did he forget about me? Did he forget about the good times?"

"He's dead, unfortunately," I say. "He died last Saturday."

"Oh my god," says the waiter, nearly dropping the menus he'd just collected from us. "He was younger than me. Oh my god!"

"Has there been anybody suspicious in the building lately?" I ask. "Anybody you've never seen before?"

The waiter looks up at St. Catherine for a moment, then shakes his head. "No," he says. "Nobody new ever comes here. Nobody suspicious, nobody unsuspicious. Mostly nobody at all, you know?" He keeps shaking his head as he plods off toward the kitchen

The three of us sit in silence until the coffee and cannoli arrive. The ancient waiter's hands are jittery as he sets down the cups and saucers in front of us. I reach for my coffee and take a tentative sip, then a longer one, pleasantly surprised to find it's not weak and watery, but rich and dark, how I like it.

Gabriella picks up her cannoli and I notice she actually doesn't look all that bad. I get the sense that she is sleeping okay. I'm a little shocked, since she's usually the most sensitive one in our family, easily spooked and always urging us to try some new method to deal with generalized anxiety, a miracle food or breathing technique that she swears has changed her life.

Even though she doesn't look visibly depleted, she seems distracted. She takes tiny bites of crispy pastry and glances around the room. She's wearing bright red tennis shoes and red velour sweatpants, which I guess betrays the fact that she is getting used to having to walk everywhere in this game. All of a sudden, her eyes light up and she grins.

"I remember the smell of this place now," says Gabriella. "Garlic, smoke, and fresh paint."

"They invented *Sea Farmers* right upstairs," I say. "They used to come down here to Little Bologna and playtest it after hours and the bartender would keep the place open. Old Eddie Rossi, who was the owner, would keep them full of free pasta and tell them they were all going to be rich and famous. Mom used to call him Eddie Spaghetti. Do you remember Eddie Spaghetti? He was tall as hell and had those long arms and hair so white it seemed like he dyed it?"

"I just remember the smell," says Gabriella with a shrug.

"I remember Eddie Spaghetti," says Alistair. "He was friends with Angelo, wasn't he? That's how they got the office in the first place, some kind of deal with Angelo's uncle. They got really cheap rent on the place."

"It was mostly just the three of them back then," I say. "Mom, Dad, and Angelo Marino. They were actually doing really well and making a ton of money thanks to *Sea Farmers*, but they didn't see any reason to expand. Angelo Marino wanted them to sell the business altogether. Mom wanted them to cash out, too. But Dad thought they were crazy. He loved making games and he was unwilling to sell at any price, not when he knew that all the money coming in could be used to hire more artists and developers."

"Are you talking about old Eddie Spa-get?" interrupts the old waiter, who had slowly approached our table. "He is dead, you know, just like your father. He was a good man. When my brother went to jail for that thing with his wife, Eddie Spa-get paid his bills and made sure he got what he needed while he was locked up. There used to be an arcade around the corner from here and your father, and your mother, and Angelo, and Eddie Spa-get would go there and they would play games for free, because Eddie Spa-get would trade the teenagers working there pizza for tokens."

"That's how Dad decided that we needed to get into video games as well," I say. "So many other board game manufacturers thought they were just a passing fad, but not Dad."

"I liked to play the Space," says the waiter. "I liked to play the Joust and the Asteroid. Eddie Spa-get was never any good at the Asteroid. He wasted so many quarters trying to beat my scores at the Asteroid, but he never got anywhere close. Well, now he's dead. And now your father is dead, and what does any of that matter anymore? What does anything matter to anyone?"

The waiter wanders away as the security guards come back down.

"We checked the place out," says Ed. "There isn't anything up there but some old rat traps and a deflated air mattress. I think somebody must have been sleeping up there, probably breaking in at night."

I look at my brother and sister.

"We'd better do it soon," I say.

"And what about Bernard?" asks Gabriella.

"He's got a life to burn," I say.

We climb the stairs to the office above Little Bologna. The air is musty, the ceilings are low, and there isn't much light, even though it is early afternoon. The walls are seafoam green. I can't remember if that was the last color our mother painted the office or if it has been repainted since.

"There's probably ten coats of paint on these walls," I tell Alistair and Gabriella. "Our mom didn't really know what to do with herself, but she wanted to be useful to the company so she kept painting and repainting the office, choosing the gaudiest and most inappropriate colors that she could find. The walls were bright orange once. Actually,

I think she might have even painted them black at one point. And neon purple."

"I like black paint," says Gabriella. She touches the wall and I can see her struggling to remember this place. I know that she only remembers what life was like after Nylo was a massive success, when we never had to worry about money again. When it became an abstract concept for us, like process art or the phenomenon of divine grace.

I've often wondered if it is the fact that I watched our parents struggle, even slightly and for only a few years, that has given me such a rapacious appetite for business. If being privy to the sweat of their early years made me so dominant.

We take out our game phones and explore the office, looking for the place where they will interface with the hidden box.

"Over here!" yells Alistair, crouching down in a corner. "It's under this window for some reason."

Gabriella and I follow his lead, squatting beneath the window and holding our phones under the ledge. They bleep in turn, informing us that we have taken second and third place.

"Now what?" says Alistair.

"Now we'd better call the cops and get out of here," I say. "They can come and investigate, just in case something goes wrong like the aquarium exploding. I want them to see for themselves that we are all in danger. Maybe then they'll start taking this whole thing seriously."

We return downstairs and leave through the restaurant, waving to the old waiter on our way out. As I say goodbye to Alistair and Gabriella, I can't help but feel a pleasant sense of satisfaction. *I am still winning the game. Or at least not losing.*

27

"Ed and I have been talking," says Mel sheepishly as we make our way back to the train.

"Oh yeah?" I say.

"We're worried about you," he continues. "We've never seen anybody in your specific circumstances before and we aren't sure that you are taking all the possible precautions to stay safe."

"Most likely not," I agree.

"First of all, we don't think you should go home right now, not while you're being targeted for attack so flagrantly."

"That makes sense," I say. "But then again, home is where all my stuff is. What about the office? Can I keep sleeping there?"

"We don't think that is a good idea either," says Ed. "It seems like whoever is doing this is somebody who knows all about the Nylo Corporation and has a grudge against it. The building may not be safe." He pauses, then looks me in the eye. "You're looking out after your kids by sending them away, and that's a good plan. You're a good mom."

I am a good mom? Me?

"But who is going to look out after you?" he asks. "That's our job. We are supposed to have your back and keep you alive. But we're in over our heads here, with respect to security, and we aren't ashamed to admit it. We think you should work just as hard to protect yourself as you are working to protect your kids."

"Alright," I say. "So what should I do?"

"Don't you have any friends who could put you up? Somewhere you could crash for a while? Maybe somebody you haven't talked to in a long time who would be happy to hear from you?"

He's trying to be helpful, but he doesn't know how deeply his words cut me. The truth is that I don't have anybody like that. When Ben and I were together, all of his friends became my friends. They were easy to impress and help out.

The central problem of most people's lives, especially teachers, is that they don't have enough money. The central problem of my life is that I have too much money. It was wonderful to be able to play god to his posse of scrappy, salt-of-the-earth Brooklyn intellectuals and artists, getting them work when they needed it in the industries that would be the most helpful to them.

It was like playing a very satisfying strategy game. I had my own Sim City to cultivate, full of fallow fields that I could dump resources into and watch thrive. Before we had kids, I treated his wild pack of college and high school friends as my ersatz children, inserting myself into every aspect of their sad lives, making them dependent on me to a pretty horrifying degree.

Ben loved it. He was like Aladdin with a magic genie and he got to dispense my riches according to his own whims, performing triage among his friends with respect to who needed what and who would benefit the most from my infinite largesse. I liked making Ben so dominant and indispensable among all of the other fellows, and I liked helping him cultivate this grungy garden of bros and bras. It was better than buying lavish real estate. I was trafficking in human souls.

Even those among his friends who were the most resistant to my handouts and charity still took advantage of the Nylo Corporation's infinite coffers when it came to trips abroad, and yacht parties, and long lazy weeks in Nantucket during the summer. That was when our gray palace on the beach became a permanent crash pad for whoever was rootless and unmoored enough to coke and booze it up with us until they collapsed on king-size beds in private rooms, central air conditioning going full blast on their tanned and well-fed bodies.

During this time, and even after Olivia and Jane were born, I managed to convince myself that Ben's friends were my friends. In fact, I told myself that they were more than just friends, even if they didn't know it. They were my vassals. They had started to belong to me in some strange, demented, dependent way.

When we finally ended our relationship for good, my final gift to Ben was to return his friends to him, even if it meant them hating me. I never told him about all the awkward, too-bold overtures even his closest friends made once we were no longer together, leveraging the fake good times we'd had into sudden propositions of sex, of running away together abroad, of drug-fueled benders, of marriage.

I never told him how his friends abased themselves to remain in my patronage and in my good graces, throwing him aside as fast as they could.

But I didn't accept any offer, even if occasionally I was lonely enough to want to. I was as cruel to his friends as Ben was to me, when I could have been the opposite and scooped them up and owned them for myself.

This was heartbreaking, but I relished the pain of it. It was one last pointless act of self-abnegation at the altar of his indifference. I had never had a group of friends the way that he did, all of whom depended and relied on each other for moving up in the world, for keeping each other sane, for challenging each other to make the most of themselves, for giving each other the space to make mistakes, and for being there for each other on the other side of failure.

Henley liked Ben's friends, too. Henley worked his way through all of the women in Ben's circle, pleased that I brought him such easy pickings. At first, each would picture herself as Henley's one and only beloved, striding along at his side at the top of the world. But then the dark reality of Henley's passions would become clearer. They would renounce him with as much cruelty and drama as they could muster, just to try and make him change his awful lizard-like expression.

Henley was sad to see this proletariat henhouse dry up, but he understood how I had to let Ben's friends return to Ben. How I needed to create a permanent firewall between his world and mine to teach Ben a permanent lesson about the limits of patience and capital in a loveless world.

My own friends from school and childhood had all been achievers and climbers, boring socialites who worshipped and feared me like a force of nature for the way that I preferred the company of men, of games, of dissolution, of narcotic despair.

I was glad to be rid of them, frankly, and avoided anything like reunions or late-night phone calls to reminisce. I had never done social media. I had never created an Instagram account or tried my hand at Twitter like Gabriella, attempting to replace the sucking void of my soul with something like a brand or a fixed identity. I relished the sucking void and had no desire to pretend that it could be plugged, that there was anything like a piece of cork that might take the shape of my wound and stop the respiration process of my shabby, sobbing pain.

"I do not have any friends who I would trust to take care of me in this situation or who I would want to burden with the danger of what might be happening right now," I finally reply.

Ed and Mel look at each other, so full of knowing compassion that I want to vomit on their shiny shoes.

"Listen," I say. "I need to clear my head and get away from all of this. I know a place in the Village where we can play very high-stakes board games. I will cover the two of you if you accompany me as my guests and not merely as my employees for the afternoon. If I am going to be murdered, I would rather be murdered there. Actually, it's probably the safest place in the city I could go. No one knows about it and there are cameras everywhere."

Ed and Mel look at each other and shrug.

"We have to go where you go," says Ed.

"Do you like board games?" I ask.

"Sure," says Ed.

"Do you like gambling?"

"When it's somebody else's money," chuckles Mel.

"Well, I'll make it easy for you. You can place side bets on the action, betting on any given player to do well. You should just place your bets on me, honestly. If I win, you'll make some extra cash that you can keep as your own rakings. You will be my personal invited guests."

"Like I said," says Ed, "we have to go where you go."

I pull out my phone, just to make sure Cardboard Struggle is open. It would be rare for them not to be operational on a Friday afternoon, but the proprietor is a cantankerous son of a bitch named Raj Pandat and he keeps to his own hours and runs his board game speakeasy according to his own sadistic whims.

"What?" he says, picking up my call.

"You open?" I ask.

"Yeah, there's five people playing fifty-grand *Sea Farmers*, about to stab each other to death over the way the coral is rolling up. Your dad would be proud as shit to see them so angry over something so stupid."

"I'm on my way," I say. "If we can get all five on board, I'd like to get a game going. Maybe Diplomacy? Or Teeth of Steel?"

"What's your bet?" asks Raj.

"I'll stake a hundred grand, just to call the game. I'm bringing some friends. Security, actually, but tell everyone not to be alarmed. I'm going to stake them, too. They don't intend to play, but they will certainly enjoy the action."

"I'm not going to bet on you today," says Raj. "You don't sound good. You don't sound steady. You sound wild and stupid."

"We'll be there in thirty minutes," I say. "Make sure they wrap up this game of *Sea Farmers* without anyone getting stabbed. Anybody who loses their shirt will have an opportunity to make it back as soon as we get there."

We take the train down to the Village.

Cardboard Struggle is in a loft apartment off Minetta Alley. I am one of the original investors, having met Raj at the Compleat Strategist long ago when we were both moody, inscrutable jerks who enjoyed being underestimated by the fresh-faced eager teenagers and old crew-cut military men who made up the city's churning population of elite gamers. He was independently wealthy like me, the son of an Indian steel baron. We both wanted a place where we could be assured of a game that would be challenging but professional, where the stakes could be as high as we wanted and where no one would flinch from the thrill of cardboard carnage.

I ring the buzzer downstairs and, after an interminable wait, the buzzer downstairs correspondingly goes off, signaling that it is okay to come up.

"I guess these are the friends I have left," I tell Mel and Ed. "Besides you two, of course."

28

Cardboard Struggle is a three-room loft with a kitchen and two bathrooms.

Two rooms are just for gaming, containing long tables and short ones. There are bars and flat-screen televisions that play video feeds from other high-stakes gaming parlors around the world. If you are bored by the slowness of a game, you can bet on the action elsewhere. Correspondingly, there are cameras all over these gaming rooms that broadcast the feed from here, if everyone agrees to make a game public.

The third room is a giant game library, which has been stocked with almost every existing board game, rows and rows of first editions and reprints. It is a circulating library of the best and the worst, of the most complicated and successful crystallizations of rule and process, arcane systems meant to provoke conflict and satisfy tenuous hierarchies.

All three rooms are wallpapered in game boards, stitched together like the skins of conquered animals. The *Tetris* tiles of these antique boards loom down over everything, giving the whole place a comforting but claustrophobic feel. Maps and tiles provide too much information everywhere you look. When coupled with the neon lighting and video feeds, Cardboard Struggle has a hallucinogenic effect that can be disorienting, like any good casino.

I love to play here, but I am also an investor, so I have an interest in the house winning. There is a much bigger, much more elaborate, much more proletarian and nerdier version of Cardboard Struggle in Vegas that Raj and I both also have a stake in. We take junkets there sometimes, but it has been a while. We both prefer the skill level and professionalism of New York—a city of strategists, financiers, and secret geniuses.

My two very pleasant and conscientious bodyguards insist on checking out Cardboard Struggle before I go inside.

"Somebody could be monitoring your calls," says Ed. "In which case, now they would know exactly where you're headed. You're telegraphing your moves."

I let them go up first and do a quick pass while I wait downstairs, pondering this warning. Am I really telegraphing my moves? I think about who in my family would be the most capable of monitoring my phone calls and movements. Alistair, definitely. But it's also entirely conceivable that Angelo Marino could have hired someone to do the same thing. His resourcefulness is undeniable and unbounded, and I have certainly benefited from it over the years.

Ed and Mel come back to me bemused and a little rattled. "It's all clear," Ed reports, holding the elevator door open so I can join them for the return trip up.

"Well, well, well," says Raj Pandat, greeting us as the elevator doors slide open. "Thinking pretty highly of yourself these days, eh? Who in god's name would ever want to do you harm?"

"Did you clear a space at a table for me or not?" I push past him and enter the first game room. "I'm here to play, and these two are here to lay bets."

Ed and Mel nod uncertainly.

"Sorry about your father and your little brother, by the way," says Raj. "I took a lot of money from Henley over the years, and your father was a legend, a true hero of games, though he wasn't as good of a player as you. Too generous—too much heart."

"Thanks for saying that," I say, shocked. I have never known Raj to be sentimental, and I have never heard him say anything nice about anyone, ever. His sudden praise of both me and my father is almost heartbreaking. I find myself tearing up and have to look away.

"Everyone is waiting," says Raj. "We'll all let you stake your hundred grand if you really want to play Teeth of Steel. You haven't won yet."

"I don't think I'll lose today," I say. "Do we draw for armies?"

"We've decided to let you pick first, on account of the trage-dies and all."

"Nothing gets my rage, skill, and dander up like sudden tragedy," I say. "You're all going to lose a lot of money if you keep being nice to me."

"Honestly, getting to choose your army is a liability in Teeth of Steel," says Raj. "You'll always feel a little bit of regret no matter which army you choose, and the regret will cripple you, as the rest of us make do with what we have, feeling no remorse, glad not to have your deci-sion fatigue. I assume you'll pick the Army of the West?"

He's trying to psych me out, to get me *not* to pick the Union by somehow implying that it is the obvious choice for me, that I am predictable in wanting Grant's army—a conglomeration of magical mechs—and taking Grant's mobility bonus in exchange for his terrible position. But I won't let him chisel me into picking Forrest's Blood Demon Cavalry or the Army of Northern Virginia.

"Give me the Army of the West," I say. "My mechs are going to crush your demons, you son of a bitch."

"How do you know I'm going to choose Forrest?" asks Raj.

"You always do," I say. Now he is the one who is rattled, squinting at me, sizing me up. Maybe this really will be the time I finally win this game.

He leads us into the back room, where the table has already been set up. It's a rogues' gallery of players, but there isn't anyone here I don't know.

There are two finance dudes who are friends of Raj, and I only know them as Shaheed and Wallace. They look exactly alike and I have a hard time telling them apart. They vape cannabis oil constantly and are so laid back that it is hard to take them seriously, even though they are both formidable strategists. They have a tendency to team up in ways that are usually felicitous, but that sometimes lock them into a homosocial death spiral that keeps them together even when it is in their interests to turn on each other. Additionally, it is such common knowledge that they will always get each other's backs that their alliance is often more of a liability when everybody else gangs up on them, especially in a six-player game.

Isabel Wu is here as well. We don't have much of a relationship, but I know that she is an M&A lawyer at one of the Magic Circle English firms and that she is cheating on her husband with Raj. I also know that Raj won't commit to her, even though she wants him very deeply.

She is hard for me to read and she doesn't let her feelings for and against Raj (they oscillate wildly) influence the way she plays. She is short and her black hair is short and her otherwise pretty face is pocked with acne scars. She dresses flawlessly in a way that I find annoying, especially since we are all just playing games here. Isabel comes from Singapore money, which I've never given any consideration to, until now. When I see her in the flesh, I can't help but have a fleeting racist thought that somehow she might be involved with whatever happened to Henley.

But she barely knew Henley. She only saw him when he followed me here to make side bets or to spend the evening hiding from his girlfriends and she happened to also be in for a night of gaming. Still, it isn't outside the realm of possibility that he managed to seduce her at some point and eventually she wanted revenge for this indignity. Except for one thing: she didn't find anything about Henley impressive and thus wasn't his type.

And then there is The Kid. We actually don't know much about The Kid, since he likes to be mysterious. He is Orthodox Jewish and can't be much older than twenty-one or twenty-two. He doesn't seem to be in college, or else he finds college so easy that he is perfectly willing to spend all of his time hanging out with people twice his age in a dingy Greenwich Village den of iniquity. We don't know where he gets his money to gamble, but he wins often enough that he isn't in the hole, so we don't have to care.

We actually all make money here every time we play, on account of the side bets and action around the world, with people logging on and watching us play games. They only really get to see the board and hear our patter, since as is tradition at Cardboard Struggle, our faces are obscured. Plenty of people have made guesses as to who the players are, but nobody has even come close. In the chat channel of the live stream I'm always referred to as Kimberly Drummond—the girl from *Diff'rent Strokes*—based on fleeting glimpses of me in shadow. I guess I do kind of look and sound like her, although anyone with an internet connection can quickly find out Dana Plato is dead.

We take our places around the table and all the bets are sorted out. Everybody meets my ridiculously high stakes. This is the kind of game that can take about eight to ten hours to play if everybody takes it seriously, and a $600,000 pot ensures that all the players will bring their maximum attention to victory.

The house rule is that performance-enhancing drugs are fine, but if somebody keels over or has to go to the hospital as a result of a bad crash or a crying jag or a heart attack, they forfeit their stake in the game and we kick them out and leave them on the curb and they can fend for themselves. Actually, except for the occasional Adderall, we've all basically learned our lesson by now and it's rare that any coke or speed or even alcohol makes an appearance, although Shaheed and Wallace are constantly high, and I once beat the shit out of everyone at Diplomacy while candyflipping by weaponizing my own empathy. But that was back in my twenties, when Raj still had some hair on the top of his head.

Teeth of Steel is a fantastic game, even though it isn't made by Nylo. It is an asymmetric war game, where there are two teams: the Nationals and the Rebels. You fight to vanquish the other side, but the winner is determined by which specific army on one side or the other is the most effective, meaning that there is internal warfare at the same time, which causes the game to mimic other kinds of political contests, like primaries leading to a general election.

The game is set in a fantasy world version of Civil War America and features Union and Confederacy generals from the real world: Grant, Meade, and Sherman versus Lee, Forrest, and Johnston. The difference is that each of their armies is composed of fantastical creatures with specific bonuses. Forrest's cavalry, for instance, consists of massive blood-drinking demons who move faster each time they feast on the battlefield carnage of their fallen opponents—or allies.

I've decided to play as Grant's steam-cyborg mech pilots, where stoic dwarves, constantly drunk and constantly chomping cigars, pilot huge and deadly eldritch machines that come on with an inevitability of purpose that I find irresistible. Plus, in this fantastical world, Grant is a short-haired redheaded woman with glowing blue eyes and I am pretty much in love with her.

29

We start playing. The hours disappear. For the first time since my father died, I feel a sense of relaxation, of relief, of camaraderie.

I end up on the same side as Shaheed and Wallace, who choose to play as the other two Union generals. I would ordinarily find it annoying to be paired with them since they are so inseparable, but I like being welcomed into their cabal this time. I don't trust them and I know they will privilege each other over me, but I like that they are at least fake nice to me and seem to enjoy the illusion of everybody being on the same team.

We are opposed by Isabel, Raj, and The Kid, and they make a formidable array against us, but in some ways, the other team is actually too good, too cynical, too strategic. They can't for a moment lose themselves in going for victory against us, and they are quite self-interested in each winning as the most impressive rebel general. Shaheed and Wallace provoke them every way they can. Being on this side of their united front, it is easier to understand why Shaheed and Wallace so often prefer the strategy of cooperation over the more cutthroat ambitions of the rest of us.

Things become dire as the early strategies of the Confederacy fail to pan out and it becomes increasingly clear that the North will win yet again in this ancient fight. Here is where the game truly gets brutal. The losing side has the ability to play kingmaker, surrendering to whichever general in the North makes the most sense in order to turn us against each other.

At first, their strategy doesn't seem to be working. We maintain something like equality among the three of us. We've already established that this will be the way forward, at least until one of the Southern generals goes out altogether.

But slowly, Raj manages to get into Wallace's head. Wallace doesn't outwardly seem to believe Raj's constant insinuating palaver, but Raj does have a point: only one of us can win, and I have managed to maneuver myself into being indispensable to the North's cause. I try to keep our fragile alliance together, but Raj's only shot is turning one or more of us on the other side into copperheads, giving the South a chance to recover.

It is well after midnight before we start to enter the last stage of the game, where captured soldiers become five times more valuable and where it costs twice as much to keep armies in the field.

"You know," Raj says to me, grinning across the table, "I'm glad you were able to join us for a game today, but I have to say: Kimberly Drummond, you look like shit. What's the deal? It actually feels kinda bad to play a game against you for money with you looking like this. Are you dying of cancer or addicted to meth now or something?"

"I guess I'm not feeling great"—I cast him a sharp glare—"and not looking great, as a result of my dad dying and somebody murdering my brother."

"Whoa," says The Kid. "Didn't know he was murdered. Just thought it was an elevator accident?"

"No, it might be murder," I say. "The whole thing is very complicated."

"Is that why you have these security goons?" asks Raj. He looks at Mel and Ed blankly and then grins. "No offense, of course. Though I'm sure people have called you goons much worse."

Raj turns his attention back to me. "Did you know that only fifty percent of homicides are ever solved in the United States? That's a pretty good rate for murderers. Way better than most countries. If you kill somebody here, you have an even chance of getting away with it."

"Hey, man," says Isabel. "Low blow."

"It's fine," I say. "I can take his charm."

And it's true. I am immune to him strategically. But when I excuse myself to use the bathroom, I find myself looking up Raj's statistics. It turns out he isn't lying. New York City has a much higher clearance rate than most big cities, but it certainly isn't anywhere close to where I thought it would be. They always figure out who did it on TV. It's actually suddenly insane to me how easy it is to get away with murder. Then I think about the cops on our case, the Midtown tunnel and elevator detectives, and it all seems like a sick joke.

"Whoever is doing this is going to get away with it," I mutter to myself. "They are going to keep getting away with it until there's only one of us left."

I start thinking about Henley and Ben and the girls. I wish Henley were here with me, giving me shit while slowly getting wasted. I wish Ben were here with me, bored with Henley's stories, waiting for me to finish up so that he could take me home and pound his frustration out in my ass like a good, patient little lad. Guaranteed he's not getting that kind of action anywhere else these days. And in this moment, I can't help but miss it. I might even miss Ben.

I choke on my own sobs.

When I stumble out of the bathroom, I am not ready to give up, but I am ready to get good and drunk.

"Somebody pour me a damn drink," I say. Mel obliges, fixing me a bourbon from the sideboard and putting it in my flexing hand as I hunker over the board.

"And keep them coming, alright?" I tell him, scowling. "What am I even paying you for? What is the point of having bodyguards if you can't get totally wasted and let them carry you home?"

Time passes in a blur. Night turns into morning. It is close to dawn before we finish the game, after several long breaks for food where we spend the whole time arguing about the state of the board. Mel and Ed went from sort of interested to so deeply bored that they are taking turns standing guard while the other sneaks a nap in the gaming library.

At some point, I pass out. I feel myself lifted up by big hands, and I throw up down somebody's big strong back. I'm pissed that they don't even care that I've ruined their clothes.

"Don't you have any dignity?" I shout. "I am a monster! Defend yourself!"

"You aren't a monster, ma'am," says Mel or Ed. "You are just very drunk. We're happy to help you out. You made us very rich tonight."

"I did?" I say.

"We bet on you to win," says Ed or Mel, chuckling. "Like you told us to. And you won."

"I did?"

"You don't remember? Everyone was very upset."

"Fuck them," I say. "Fuck Henley. Fuck Bernard. Fuck Gabriella. Fuck Raj."

"Here we are, ma'am, your bed," says Mel or Ed. We're in my bedroom at Nylo Corporation. I have no idea how we got here. My room swims out in front of me and then everything goes black. It is the first oblivion I have tasted in far too long.

I dream of my childhood home, of the White Room, covered in blood. My mother is there, grinning at me, dressed all in white, but drenched in red. I look down at my hands. They are alabaster, lacking all my normal blue veins and tan freckles. They are too white, except where they are also smeared with blood.

I wake up in stages, struggling for consciousness half-heartedly, eventually falling from an exhausted state of panic into something like restful annihilation. I forget why I should be awake and instead luxuriate in the healing darkness.

I finally sit up, no longer feeling tired. My whole body aches, but in a good way. I stumble to the sink and wash my face. I put on a sleek red Adidas tracksuit and enter my office.

The light streaming into the room is mellow and dry. It isn't just another typical gross, humid New York day. The day feels caramelly and mellow. I feel good. It is so rare for me to feel good that I make a note of it. How did I get to feel good? I try to chart the path of it, thinking back, hoping to somehow replicate it.

Ed comes into the office, his face long.

"The general rises," he says.

"How long did I sleep?" I ask.

"A long time," he says. "People wanted to wake you up, but you told us not to let them. You said to let you sleep, whatever the cost."

"I said that?" I say, starting to panic. What time is it? I move the mouse on my computer to wake it up.

"Oh fuck," I say. It's 4 p.m. I missed the twelve o'clock call.

I run back into the bedroom and rummage around in my purse for my game phone. It doesn't show anything but the newest clue, swimming over a sea of flying toasters: "If you want to run everything, the first thing you've gotta do is run."

I know this one. It means the gym where Mom used to go at night. The New York City Women's Strength and Fitness Club.

I feel sick to my stomach. I call Alistair, but he doesn't pick up. I call Gabriella, but it goes to her voice mail. I even call Bernard, knowing he won't answer either.

Except for Gabriella, we all have one life left. We all know our lives might be at stake if we lose. My siblings no doubt all know the answer already, and they won't need my help. They've had a four-hour head start. It will be me who dies this time.

"Let's go," I tell Ed and Mel. "Did you guys get enough sleep? Never mind, could one of you go grab me a plate of muffins and a cup of coffee? Who came by? Did Alistair come by?"

"Your assistant," says Ed. "He came in around 11, even though it's Saturday. Said it was urgent. We had to put the fear of god in him. You

made us more money last night than we make in a year. We were glad
to do it. Also that lawyer came by. Wouldn't take no for an answer. But
we don't work for him. We work for you. He said he was gonna get us
fired, but I guess he hasn't managed to pull that off yet."

Mel chuckles.

I am annoyed with them, but it isn't their fault. It's mine. What was
I doing, staying out all night gambling on the Civil War and drinking
to oblivion when I should have been solving my brother's murder or
at least waking up in time to play the game on which my life depends?

As soon as Ed returns with coffee and pastries, we get in the elevator and head down to the ground floor. I practically run to the subway.
My bodyguards have no trouble keeping up. We take the train to the
Financial District, transferring to the R from the F. I am silent the
whole time, reading articles on my phone speculating on Nylo.

There are still people wondering about our father's death. Now
there are reporters questioning what happened to Henley. Was he next
in line to take over the company? Was he killed in some ruthless shareholder power play?

"Fucking ridiculous," I say. The only company that Henley has ever
understood was paid company.

"You don't pay them to fuck you," he used to say. "You pay them
to leave."

I can't help but wish he were here right now. He was a hedonist
without any kind of moral compass. But he was fearless.

Which I am not. I want to win, but now, more importantly, I don't
want to lose. I don't want to find out what losing means.

30

The New York City Women's Strength and Fitness Club is a city institution. It has been open for a hundred years as a private twenty-four-hour gym just for women. It also serves as a social club. It was once a hotbed of progressive activism, where the ladies of society used to meet up in order to figure out the problems of the poor, such as how to implement broad public health changes to the city in order to reduce communicable illnesses. Their secondary goal was to improve the lives of women all over America, generally.

The club also has a dark history involving eugenics and testing experimental drugs on prisoners, along with fairly entrenched institutional racism. By the time our mother joined up, all that was mostly in the past and it was just a very good place to run on a treadmill without being bothered by men.

We get off the subway near the ferry. I run to the club, flanked by Ed and Mel. Before I go inside, I call my siblings again, but none of them answer. I do have a message from Angelo Marino. He tells me that Henley's memorial service will be tomorrow morning, in accordance with his wishes. It will be a low-key affair held at his favorite dive bar, Ugly American. The bar has generously agreed to let us have the run of the place before it opens.

The club lobby is full of women coming and going, their hair swept back in fashionable ponytails and wearing the trendiest Lycra athleisure. I think about calling the cops, but what good will they be at this point? They don't care about anything that is happening to me or my family. They don't even seem to think anything is wrong or out of the ordinary. At least I've got my bodyguards, even though I obviously can't bring them in with me.

"I hate to say it," I tell Ed and Mel, "but you guys need to wait outside. I won't be long. If something crazy happens and I find myself in trouble, I'll text you."

"We aren't supposed to let you go anywhere on your own," says Ed. "Especially if your life is at risk."

"Yeah," adds Mel. "This is really when we should be at your side."

"That's true," I say. "But they aren't going to let you in. We could wait for your security company to send us some female agents, but we really don't have the time. We're just going to have to risk it."

Neither Ed nor Mel is happy about this, but there isn't much they can do. They are bound to obey my orders.

I walk past the front desk with purpose. I act as if I am meant to be here so that no one will dare question me. I'm already dressed the part in my red tracksuit, a lucky choice this morning, as it turns out.

"Uh, excuse me, ma'am?" says a young blond, grinning and running up to stand bashfully in front of me. "We need to sign you in."

"Of course," I say, reluctantly following her back to the desk. "But wait"—I pretend to search my purse—"I left my fob at home."

"Oh, okay, that's fine," she says. "What's your last name?"

"Nylo," I say.

She looks at me, recognizing the name. She frowns, scanning her computer.

"Oh, okay, it actually looks like you already signed in and left," she says.

Gabriella must have a membership here. It is definitely the kind of place where she would enjoy hanging out, looking for validation and camaraderie.

"Yeah," I say. "I did the hard part first and then grabbed a quick, early dinner and now I am going to do my long run for the week."

"Enjoy your workout!" she says sunnily, not really hearing my lame excuse.

I at least know that I'm behind Gabriella, which makes sense. She would remember where Mom used to work out, especially if she now has a membership here herself.

I take out my game phone and hold it in my hand as I peruse the main floor of the gym, where people are lifting kettlebells, running on treadmills, stretching, and riding stationary bikes while watching the business channel.

Mom liked to exercise late at night. She would leave at one or two in the morning, frustrated and yelling, letting us all know that she was tired of our bullshit and that she needed some time alone.

She wasn't subtle about it. She would tell us that we were the ones who were making her crazy, that it was our fault she was leaving and that maybe she would never come back. She would usually return early in the morning, sweaty and ashen. We always assumed she went out drinking in her workout clothes rather than to the gym. And yet, she must have been exercising at least some of the time. What else could explain her perfect figure, despite how much she ate and drank?

I head to the treadmills, holding my phone up beside each one, pretending to check a series of texts. My heart is beating fast.

What if I'm the last one here? What will happen to me? Will I be electrocuted? Will someone smash in my head with a twenty-five-pound plate?

None of the treadmills trigger the game phone. I walk around the perimeter of the club, growing increasingly frustrated.

I corner one of the towel girls, almost pushing her up against the wall.

"Listen," I say. "Have the treadmills always been right where they are now?"

"Yes, ma'am," she says, as she puts a hand up to steady the stack of white towels in her arms. "I think so. They've been right against that wall ever since we moved them up here from downstairs."

"From the basement?" I ask.

"Yes, ma'am. That was before my time. All the treadmills used to be down in the basement and all the showers used to be on the third floor, but we switched everything up after the hurricane."

"After the flooding," I say, as if I have been coming here for years.

"Yes, ma'am," she says, looking relieved to have appeased me. "They say nothing ever changes here, but I guess sometimes things do get shifted around."

The basement. Fine.

As I walk down the short, sharp stairwell to the lower floor, I have all sorts of fantasies for how I might be exterminated in the basement of this gym. I might be drowned, or attacked by a plague of rats, or walled up in some dark corner—asphyxiated—my bones left to molder and dissolve in the humid walls.

I take a deep breath and grip my game phone so hard that my knuckles turn white. Either I am the last Nylo here, or I am not. There's nothing I can do about it.

I walk around the perimeter, holding my phone up like a metal detector. The space is relatively empty. There are showers and lockers, but not many women taking advantage of them. I try to be discreet so that nobody will think I'm snapping inappropriate pictures.

I walk all the way along one wall, then another, then a third. On the fourth wall my phone starts to vibrate and then it plays the Nylo Corporation theme song. My whole body clenches up in a paroxysm of fear and stomach acid, like a reverse orgasm.

I look down, afraid of what I'll find. And then I heave a huge sigh of relief.

I am in the third spot, behind Gabriella, who came in first, and Alistair.

I cannot believe my luck. It is almost 6 p.m. How did I beat Bernard?

Even though I should feel safe, I still wait a moment for something terrible to happen. To be scalded by boiling water pouring from an exploded pipe. To be shot at point-blank range by a sulking towel assistant. But nothing happens. I walk back up the stairs to the first floor, salute the blond girl at the front desk, and then go outside, my brain abuzz with the madness of this crazy game.

What does it mean that all the clues revolve around how much we know about our dead mother? What is Dad trying to say to us? Is he trying to say that the person who should inherit the company is the one who paid the most attention to Mom? Who absorbed her qualities instead of his? Is he trying to say that he wants the company to go to the one of us who loved what he also loved: our poor, broken, mean, cruel, suicidal mother?

Or is this a confession? Of something dark and transparently sinister? Is he admitting a role in her death? What if all the rumors were true, and our father killed our mother for breaking his heart and then used all of his strategic skill and money to cover it up? What if his last message to his children is a cry for absolution?

Or what if his last will is somehow to extinguish us all just like he extinguished her?

I shake off this dark feeling. In the same way that I know our father didn't kill our mother, I know he didn't kill Henley either. I know that he wasn't the one who tried to kill Alistair and me at the aquarium.

"Is everything okay?" asks Mel as soon as he sees me walk out through the club's front doors.

"I mean, as far as it can be," I say and give him and Ed a wan smile.

There is a sudden noise right above us that sends all the trash in the street spinning. People scream and point, running out of the way. Are we being attacked?

I look up and see a helicopter breaking the law and heading right for the ground in the middle of the small triangular park.

Who is it? The fucking president?

No, it's just my brother Bernard, trying to win twenty billion dollars.

People are running in all directions, pointing and taking pictures. How much money did Bernard spend to bribe the city into letting him land his helicopter wherever he wants in Manhattan without getting shot down? A few cops race to hold people back. I can hear them loudly explaining that everything is fine, everything is normal.

A trash can blows over and a cop races to put it back to rights. That is the only real damage done, except for some tulips that get flattened by the whipping air. Luckily, the Financial District is mainly closed to traffic and so there aren't any car accidents as people stop and gawk.

Bernard's security detail gets out first. They shake hands with the cops and check everything out from the park to the door of the gym. Finally, Bernard gets out, eating a Zero bar, wearing sunglasses and a red silk shirt under his suit jacket. He looks like the devil himself.

He walks right up to me, his hands held out at his sides as if in embarrassment. It's like running into a friend at the same brothel.

"Hello, big sister," he says. "This was an easy one, wasn't it?"

"Bernard," I say. "What took you so long?"

"I had to make a few calls before I could land the copter here. Do you know how hard it is to reach city officials on a Saturday? Fucking bureaucrats. I finally made it, though."

Should I tell him that it won't matter? That down in the gym basement someone will try and kill him? Would he tell me?

31

ernard brushes past me, stabbing a finger at one of the cops. I almost let him go inside. I hate myself for doing it, but I almost let him jauntily run down the stairs to his doom.

"You are the last one," I blurt out, right before he disappears inside. He stops on the threshold, then looks back at me. He takes off his sunglasses. A woman elbows past him on her way out of the gym. He returns to stand in front of me.

"You are the last one," I say again. "If you go inside there and use your phone, something terrible will happen."

"What?" he says.

"I don't know," I say. "I wish I did."

He stares at me for a long time before finally nodding.

"If it was any of the others, I wouldn't believe them," he says. "But you don't like to win like that. You don't pick favorites. You don't lie or cheat. You like the feeling of everybody always knowing that you have beat them because you are better than they are. You get off on it. And for that to be true, you need to always be incorruptible and always play with perfect, hateful sportsmanship. So I believe you."

"You don't have to believe me," I say, showing him my phone. He looks at it, frowning.

"So what? What now?" he says, gritting his teeth.

"I don't know," I reply. "We all could have been coordinating before this. We could have all gone on strike."

"Fuck that," says Bernard. "I had a shot. I could have beat you. It was a fair game, not one of your dumb puzzles. I liked my odds. I got the helicopter."

"Well, you've crapped out," I say.

"You guys formed a cabal against me," he says. "Despicable, though I will admit not technically cheating."

"Yesterday we formed a cabal," I say. "But not today. Today everyone was on their own. The stakes are just too high now, I guess."

"I'm gonna get in that helicopter and fly away," he says. "I don't even know where I'm going to go. Nobody can find me if I don't know where I am going myself. I'll roll the dice against the alphabet and pick a random city. I'll mail you a letter from wherever I end up. Then you can mail me back some money when you win. When this all blows over."

I don't know what to tell him. It actually sounds like a pretty good plan.

"We'll catch whoever is doing this," I say. "And then you can come back. If I win, I'm going to make sure that nobody goes broke and nobody starves. Like I said."

He nods. He glares at me and I smile at him, hoping his icy stare will soften. He isn't the smartest of us, or the nicest, or the funniest, but he may be the shrewdest. He has never been able to tolerate nonsense. He almost has a physical aversion to it.

"Alright," he says. He pats me once on the shoulder before getting back in the helicopter. He turns around to the pilot and twirls his finger. The rotors start spinning, faster and faster, and then the helicopter takes off. The trash can falls over again and this time a cop doesn't bother to put it back in its place. The cops disperse, no longer needing to cordon off the tiny park from lookie-loos.

I call for a car while Mel and Ed commiserate with their counterparts.

They all smoke cigarettes until our Uber arrives. We crowd in and head back across the bridge to Dumbo.

"He ditched his security detail," says Ed. "But we'll find him. Don't worry. He'll be safe."

"I kind of hope you don't find him," I say. "I kind of hope he's unfindable."

I text Pez and tell him to meet me at my office. I call my favorite Indian restaurant in Jackson Heights and order chicken tikka masala, lamb korma, vegetable biryani, and a big plate of naan to be delivered. My stomach is growling. My hangover is basically gone and I am hungry as hell.

Pez is waiting in my office when I arrive.

"You look better," he says. "You got some sleep. Good. I was worried about you."

"Listen," I say. "I need you to figure out another very important mystery for me. And I need you to do it basically by tomorrow."

"What do you need to know, kid?" asks Pez.

"I need to know if my dad killed my mom," I say. "I need to know if he is some kind of psychopathic murderer and if this is all his fucked-up revenge from beyond the grave. He has moved onto the top suspect list."

"Jesus," says Pez after staring at me for a while. "You aren't kidding."

"No, I'm not," I say. "There are only three of us left in the game now. I managed to warn Bernard before he triggered some kind of death trap, but the other two aren't returning my calls."

"Your dad didn't kill your mom," says Pez. "There's your answer. Okay?"

"How do you know?" I ask. "Do you know that for a fact?"

He doesn't say anything. He sighs, looking at the desk. I feel like he wants to get mad at me. I feel like he wants to tell me off for even insinuating something so insane, so cruel. His brow furrows and he starts to get red under the collar. But he is saved by the arrival of the food. The weekend building assistant, Jennie, sets up a giant spread on a table behind us, and Pez is momentarily mesmerized by the warm spicy funk of cardamom and curry.

We fix ourselves giant plates of chicken, lamb, and rice. I pour us bourbons. He nods at his drink like an old friend.

"I knew your mom and dad very well," says Pez, after taking his first bite and chewing it thoughtfully. "They loved each other very much, in their own awful way. That's how everybody does it, you know. They do the best they can. It isn't ever easy. They had five children together. You have to like each other to have five children with each other, don't you? There's just no getting around the logistics of that."

"I'm not sure my mother ever wanted to have one child, much less five," I say. "I don't think she liked being a mother very much. In fact, she hated it. Sort of with a rare psychotic fervor, in fact."

"She doted on you all," says Pez. "She fretted and worried about you and she gave you the best parts of her. Especially you. You are so much like her, you know? You have your dad's head for business, but you bend people to your will like she did. You both had Prescott wrapped around your finger. And you both had a hard time respecting the men who chose to love you."

"I don't need any therapy," I say. "I need answers. I want to know for sure, one way or the other, whether my father killed my mother. You are going to find out for me, or at least tell me what you know. You are going to tell me every dirty secret that my father ever kept from his children."

Pez shakes his head in defeat.

"Well, I do know by now that your father was involved at least on some level with the planning of this game," he begins. "He was an integral part from the beginning, and I have tracked down that he was the one who stole people right out from under Alistair and redirected them to begin developing the game using already existing technology."

"How do you know this?" I ask.

"I interviewed some of the engineers who did the developing in house," says Pez. "They finally cracked. Members of Alistair's team.

They said that the only person who ever dealt with them directly was your father. He wouldn't tell them why they were working for him. He swore them to secrecy to the grave. However, they broke down and told me the truth when I explained what their work was being used for. That Henley was dead."

"Did you tell the police to interview them?" I ask.

"Yeah, and those detectives said they would 'get right on it.'" He curves his fingers into air quotes and shrugs. "I didn't hear very much enthusiasm. I don't think they're taking any of this very seriously."

All of a sudden, the muffled yet unmistakable sound of the Nylo theme song emanates from my pocket. I am seized with an overwhelming sense of dread.

"Henley's funeral is tomorrow," I say, warding off whatever is coming from the game phone, hoping that if I don't answer it, I won't have to deal with the latest horror it wants to show me.

"I will definitely be there," says Pez, raising an eyebrow. "Um, Caitlyn, your phone is ringing."

"I know," I hiss. I gingerly remove the phone from my pocket, letting the jingle repeat until I'm ready to commit to the inevitable.

The screen shows a grainy, shaky video of Bernard's helicopter flying over an empty field. It is Middle America, probably Pennsylvania farmland. I wonder for a moment if it might literally be Gettysburg.

The bottom drops out of my stomach.

Pez sees me stricken and maneuvers out of his seat to come stand behind me. We watch as the helicopter rotors stall in the sky. The helicopter starts to wrench sideways, advancing jerkily in first one direction and then another. Then the camera zooms in, so the helicopter takes up the entire frame. I think I can even see a pale white face looking out. Suddenly the helicopter snakes out of view and there's a mishmash of blue sky and green field and the sickening boom of a crash.

The helicopter doesn't explode. Nothing so dramatic as that. When the camera finds its target again and pans back, we see the helicopter crushed beyond recognition in the field, smoking, silent, motionless.

Pez and I stare at the screen, willing someone to climb out of the wreckage, to stumble from the crumpled mess and then to run toward whoever is holding the camera and snatch it from them and punch them in the face.

But no one gets up. The camera zooms in close again and I see bodies in the belly of the ruins, twisted and lifeless. We watch for what feels like a solid minute. And then the feed goes dead, returning to the character-creation screen, which shows me that I have only one life left.

"Call the police," I say. "That has to be Pennsylvania. Surely the helicopter has some kind of GPS chip or something? Maybe call the helicopter company first. That's what the police would do. Maybe somebody saw it go down. They could still be alive."

Pez nods. He runs out the door.

I feel sick. I fumble around under my desk for the tiny wastepaper basket that is largely ceremonial, since my office is cleaned several times a day and I do all my work at the computer, generating basically zero paperwork. Every so often I toss a bag of chips or a takeout clamshell into it, but thankfully right now it is empty.

I heave out my guts into the tiny trash can. I puke up my hangover and the Indian food and the toxic swirl of anxiety and despair overtaking me. Bernard is dead. I know it. Even if he managed to survive the crash, the first person to arrive on the scene will be whoever was taking the video, and it won't be much work to make sure that whatever is left of Bernard doesn't make it to a hospital.

Three Nylo men dead in one week. The contractions of my stomach turn into sobs and I don't give a fuck if anybody hears me or not.

32

wimp out and let the cops go to Bernard's house to break the news to Phoebe. It should be me who tells her what happened, but I am simply not brave enough. I want to talk to her, but I don't want to be the one who tells her that her husband is dead.

And he really is dead. I got a confirmation from the tunnel and subway detectives within an hour of seeing the video. The police are still trying to figure out what happened. Perversely, against all circumstantial evidence, they think it was some kind of pilot error. They see no reason to assume that it was murder.

Even though he's the third Nylo to die this week.

So the police are clearly not going to help. At this point, the FBI should get involved. If I wanted, I could bring that kind of pressure on the city and make it happen. But I can't stand the idea of the agents' smug faces as they go through our phones, our computers, our lives.

I don't want to travel in a helicopter to Long Island. Not after what happened. I can't land on Bernard's lawn in a helicopter and give Phoebe even a fleeting glint of hope that it might be him.

Plus, I don't think I could bring myself to climb aboard a helicopter right now. Instead, I take a car. I arrive with Ed and Mel an hour or so after the cops. On the way I try to call Gabriella and Alistair, but they are still avoiding me, possibly afraid I might try to bend them to my will, like Pez said I do to people. But didn't they see the video? Bernard is dead, for fuck's sake.

Phoebe's au pair answers the door, a dowdy Irish woman in her fifties. She shakes her head when she sees me and opens the door wide. I hear wailing from deeper inside the house. The two boys are standing by the foot of the stairs. The littlest one runs up to me and hugs my legs.

"Make it stop," he says. "Make her stop."

"I can't, little guy," I say, rubbing Julian's back as he clings to me. "I can't turn this one around."

"Yes, you can," says Maxim with a sneer. "Yes, you can! You can do anything you want. You need to bring our dad back here and make Mom go back to normal."

I leave them at the stairs; there's nothing else I can do. They let me go, unsure whether my silence is acquiescence or defiance. I suppose they are going to have to get used to the ambivalent feeling of absence from the ones they love. This won't be good for either boy, but it will be especially bad for Maxim, who is already a toxic soup of behavioral problems.

I find Phoebe in one of the small libraries on the ground floor. There is a packet of papers on the table in front of her. It looks like a printout of grief counseling phone numbers and meeting times that the cops must have left behind.

She sees me and stifles a sob, then offers a half-smile. Even after her world's been turned upside down, she's still trying to be nice to me.

"What happened?" she says. "How could this happen?"

"It's all so horrible," I say. "And so sudden."

"Where was he going, that bastard?" she says. "Was he going to one of his women? Without even bothering to lie to me? Just taking off for the night to visit some piece of ass in another state? Without so much as a phone call?"

"We don't know where he was going," I say, which is the truth. He didn't tell me which city he had picked at random.

"I know he was cheating on me," says Phoebe. "I mean, he never actually started being faithful, so it was just a continuation of the cheating he was doing before we were married. But he was usually discreet about it. He would give me a lie. Why didn't he bother to give me a lie this time? Do you think it was some kind of suicide? I know he wasn't happy. But he couldn't be happy, could he? That wasn't in his character. He was happy enough, though, wasn't he? Why was he running away?"

"It wasn't suicide," I say. "I know that for a fact. He loved you. He loved his boys. Whatever he was doing was business related. I can tell you that much. I won't lie and tell you that he never cheated on you. But this wasn't about that. I know that for a fact."

"How can you say that?" says Phoebe. "You don't know his mind any better than me. How can you stand there and pretend like you knew him?"

I move closer to her. It doesn't feel right, but I guess it will never feel right. My family has been basically cut in half in one week. I do something I never would have done a week ago and put my arms around Phoebe, hugging her as tightly as I can.

"We are going to get through this," I say, not really believing it myself. "We are going to keep each other strong for our children. Whatever is left of Bernard is in those kids. They need their mommy right now."

Impossibly, she nods at me, somehow soaking up my bullshit. In situations like this, it really doesn't matter what you say, as long as you say it with sufficient zeal and gravitas.

"I want you to know, first of all, that this changes nothing," I say. "You will be taken care of just as if Bernard were still alive."

She looks a little shocked at this.

"Of course I will be," she says. "What do you mean?"

"I just mean, in case you were worried," I say. She thrusts her jaw out at me. She wasn't worried before, but now she is.

"Nylo will always take care of you," I say. "No matter what."

"They are supposed to send the body back tonight," says Phoebe.

"He broke his neck in the crash. That's what they say. At least he didn't suffer."

"Bernard never suffered," I say. "Not one day in his life."

"That's true," says Phoebe, smiling ruefully. "He didn't know how."

"Listen," I say. "I need to know something."

"Yes?"

"I don't quite even know what to ask. But have you seen anybody new around lately? Anybody suspicious, watching you or making you feel uncomfortable? One mother to another: sometimes we have a sixth sense about these sorts of things. Was there anybody who sent hackles up your neck? Anybody who didn't belong?"

To her credit, Phoebe doesn't dismiss me immediately out of hand. She thinks about it for a moment before shaking her head.

"Everything has been pretty quiet around here," she says. "Nothing exciting at all. Just the same daily dramas. I give the kids everything I possibly can, and Bernard fucks any old slut that comes into view, and I pretend not to see and we don't talk about it."

I nod, not wanting to let her pull me over to her side quite yet. My loyalties remain with my brother. I always told him that getting married was a bad idea, especially to someone so self-sacrificing who would seemingly let him get away with anything, but who was secretly bearing all of his insults and neglect like a metastasizing cancer. Eventually, one day, she would overwhelm him with pure righteous fury. Better to marry someone as awful as him, I said.

I almost feel bad for Phoebe that Bernard has denied her a cleansing final moment of rage, but I assume that in six months or so she will smash his convertible with his golf clubs or deck one of his many mistresses in a Wegmans or something and then she will write a cathartic "friends only" locked social media post about it that will have a similar effect and will let her begin the process of demonization that will fuel her spite tank for the rest of her life.

Not that Bernard wasn't an awful bastard. But he was my brother. And I am an awful bastard, too.

"It can't possibly have been easy being married to my brother," I say, standing up. "But you have been a good and loyal wife to him. I have always admired you for that. You were a really good team together, despite your differences. I hope now that he is gone we will be able to become closer, you and I, now that we are no longer divided by something so lame as a man."

She bursts into tears, nodding. It would be so easy to capture all of her self-abnegating, submissive energy and make it my own. But what purpose would I bend her toward? For now, it's good enough to keep her docile, to keep her from hating my brother for dying for just a little while longer as a gift to his memory.

"Henley's funeral is tomorrow," she says.

"Yeah, or whatever," I say. "Listen, you are in no shape to go to anything such as a funeral right now. I get it. You just stay here with the boys and take care of yourself. No one will blame you for not showing up. I guess we have to stagger our grief right now."

"Bernard was going to give a speech," she says. "He was working on it last night. It wasn't much, but maybe you can read it for him instead?"

"Yeah, okay, maybe that will be nice," I say.

"He sent it to me to proofread," she says. "Hold on, I'll text it to you."

I let her cry as she works her phone and then I give her a bottle of lorazepam. She smiles and tells me that she already has her own, but I leave the bottle anyway. You can't ever have enough.

I go looking for Ed and Mel. I find them playing with my nephews, letting Maxim and Julian climb all over them and giving them piggyback rides where they almost scrape the vaulted ceilings. Their insane levels of inhuman patience are proudly on display, and I envy their easy, laconic way of existing in the world.

I'm glad that Bernard dismissed his security detail before getting in that helicopter. I make a note to make sure that the helicopter pilot's family is generously compensated beyond whatever insurance claims they'll be able to make from the company and beyond whatever whole-life policy helicopter pilots must surely get for themselves as a matter of course. Whatever his family is paid, Nylo will match it.

"Aunt Caitlyn, did you make her stop crying?" asks Maxim as I pry my nephews off of my security guards. "Is everything back to normal?"

"Well, little guy," I say, "it isn't. But that doesn't mean you won't get used to the way things are now. You have to grow up a little bit faster, that's all. I wasn't much older than you when your grandmother died. Did you know that? Right now, I have to get back to the city, but when this is all over, you and I are going to get together and we are going to have a real special grown-up talk, okay?"

He nods at me, satisfied.

33

omehow, I manage to sleep. When I wake up, I check to see if Alistair or Gabriella has texted, but they still aren't responding to my messages.

I hop into the shower and let the hot water rain over me, steeling myself for Henley's funeral, followed by another round with the Game Master. I throw on a nice black dress before getting a car to Ugly American.

Maybe Alistair and Gabriella will bother to show up. Or maybe not. After all, any one of us might be next. Whoever is running the game has proved that there is nowhere to run and nowhere to hide from what is coming.

For the first time, I start to wonder what people will say if I win this horrible game. How will I spin it? Won't people be suspicious if I am the only one left alive and therefore have total control over my family's fortune?

I start to think about the Netflix documentary on this whole sordid affair that I will have to produce myself. I start to think about the way in which the police will be blamed for bungling the case and letting my siblings be killed by a terrorist one by one.

What will people say about me when they are asked? Will they tell the police that I would never be capable of something like this, of something so brutal and calculating with so many moving parts? Will they tell the police that they could never imagine me doing something so ruthless and diabolical?

Of course not. They'll tell the police that I am the only person they know who could actually pull something like this off.

Even Ben won't be able to spin a yarn that makes me heroic. My little girls will wonder about their mother. They will slowly become certain that I'm a murderer as they become rebellious teenagers. I don't exactly project warmth.

It dawns on me that my only way out is to pin it on Angelo Marino. He is just as much of a possibility as me. He would have had the same access to our father in order to make this all happen. *If I go down, he will go down, too.*

I get to Ugly American shortly before 10 a.m. One of the bartenders lets me in. The caterers have put out a spread of Henley's favorite foods in accordance with his wishes: SpaghettiOs, incredibly expensive French cheeses, rosemary and cracked black pepper crackers, kolaches, marzipan. There is a giant bong and a crystal bowl full of weed.

At first, I'm afraid no one is going to show up, but then Henley's dirtbag friends start to trickle in. It is a motley collection of posh-looking private school sneaks and paunchy local scumbags. My Midwesterners arrive as a pack, looking like they've been up all night. When the one with the new chin sees me, he gives a wave. Everybody begins eating and drinking, periodically hitting the bong. It is a relatively upbeat and festive affair. Henley has always mocked anyone who worried about life, death, or anything in between. He didn't learn that from our mom and dad. He got to that particular wisdom all on his own.

Pez and Angelo Marino arrive one after the other. Pez has his arm around a weeping woman dressed in skintight leather, whom I assume is Henley's ex Sheila.

We are just about to start giving speeches when the tunnel and subway detectives slink up to me, sizing me up, both of them eating electric blue freeze pops. Their tongues are bright turquoise. They must have gotten them from the cart down on the corner, which also sells dirty-water hot dogs and probably cocaine.

"Detectives," I say. "I'm glad you could both make it."

"It's official NYPD policy," says Detective Jay.

"We're supposed to attend the funerals of every homicide victim that we're investigating," says Detective Rutledge. "You never know. The killer might show up just to gloat, or else show some kind of weepy melodramatic remorse in public to throw us off the scent."

"Well, it's a nice gesture just the same," I lie.

Peter shows up and gives me a weary but sympathetic look. I have been trying to keep a firewall between my business and personal lives. Of course, that means I've been keeping him in the dark about the game, not letting him help me.

"I brought what you asked for," he says, shrugging a cooler off his shoulder. "I packed the cooler full. The bottles were just where you said they would be."

I take the cooler and open it up. Should I make an announcement? Should I tell the bar what this means to me, sharing from my personal stash?

His whole life, Henley bugged me for a taste and I always denied him. My White Coke was the one vice that I refused to share with him. Now, perhaps by filling his friends and lovers with White Coke, some of it will spiritually reach his spectral essence. I tell myself that ghosts surely attend their own funerals.

I decide that the people here will not enjoy the White Coke as much if they realize how precious it is. It must be a quiet novelty, something fun and frivolous.

I grab a bucket of ice from the bar and fill it up with clear bottles sporting red stars. Peter looks at me plaintively, like a kicked puppy. I nod at the bottles in the bucket and smile at him. He eagerly reaches out and takes one. He cracks it open and takes a long, luxurious sip.

"Tastes like freedom," he says with a happy sigh.

I grab a bottle of my own and tap it with a spoon to get everyone's attention and then I deliver Bernard's short speech about Henley. It is all wooden pleasantries, the kind of eulogy that you would write after Googling "how to write a eulogy." It is well-received. The gathered throng claps at the end. A few people make themselves cry.

Alistair enters the bar just as I am finishing. His face is gray. He is wearing the official Nylo Family Scavenger Hunt T-shirt that came with the phone in the steel suitcase. He is followed by Gabriella, wearing a pink tube top and fishnets. She looks like she has been out all night carousing. We make eye contact across the bar. *What is this? An armistice?*

I check my game phone. It is fifteen minutes until we get the next clue. At least we will all be together this time.

Alistair approaches me first. But he is interrupted by one of the Midwesterners, who claps me on the back, tears streaming down his beefy face.

"He was the best," the huge man gushes. "The best there ever was."

"There will never be another like him," I say.

"I heard your other brother was tragically and accidentally killed as well," he says. "Oh my god. How are you holding up? How are you bearing it?"

"I am not handling it particularly well," I say. "In fact, I am choosing not to really think about it yet. I am choosing not to process anything at all for the time being. I just want to do right by them the best I can. To do right by their memories."

"Hey, did you know that those bottles on the table aren't vodka? They taste like Coke—Crystal Coke! Isn't that crazy? Do you think the bar knows? Do you think they got swindled?"

"I'm sure I don't know," I say, smiling.

Alistair cuts in. He stands awkwardly in front of me for a moment and then hugs me. Gabriella follows behind him, embracing both of us in one of her too-warm, too-sexual hugs.

"We can't fight each other anymore," she says. "We have to all work together now. The stakes are too high. I know I am in the lead right now, but any one of us could be next."

"We talked it over," Alistair says to me. "We'll do whatever you want. You're in charge, sis. We are in your hands."

My eyes flash and I see a vision of both of their dead bodies, broken and bleeding. Even though Gabriella has two lives left, I know that Alistair is really my last rival here. If I can just beat him, I will win everything.

I chase the thought out of my head. The only rival I have is the game itself. We all have to work together if the three of us hope to survive and to catch whoever is doing this to us.

"It's almost time for the next clue," says Gabriella. "May I?"

She points to the bottles of White Coke on the food table. She certainly knows what they are. I nod.

"For Henley," I say. "And for Bernard."

Gabriella gets a bottle for herself and one for Alistair, and we clink in camaraderie. It feels good to share this with them. Almost as good as it has felt denying it to them all these years.

34

Everybody shares their final thoughts about Henley. It is fairly cathartic, and I know that all of these people will be drinking and partying here all day and all night, involving any strangers who wander into the bar in this celebration of my dead brother. But the three of us have other plans.

At noon, Pez, the detectives, my brother, my sister, and I gather in a quiet corner.

"It's time," says Gabriella.

"The two of you still have your superpowers," I say, just remembering.

"They haven't helped us out at all," says Alistair. "I can open any lock. Great."

"Yeah, and I am impervious to bullets," says Gabriella. "I put a gun in my mouth and tried to blow my brains out last night but nothing happened."

"Did you really?" I ask, ready to believe anything at this point.

"No," says Gabriella, shaking her head. "Not really."

The Nylo Corporation theme song starts to play. *Here we go.* The three of us hold up our phones to get the next clue.

This time, the Game Master is wearing a mask that looks like a fabricated vinyl reproduction of our father's face. It is ghoulish.

"You fucking monster," I say. "You piece of shit."

The detectives look at me knowingly, as if I have revealed too much. They seem pleased that my facade of decorum has been pierced.

"I am no monster," says the Game Master in a voice like a strung-out chipmunk. "I am merely in charge here. And it is time for the next clue. There are only three of you left, which means that the stakes are high."

"We aren't going to play your game," I say. "We are banding together. We are unionizing. We are going on strike. Are you going to kill all three of us at the same time?"

"I'm sure I don't have any idea what you are talking about," says the Game Master. "This is all just good corporate fun. Your next clue is: 'In a white room with white curtains.' That's it. Good luck, all of you!"

The Game Master's face disappears from the screen. The three of us look at each other. We all get it immediately. This one is even more obvious than all the others. It's as if the Game Master isn't trying to trick us anymore. Instead, they are trying to turn us against each other, to put us in an impossible pressure cooker of panic and resentment.

The clue swims on our game phones, shimmering over a field of red rain.

"You all seem like you know the answer to this one," says Detective Jay.

"Yeah," says Gabriella. "We know this one."

"It's down in Ditmas Park," says Alistair. "Where our mom killed herself. Our old summer house in Brooklyn. We sold it, of course. But the house is still there."

"We should have burned it to the ground," I say. "We should have capped it with concrete like a tomb."

"So, should we get a squad car there immediately?" asks Detective Rutledge. "That's where the next terrorist attack will be?"

"We don't care what you do," I say. "Send the police or not. But we are going. And we are going together." I turn to Gabriella and Alistair. "We can take the train. I can use my pass for all of you."

"But it's such a nice day," says Gabriella. "And we should give the cops a chance to check the place out."

"I don't have any plans," says Alistair. I realize that none of us are in any hurry.

"Then we'll walk," I say.

Alistair, Gabriella, and I each take a somber shot of bourbon before leaving the dark bar behind and venturing out into the sunny June afternoon. Gabriella has sunscreen in her bag and we all slather up as best we can, making sure to get the backs of our ears and the backs of our legs.

Just as we are about to take off, Angelo Marino steps outside and grabs me by the shoulder, pulling me aside.

"You'll meet us over there?" I ask him.

"I will," he says.

"How can any of this be legally binding at this point?" I say. "As a last will and testament?"

"It isn't," he says. "But that's not why you are doing it now. Is it?"

"No," I say. "It's about something else now. Pride. Not being afraid. Confronting this asshole. And staying alive, obviously."

"I need to tell you something," he says. "Something I've been meaning to tell you for a long time. I never could do it before, not while your father was alive. First of all, he wouldn't let me. And second of all, I was deeply ashamed. I want you to know that everything was fine between your father and I. He hated me once upon a time, it's true. Hated me for a long time. But in the end, he forgave me. And in the end, the fact that we both had the same love, the same grief: this fact united us. It kept us together. Even when we should have run from each other, we ran toward each other instead."

"What are you trying to tell me?" I say, knowing exactly what he is trying to tell me.

"Your mother and I," he says. "At the end. We were together. Intimately. It wasn't good for us. We were going to stop what we were doing. But she was lonely and I was lonely. And I had always loved her. It didn't feel wrong. It was she who started everything. I think she was trying to get revenge, but I don't know why or what for. But I also think it was more than that. She just wanted to change herself. To become something new. She was tired of her life and she didn't know what to do about it."

"How long?" I ask, not sure I want to know the answer.

"It was years," he says. "But it wasn't like you are thinking. It was sporadic. I loved her, but I don't think she ever really loved me back. She was just taking from me. Sucking my blood to stay alive. Anyway, I wanted you to know that. I loved her and I loved your father as well. Losing her was the worst thing that ever happened to both of us. I blamed him just as much as he blamed me. But in the end, it was both of us who were wrong. And her role can't be ignored either. After all these years, the person I blame the most for her suicide is her."

I raise an eyebrow at this last bit, which he says with unbelievable venom, but I know he is right.

"Thank you for telling me," I say. "It can't have been easy for you."

"No," he says. "I just wanted you to know. I needed to get it off my chest."

"Just in case I'm murdered," I say. "And you never get a chance to unburden yourself."

He nods.

"You are so much like her," he says. "Sometimes I forget that you aren't the same person."

He looks like he wants to say something else, but he doesn't. He opens his mouth and shuts it and then turns away, back to the door of Ugly American.

As my siblings and I walk, three security guards follow us and three move in front, clearing the way. We are in a bubble of protection. It is unnerving and feels almost biblical, like Palm Sunday, with Jesus riding into town on an ass for one last week of glory. It feels right to walk. To strut through our city.

We reminisce as we stroll, talking about the old days, talking about our father and our two dead brothers. Gabriella asks me about Phoebe and the children.

"I want you guys to promise that you will take care of all of them," I say. "I know Bernard wasn't the greatest husband or father, but he really did love them and he would have wanted for us to provide for them all, just as if they were our own kids."

"They won't want for anything," says Alistair.

"Nothing but caviar and Harvard for everyone," says Gabriella. "Truly. We promise."

This comes as a relief. I think about Bernard's indiscretions weighed against our mother's cheating heart. He was faithless, but was it really his fault? I remember back when he was a boy and he used to cling to her, much more than Alistair, who was enamored with our father. It was only Henley who didn't seem to need anyone at all.

We cross the bridge into Brooklyn and then make our way down Coney Island Avenue, past the endless car wash stations and fast food restaurants. This is the part of New York City that feels the most like any other place in the United States: a hollow, bombed-out hellscape where brands meet cars and where freedom shrinks down to what you can buy and where you can drive.

We are exhausted by the time we make it to Ditmas Park. I am now fully sober. I wish I had brought a hat. I am fairly certain I have managed to burn myself along my scalp, where my hair parts down the middle.

We weave through the blocks to our old summer house by muscle memory. I remember these streets well, like creases in my own brain, cut deep by paranoia and obsession. The security guards fan out to protect us, joining the security staff who are already there. They sweep around the perimeter of the house, jogging into the backyard.

"The cops came and went, but they only barely checked the place," Mel informs me.

"Let us go in first," says Ed. "I don't trust the cops."

I give the okay and our security detail checks the doors, both front and back. Then they pour into the house like an enema.

I don't know how many times this property has changed hands over the years and I don't know where the deed has ended up. I expect that Angelo Marino will be able to tell us once he arrives, but he isn't here yet.

The White Room in the front will just be a normal living room now. The bloodstains won't be on the walls and on the carpet and on the curtains. It will just be an empty front room, like any other room in the world. I still can't quite imagine what it will be like to step foot in there again, to test myself against the worst memory that I have.

Angelo Marino pulls up in an Uber. He steps out of the car, looking contrite and embarrassed. I'm sure he is wondering if I have told Alistair and Gabriella about his dalliances with our mother.

"Just in time," I say as he morosely walks up to us. "We need to know who owns this house."

"Actually, you own it," says Angelo Marino. "Or rather, the Nylo Corporation does. It was purchased by a shell corporation two years ago. I had nothing to do with it. It was something that your father did on his own."

"So he sold it and vowed never to return, and then he bought it again just so he could send us on this sick quest?" I ask.

"Seems so," says Angelo Marino.

While the security guards scour the inside, we wait on the front lawn, smoking cigarettes and trying to find shade among the big trees of the neighborhood. Eventually, they come back out, shaking their heads.

"There's no one in there," says Ed. "It's completely empty. It looks like there hasn't been anybody inside in a long time. There's dust on the walls, on the staircase, on the doorknobs."

"Whoever set this up might have done it months ago," points out Alistair.

From the lawn, we can see the front room, surely where we are supposed to go.

"How should we do this?" asks Alistair. Gabriella can still afford to lose a life, whereas neither Alistair nor I can. We both look at her.

"I don't want to go in there," says Gabriella.

"We'll take your phone in for you," I say. "You can just wait here on the lawn."

I tell the security guards to expect anything. They make a wall around us as Alistair and I step toward the house, blocking us from all sides.

"The Game Master is probably watching somehow," I say. "Like they were watching Bernard fall out of the sky. They must be here somewhere. Well, let them watch."

Alistair and I enter our old house. I breathe deeply, shuddering as I cross over the threshold. He puts his hand on my shoulder and I nod, letting him know I am okay. We move into the White Room, just off the foyer. Against all odds, it's still white. The carpet, the curtains, the walls. All white. A shiver runs down my spine.

We walk all the way in, but nothing happens. We move together around the sides of the room, our hands grazing the walls, but it isn't until we reach the big front windows that the Nylo theme starts to play. Alistair wins. I come in second.

"I'll go get Gabriella's phone," he says to me. "Are you okay in here?"

I am having a hard time being in this room again, but I don't want to leave until I can handle it. My brain is screaming and I feel like running in thirty directions at once. Instead of exploding into a flesh-colored mist, I smile at Alistair and nod.

I watch him jog outside and retrieve Gabriella's phone. She waves to me where I stand in front of the big White Room windows. I wave back. Alistair comes back in and presses it to the wall beneath the window where the box must be hidden behind the baseboard. The Nylo theme begins to play on Gabriella's phone.

The theme is still playing when we hear a screech of tires from down the street. Two black vans come speeding around the corner. Security guards pour into the house. I am tossed to the ground as Mel and Ed cover me. My face presses into the White Room carpet just as the gunfire starts.

All around me I hear screaming. I try to fight Mel and Ed to see what is going on, but I only manage to turn my head to the side. The noise of gunfire is deafening.

I hear the vans speeding away, tires squealing.

"Somebody follow those vans!" shouts Ed.

"I'm already on it," says Mel, leaping to his feet and running to the cars parked in front of the house.

I sprint outside to the lawn, expecting the worst. Alistair is right behind me. Gabriella is sitting cross-legged on the lawn. Her eyes are wide.

"They shot right at me," says Gabriella. "Doors opened up on the side of the vans and they unloaded at me. They were wearing masks. My ears are ringing. I can't hear my own voice."

She puts her hand to the side of her jaw and opens her mouth wide, as if trying to pop her ears.

"Impervious to bullets," she says, almost to herself.

"Is anybody hurt?" I shout. Nobody on the lawn says anything. One of the security guards who didn't chase after the vans answers his phone when it starts to ring.

"Mel caught them," he reports. "They weren't even really trying to run away. He caught them on the next block over."

The Nylo music sounds again and all three of us take out our phones. Video plays. We see Gabriella's back as she stands on the lawn like Superman as starburst flashes from automatic weapons light up the afternoon all around her. She drops to the ground, her athleticism showing. The vans squeal away and we see the security guards scrambling.

Alistair and Gabriella and I look at each other. Then we look up at the top window of the summer house.

The angle of the video was taken from up above and behind us. The camera in the video was shaking as it panned: a person was holding the camera. Which means that whoever was taking the video is somewhere inside the house.

35

"**A**ctors," says Mel, after returning in his car and walking up to us slowly. "It's a bunch of actors. They're staying put until the cops arrive. Somebody hired them to shoot at us with blanks."

I wonder what would have happened if one of us had actually lost. Would we have been taken out by a sniper bullet from upstairs?

"The Game Master is in the building," I tell Mel and Ed. "On the top floor. Waiting for us. They want us to know they're there."

"Then we've got them." Mel's eyes dart to the top window, then scan the area around the house. "We'll cover all the exits and wait for the cops to take them out."

"Somehow I don't think it will be that easy," I say with a sigh.

"They're trapped," says Alistair. "There are people everywhere here now."

It's true. Neighbors are coming out of their houses up and down the street to see what is going on. We can hear police sirens on the way, surely brought here by reports of gunfire.

Our game phones all begin ringing again. Gabriella, Alistair, and I press our heads and shoulders together in a huddle and hold up our phones to see what comes next.

It is more video feed. The Game Master is wearing a *Sea Farmers* mask. He or she looks just like the iconic trident-wielding Atlantean on the game box. They are holding what appears to be a detonator: a big box with a plunger, right out of a cartoon.

As we watch, a taxi pulls up and my two little girls and Ben get out. I snap my fingers at the security guards and they run over to shield them.

"Keep them back," I yell to Ed and Mel. Then to Ben, Olivia, and Jane, who should be safely tucked away in an Airbnb in Nantucket, I call, "Why are you here?"

"Mom," shouts Olivia. "You texted us and told us to meet you here. You said it was an emergency. We flew here on the afternoon plane. What's going on?"

I didn't text them. But someone did.

"Everyone's here then," comes the Game Master's modulated voice, blaring tinnily from the three game phones. "Fantastic. That means we can begin. As you might have figured out by now, this entire building is wired to explode and I am holding the detonator. If anybody tries to leave, I will blow the whole place up. Since it is now down to three of you, we can move on to the final challenge. It's an easy one. The three of you just have to come inside, alone, and come upstairs, where one of you will find your destiny and the others will not. Come unarmed or I will blow everything up. Come right now or I will blow everything up. If anyone tries to leave, I will blow everything up."

The Game Master is obviously bluffing.

But what choice do we have? We have to end this thing. We have a chance to meet this person in the flesh. To be in the same room with them. To rip the mask off their face and get justice.

I look at my brother and sister. They see the fire in my eyes. My resolve.

"I don't want to go in," says Gabriella.

"You have to come," I say. "We all have to go." Alistair nods his agreement.

Gabriella chews her lip as her face turns red. She takes a few pills from her purse, shakily shoves them in her mouth, and swallows them dry, then nods vigorously.

"If you're going," she says, "then I'll go, too."

The security guards don't want to let us reenter the house at first. But they aren't cops. They can't actually stop us. In fact, they work for us. They must do what we tell them, so in the end they get out of the way.

I walk back up the steps and go inside first. I am purposeful, determined. I don't care about this contest. I am going to find the Game Master and tear them apart with my bare hands.

I hear Alistair and Gabriella creeping into the house behind me. I immediately look over into the White Room again. I half expect to see it covered in blood. To see our mother's corpse spread out on the floor. But the room is empty.

"I think we're supposed to go upstairs," whispers Alistair. I nod.

We make our way up the stairs one after the other, me, then Alistair, then Gabriella, none of us wanting to admit that we are afraid. I know Alistair well enough to know that we are both in silent accord: we are going to get revenge for what has happened to our family. We are going to get revenge against whatever butcher has cut the Nylos down, even if it means that the entire Nylo family is extinguished from the Earth forever.

At the top of the stairs, we walk down a long hallway to a door with light coming from underneath. This used to be our parents' room. We push open the door.

The Game Master is sitting at a card table. Where did they come from? How did the cops and our security team miss them? On top of the card table, *Sea Farmers* is set up and ready to be played, a bottle of bourbon and three crystal glasses full of ice sitting alongside it. Three empty folding chairs await us.

"Sit," says the Game Master in his or her strange, digitally altered register. "Please, sit down."

We do as we are told. I look to the window and realize that the way we are positioned around the table will prevent anyone outside from getting a clear shot at the Game Master. We are being held hostage quite effectively.

The Game Master gestures to the bourbon and glasses. "You may drink if you like. It might help for what comes next."

"What comes next?" I ask, my voice steady despite my raw nerves. As if I don't know.

"You will play," says the Game Master. "And one of you will win."

That's when I notice the revolver in the Game Master's lap beside the detonator. They are cradling it gently, like an infant.

"Caitlyn, you are the current CEO, and Alistair, you are the brains behind developing Nylo's most successful games and diversions. But only one of you is leaving this room alive. Gabriella, you have just as much of a shot as your elder siblings. But only one of you will walk down those stairs as the inheritor of twenty billion dollars and control of the Nylo empire. If you don't play, I will blow everyone up. If you try to kill me, I will obviously blow everyone up. It will be best for you if you each see the logic of what must happen as quickly as possible and begin the game."

"This is insane," I say. "We aren't going to play *Sea Farmers* while you're holding a gun on us."

The Game Master is implacable. They sit silently behind their mask, watching us.

"It should be you," Alistair blurts out, turning to face me. "You know what you're doing. I would never be able to run the company without you. There is no Nylo without you. I can be replaced. There are members of my own team who are better than me at this stuff. Designers like me are only good when they're young, anyway."

"Oh, shut the hell up," I say. "Don't give this psycho the satisfaction of taking this game seriously."

"It should be you," Alistair says again. "Can't I just give up without having to die?"

"Yeah," says Gabriella, hope shining in her eyes. "Can't we all just walk away and let Caitlyn win?"

The *Sea Farmers* King shakes their head.

"Alistair, you know you are the only real genius in the family," I say. "You inherited all of Dad's creativity and smarts, and you are the reason this company has been successful for the last decade. You're the only hope for the company being successful for ten more decades. Trust me: you can learn to do what I do. And if you don't want to bother, you can hire someone just as capable to do my job."

The Game Master crosses and then uncrosses their legs, cocking their big foam *Sea Farmers* head to the side.

"Enough table talk. Play," they goad. "Play the game."

The Game Master is right: there isn't anything else to do here. Playing the game seems like it might buy us some time to think. To make a silent plan. Plus, there is nothing more natural for the three of us than playing this board game.

And so we begin.

The first thing we notice is that although it's the normal *Sea Farmers* game board, the rules have been modified. This game includes the Kraken from the expansion pack, but not deployed in the same random way as in the expansion. In this version, the Kraken can be lured by sacrificing hatchling workers. It can then be used against your opponents in a way that directly harms them.

"An interesting modification," Alistair says after we play a few rounds. "It actually seems very intuitive."

"It was always this way," says the Game Master. "These are the original rules, before they were neutered."

What the Game Master says has the ring of truth to it. It feels very natural that this would be the first incarnation of *Sea Farmers*. I can also see why it was jettisoned. Our father's gaming philosophy was always one of non-hostility—of safe and gentle family fun. I can't help but wonder if *Sea Farmers* would have been as successful if it had such an aggressive mechanic from the very beginning.

As we play, Alistair and I keep making eye contact and looking at the gun the Game Master is holding. If we could manage to distract them, possibly one of us could make a grab at it and try to overpower them. But the problem is that we can't tell where exactly the Game Master is looking, because of the mask. Surely their peripheral vision must be significantly weakened, but it is still too risky.

Just as we are both coming to the conclusion that we will have to charge the Game Master at the same time—detonator be damned!— they stand up and move to one of the room's far corners, covering me from behind.

"Play," they say. "Don't mind me."

"There's not really a bomb, is there?" I say, looking over my shoulder. The gun is leveled at me and it does not shake. I turn back around and consider the board. I roll the dice and then choose to cultivate my kelp field.

Neither Alistair nor I have the heart to put much strategy into the game. We both find ourselves sending the Kraken at each other, letting Gabriella off the hook, which means that she quickly takes the lead. There is something instinctual about this. She is the baby and we are the older siblings. Neither of us wants to be the one who kills her. We both find ourselves subtly striving for second place. This means that Gabriella is able to play the best game of *Sea Farmers* of her life.

It almost isn't enough to put her over the top. As the game begins to wind down to its ultimate conclusion, Alistair and I are doing the math in our heads, counting who has the most cultivated fields, who has the most hatchling workers in seasonal rotation, who has the most stories on their Coral Castle. It will be tight between all three of us: Gabriella isn't selling enough kelp to buy pearls. She never did understand this game very deeply.

Finally, I can't stand it. The next time her turn rolls around, I point to the Oyster Bed and lock eyes with her. She gets my meaning. All she has to do is sell her remaining stock of kelp, turning it into enough pearls to hire all the dormant hatchling workers. If she uses her remaining action points to finish digging her last trench, she will beat me by forty points. If she doesn't, Alistair will lay his last trench and they might actually tie.

I don't mind losing to Gabriella, but I don't want to be the one who clearly loses to both of them. I trade her kelp cards for pearl jewels from the box and then lay her trench for her. She squints at me, frowning. Alistair sees what I'm doing but doesn't stop me.

"Okay, that's it then," says Gabriella, trusting that I know what I'm doing. "Everybody count up your score."

We go through the motions and it slowly dawns on Gabriella that she has won. Has she ever won a game of *Sea Farmers*? I can't ever remember her beating us. She seems perplexed.

The Game Master walks slowly back to the table, looking at the board.

"That's 180 for me, 140 for Caitlyn, and 130 for Alistair," says Gabriella. "I guess that means I win."

Now is our chance to rush the Game Master. Alistair and I both tense up.

Gabriella pushes back her chair and stands up. She grins. She crosses her arms.

"I won," she says, turning to the Game Master. "Just like you said I would."

What the hell? I flick my eyes at Alistair.

"What are you talking about?" Alistair demands. She grins at him and opens her mouth to speak.

That's when the gun goes off. Gabriella flies backward against the wall with a giant bullet wound in the center of her chest. The hydrostatic shock bursts blood vessels in her eyes and she chokes on the blood that pours out of her mouth as her body slides down the wall.

I am frozen in place. Alistair takes a step toward Gabriella's gasping frame and the Game Master shoots him next, firing twice, hitting him in the side under his arm and then in the neck. He falls across the card table, sending pieces flying. The bottle of bourbon crashes to the floor and shatters.

I whirl around just as someone new runs into the room. It's Angelo Marino, coming from the bathroom across the hall. Has he been in there the whole time? My ears are ringing and I don't know which way to turn. I feel so vulnerable. So porous. So shootable.

Angelo Marino runs to Gabriella, shouting at the Game Master. "What are you doing? Why did you shoot her?"

He skids to a halt on his knees beside my baby sister and wraps his arms around her, glaring at the *Sea Farmers* King with furious eyes. The Game Master doesn't respond. They lower the gun, but only for a second, and then raise it back up again, firing three bullets into Angelo Marino's back. At least one of them travels through his spine and hits Gabriella in the torso, knocking her head back one final time. She stops breathing.

I am covered in blood and bourbon and glass fragments. I am paralyzed, standing between the three dead bodies and the person who filled them with bullets. The Game Master fishes in their pocket for more, then snaps open the revolver and reloads the gun.

They walk over to Angelo Marino and roll him over. Finally, the Game Master takes off the mask, shaking out a smooth mane of hair. It's blond like mine, cut at the shoulder. The woman spits in Angelo Marino's face and then turns around.

Somehow I know even before I see her sparkling green eyes, her familiar jaw. It is my mother, Misty Lynn Nylo. Her makeup is immaculate. She looks good. She looks healthy. Definitely not dead.

"Hello, Caitlyn," she says.

36

"That was the hard part," she continues. "Now that we are done with all of that, we can get to the easy part—the sorting everything out, darling."

"M-mother?" I stammer. I want to scream. I want to weep. I want to throw my arms around her and hug her until my shoulders go numb. I want to smash her face in with my bare hands until all the bones in my fingers and wrists are broken.

I take a step toward her and she raises the gun again.

"Why don't we both sit down?" she says in a calm, listen-to-your-mother kind of way. "I can only assume you are just full of emotions. We can have a little chat. You look ragged. You aren't getting enough sleep, huh? I suppose that is probably all my fault. Sit down, Caitlyn. Stay a while."

I don't feel like sitting. I don't feel like doing what I'm told. But she sits down first and I feel awkward standing there with my fists balled while she points a gun at me. I pick up one of the fallen chairs and right it, then lower myself slowly, feeling nauseous and confused.

"You killed Alistair," I say. "You shot Gabriella."

"Yes, I suppose I did," she says. "I have a little secret to tell you: she was only your half-sister. She was Angelo's daughter, and that's why he helped me with my little game here. That's why I had to shoot him, too. You know, I didn't expect you to let her win like that. I suppose you are just a better person than I am. But I guess that's what this is all about. You have so many admirable qualities, darling. I guess I had to put my thumb on the scale there at the end, but I think I made the right decision."

"You killed Dad," I blurt, a fuller realization of the big picture settling in. "You killed all of them."

She stares at me, almost smiling. It is really her. Not some actor or a hologram. I feel warm and tranquil, narcotized somehow. I hate her so much that I feel floaty. And I also realize just how much I have missed her.

"You are a monster," I say. "You are a fucking psychopath."

"Yes, I suppose I am," she says, smiling slightly. "You have every right to feel that way. I have indeed killed them all, just as you say, one by one. Everyone who stands in your way. It's not something you asked me to do. The truth is, I had planned to do it a long time ago. It would have been harder back then, back when you were all children. I suppose I am a bit of a coward. I always hoped my feelings would cool. That my hatred would settle down. But it never did, darling. And when Angelo came to me and told me about your father's will, well, I knew I had to finally do something."

"You were working together," I say. "You and him."

I gesture to Angelo Marino, who is bleeding out on the floor.

"Yes, well, we have a long history of using each other," she says. "He helped me disappear all those years ago, back when you were all children. He relied on his connections with the police and mafia to help me fake my own death and start a new life in China, and he made sure that I never wanted for money. The walls of this house have secret doors that lead to secret tunnels. Angelo built them in the off-season and I used them to escape. He found some other corpse with my features, my proportions. In return, I let him love me in his way, even promising to help his daughter ascend to the top of the Nylo empire. It was a lie to be sure, but he didn't have to suffer long with the—what did he always call it—the sting of my betrayal. Oh well. Can't be helped."

"But why?" I ask. "Why did you do it? How could you kill all of us? How could you kill your own children?"

She smiles at me knowingly. "Not all of you. You have always been my favorite, sweetheart."

I think of Olivia and Jane and my mostly ambivalent feelings toward them. I'm not exactly the epitome of maternal and I don't think I've ever had a favorite, although I'm sure there have been moments when I've liked one more than the other. But as I think about my mother's actions, I am overcome by a feeling of darkness, recalling all the times when I have hated them or wished I hadn't been so naive or stupid as to think they would make my life easier or change me for the better as a person.

"I never wanted to get pregnant," she continues. "What do people say now? That relationships ought to be consensual? Well, you were not the product of a consensual act of sex, my darling. I was a very heavy drinker once upon a time—damn near an alcoholic—and your father had a taste for incapacitated women. We were dating, or whatever you call it where a man takes you out drinking and watches you like a hawk until you pass out and then does whatever he wants to you."

I swallow hard. This is a more specific and deliberate version of the same story she has told us ever since we were children. About how she never wanted to be a mother. About how she was tricked into it. We always assumed that she was exaggerating. But I suddenly realize that she may have actually been softening the truth.

"I hated myself so much back then," she says. "I hadn't made peace yet with the way that I am. I wasn't anything like my sunny, self-actu-alized current self that you now see before you. I hated myself so much that I let my relationship with your father keep going, far longer than it should have. I think I made up my mind to kill him very early on, possibly after the first time he stole a kiss from me in that elevator. I came up to the city to get away from an investigation back home in Alabama, where I had gotten rid of a similar nuisance in my life, a pastor in our church who just wouldn't take no for an answer. But before I had a chance to rid myself of your father, I came up pregnant. Obviously, my first instinct was to get rid of the child. What do you call it up here? The fetus. But I made the mistake of telling your father my plan and not following through quickly. And that's how he got me. He found my weak point. He was always a very good game player. Not better than me—not when I was sober, anyway. But back then I was rarely ever sober."

I can't remember my mother ever playing games in her life. She would watch us from afar, drinking and smoking, a look of loathing in her eyes. Much like the look she has now, recalling my father's tactics.

"He got to my family, is what he did. Before I could run out and get you scraped clean out of me, I was getting phone calls of congratulations from my mamma and daddy and my cousins and brothers and aunts and uncles from every trailer park and pig wallow in Alabama. He used his inheritance and bought them all houses and jewelry and paid their debts and sent them gambling money. He asked my father for my hand in marriage, contingent on us having this baby and many more babies. And in return, he was going to keep my family set up forever with his Nylo family fortune: a fortune that he wanted to use to make fucking board games and novelties. I was trapped."

She shakes her head in defeat, and reaches into her pocket to pull out a pack of cigarettes.

"He made it so that my family would hate me for the rest of my life if I spurned him. He solved all of their problems, joining us with capital in a way that would never work with mere feelings. I guess he really must have loved me back then, before he knew completely what I was like. Maybe he never knew completely. To drag my whole genome out of the filth and into the glory of Yankee wealth, all I would need to do was have his babies. He attacked me where I was weak: my pride. And so I let you be born. I regretted it instantly. But I did it. I did it knowing that I could always take it back if I really wanted. I wanted my family to be strong. To be rich. To prosper and to thank me for it. Pride. Pride is all it was."

She slips a cigarette from the pack and lights it. I reach into my jacket and pull out a pack of my own. I realize that we both smoke Dunhills. Of course we do. My first pack was probably one of hers that I found after she died.

After she didn't die.

"The years slipped by," she continues, after taking a deep drag and sending a puff of smoke wafting across the room. "Your brothers came next. I realized that having children isn't so bad when you're obscenely wealthy. You didn't seem to need my love. Those early years were actually kind of a blur. Your father struggled with his game designs, trying like hell to have some kind of independent success so he could wrest himself from his family's purse strings. He was rich as hell for Alabama, but for a Yankee scion he was woefully dependent. Which meant that I was also crippled by his failures, forced to travel with him to beg his mother and father for infusions of cash, or to accompany him to banks to look pretty while he wheedled out loans. He needed a success and so I gave him one."

Her eyes flick to the ground, where all the pieces of *Sea Farmers* are scattered on the ground.

"I had never invented a game before or studied game theory or anything like that," she says. "I just based *Sea Farmers* on how people live back home: pretending to be all social and caring and Christian while trying to destroy each other and buy each other's land out from under bank debts and render curses unto the seventh generation and all that. Basic human evil and primordial shittiness, the kind that's always right there in front of you if you ever choose to look. My original had the Kraken from the very beginning, but your father didn't like how brutal the game could become that way. He changed the rules, and *Sea Farmers* was an instant hit."

She smiles ruefully and brings the Dunhill to her lips for another pull. "Of course, your father said that no one would ever buy it if they knew that the game was invented by a woman. As if they really would have cared. I was allowed to come into the office, but the game's origins had to stay a secret for his own pride and vanity, for the good of the company, he said. There wasn't much for me to do in those early days, since I had no interest in developing follow-ups or marketing the damn game to all the rubes of America and Europe. Your father was very sensitive to the smell of paint, so I repainted the walls of the office over and over again to torture him. He had a constant headache back in those days. It kept him away from me as effectively as cold showers and saltpeter. It's the little tactical victories that one savors the most."

She flicks her ashes onto the carpet and takes another drag.

"I'm sure you can figure out the rest. Angelo started courting me and I let myself be courted, mainly just to hurt your father. Eventually, however, I couldn't stand any of you anymore. I didn't want to divorce Prescott and divide the fortune, nor did I want to see the rest of you brats ever again. I told Angelo how I was thinking about murdering you all and then killing myself. He said that there were easier ways to end things. Less drastic ones. He cooked up the plan of faking my death. And that was satisfactory. For a while."

She sighs.

"I thought that if I never saw any of you ever again that my resentment—my hate and loathing—would fade. Disappear, perhaps. That it would be dissolved by my own lassitude and languor. But, darling, no. It only grew and deepened. I couldn't stand how I had been used to bring all of you into the world. I couldn't stand how useless you all were. And so I began to connive to destroy you all, beginning with your father. Angelo told me what your father wanted to do with his will. How it would be a game. Angelo was worried about his own daughter, about Gabriella's future. And so my plan started to come together. I hijacked the game and replaced your father's clues and questions with my own. I told Angelo that if he helped me kill off Prescott's children, Gabriella would be left alive at the end and she would inherit everything. He trusted me. I think he really did love me, in his way. Gabriella also agreed to be part of our little cabal. With a mother like me and a father like Angelo, what chance did she have to be even the slightest bit normal? So the three of us conspired to kill you all off. And then at the end... well... "

"You chose me," I say.

She smiles.

"I chose you."

37

"I didn't expect to become so fond of you," says my mother. "After all, you ruined my life. But then again, there is so much of me in you. Your hair color. The shape of your jaw. The way you walk. The way you command a room. Even when you were a child, I had an affinity for you. Nonetheless, I thought it would be easy to kill you eventually for the humiliation you caused me by being born, but, darling, I must admit: watching you these past few months has really made me reconsider things. Accepting you the way you are has become a way for me to cherish myself more. Is that crazy?"

I give her a wry smile. "Actually, I think it's fairly normal. Possibly the definition of motherhood. Every other fucking thing you have ever done or said so far is crazy, though."

She snorts, laughing.

"I wouldn't know anything about motherhood," she says. "My own mother, your grandmother, was a bit of a nightmare horror show. We come from slave owners, you know. Not everyone had what it took to be a slave owner. You had to love it. It had to give you a real thrill."

I shudder. She grins, leaning toward me. I feel a chill down the back of my neck but also a longing. I want her to love me. Even after everything that has happened, I want her to take me in her arms and tell me everything will be okay. I am so fucking happy to have my mother back. I am relieved that she wasn't the weak part of me, the part willing to sacrifice myself to let Gabriella live. Instead, I now know that she is the other part of me, the part with killer instincts in the board room and at the gaming table.

I am covered in blood and glass, and I am scared out of my mind, but for the first time in a long time, I feel whole.

Of course, I can't let her get away with what she has done. She's come back into my life in the worst, most temporary way possible.

So good to have you back, Mother. And now you must fucking die.

"I don't expect to get away with what I have done," she says, as if reading my mind. "The world will look at me as the worst kind of abomination. I am a Medea, a woman who kills her own children. I have hunted them down one by one after deeming them unworthy. The world doesn't respect the rights of mothers. A father might send his own weak children off to die in some impossible, stupid war and be lauded for it as a patriot. A mother who kills her failed children is a monster because she shows agency. And so children bend toward the traits of their fathers, not fearing their mothers as they should. Do your own children fear you?"

Of course not. The strongest emotion I elicit from them is contempt, which I am sometimes able to twist into benign fondness. But I hate my mother. I know that for a fact. I also love her. And yes, I fear her very deeply. How could I not, as she confesses what she has done while pointing a revolver at me?

"No, I don't expect anyone to forgive me for what I have done, and I don't expect to get away with it," she says. And here she smiles at me shrewdly. "But do you think that they will forgive you for what you have done?"

I don't know what to say to this. I smooth my pants down. What does she mean? I open my mouth to ask, but I don't even know how to phrase the question.

"There are many ways that this could go," she says. "Let me lay them out for you and then let me tell you what I think will be best. I am sluggish, glutted, and satisfied with my revenge so far. I am old and tired and have lived a very good, very full life. I am ready to retire."

I nod, blankly, unsure what else to do. Outside, I can hear people shouting and the noise of police sirens and barking dogs. How long have we been up here in this musty second-floor room? Flies are starting to circle around the dead bodies. It is growing dark as the evening comes on. My mother lights another cigarette, and the glow from her lighter momentarily blinds me. I look away, starting to get a headache from the smoke and tension in this close room.

"I could blow my brains out," she says, holding the revolver up to her temple. My gut tenses up. I have imagined seeing my mother kill herself so often over the years. I am shocked to discover that I don't want her to die, even though just moments ago I thought I was ready to kill her myself. Something primal in me would be devastated. I already mourned her once. I couldn't do it again.

She lowers the gun, seeming to sense my panic.

"I don't want to die," she says. "And the cloud would fall on you. The company would fail. You would be blamed for killing the lot of us, I'm sure. So many bodies and no one around to corroborate your story."

She smiles.

I know she is telling the truth. Goddammit, she has all the power here.

"Or I could stay alive and blame you for everything," she says. "I could tell the world that you and I set everything up together so that you would be able to rule your father's empire uncontested. I'm not sure that anyone would believe me. But I could plant the seeds of doubt. I am very persuasive. You might not go to prison, but I think I could very easily make it so that the shareholders could not in good conscience leave you in control of the company. Nylo is a family business after all."

What she is saying is absolutely true. Nylo would become as lurid as the Manson Family. It probably will anyway. I can't imagine any way that the company will come out of this unscathed. Everyone is dead.

My mother smiles at me and her blue eyes glitter. She sees that I am working it all out in real time.

"Or I could confess," she says. "I could tell the truth. I have videos and recordings of what I have done. I could make the world believe that I did it alone. And you could try and understand and forgive me."

"I will never forgive you," I say instantly. And we both know that this is true. But I have overplayed my hand. She has asked for the moon and already she has the compromise she wants. Already I am trying to understand her. Already I am trying to see the world how she sees it.

And then I suddenly realize that this is why my murderous bitch of a mother has chosen me and not Gabriella. Because I will be able to understand her someday. Maybe not now. But eventually. And she knows that I will want to understand her. That I will need to know why she has done what she has done. That I will be more fascinated than revolted.

"There is something strong about you," she says. "Stronger than me. You are just as much of a monster as me, of course—just as much as Angelo, your sister, and your father. But you keep it in check. You keep it down, like vomit that will not rise. It poisons you but you hold it anyway. Wouldn't you like to know more about what you are swallowing? How to use it?"

My heart is beating wildly. She knows that she has me. That my wild love and hate for her will see us both through to the very end of her plan.

"You will come visit me," she says. "In prison. You will visit me often. And in return, I will take all the blame. I will tell all the world what I have done and why I have done it. In public, you may deny me. You will get all the sympathy that you are due as the victim of an impossible tragedy. An inexplicable, decades-spanning horror. I will see to it that the world is on your side. You will be the hero. You will rise from this, stronger, with all the control over your own designs that I never had. Did you know that for the past few months I have been watching you play board games on the internet at your little club? I have bet on you and I have bet against you. You are a canny player, but there is still so much you can learn about business and strategy from a superior player. Nylo was built on my stolen ideas. My body was used against my will, and that's where you have come from. But I will do this deal with you, because I think that you of all people might be able to understand me somewhat before I lay down my weary head."

She takes my hands in hers. My mother's touch, after all these years, after all the madness of the past hour, the past week, brings tears to my eyes.

"I don't want to have an unrequited life," she says. "I want to tell you everything. I want to be your rabbi, your consigliere, your secret source of wisdom and strength. Will you let me be your mother? After what I have done? Because of what I have done?"

What choice do I have? Letting her confess is both the right thing to do and the most self-serving thing to do. I know that if she dies, no one will ever see any of her videos or recordings. I sit across from her silently, my head and heart pounding.

I stand up abruptly and walk to the window, flinching as I look down into the yard where I can just make out Ben, Olivia, and Jane surrounded by police officers, illuminated by flashing lights from cop cars and ambulances. They obviously heard the gunfire. Do they think I am dead? What sign are they waiting for to rush in and save me?

"Give me the gun," I say, turning back around to face my mother. "If they storm in here and see you holding the gun on me, they'll shoot you."

"And you don't want them to shoot me," she says, her voice confident, but also tinged with hope.

"No," I reply, and I mean it.

She empties the bullets from the chamber and hands me the revolver. I set it on the ground by my feet and stare at my mother as an equal. I collapse into her and hug her fiercely, luxuriating in her smell, in the comfort of her arms.

"I can't believe what you did," I say. "I don't understand it. I will never understand it. I'm not like you. I never was and I never will be. You can't possibly understand what you have done. And what you have lost."

"I know what I have lost," she says, looking me in the eyes as she releases me from our embrace.

She bends down and kisses Alistair on the forehead and then Gabriella. She closes Alistair's eyes. There is blood on her lips, which she blots with a Kleenex from her pocket.

"I gave them all their life and then I took it back," she says. "And now it is you who has everything. All of my love. All of my attention. Didn't you ever wish me back to life? Well, here I am. What will you do with me?"

I don't know what to say. I want to scream. I want to jump out the window.

"Never mind," she says. "We will figure it all out together, darling."

I have won. But what have I won?

My mother seems eerily calm as she grabs my hand and leads me down the stairs. We pause together by the White Room, where she squeezes my hand and pats my cheek, and then she throws open the front door and we move outside together: her, an unforgivable monster who has satisfied a lifetime's worth of revenge, and me, the one she has left alive to tell the tale.

Dani Lamia Collection
(Elevated Horror and Supernatural Thrillers)

ISBN: 978-1-933769-70-7

When a dream world stalker begins killing her tormentors in a world where dreams and reality overlap, a bullied high schooler must stop The Raven's attacks on her behalf.

ISBN: 978-1-933769-68-4

When an idealistic priest learns in the confessional that a psychopath is murdering locals, he must find a way to stop her, without giving up everything he believes in.

ISBN: 978-1-933769-62-2

When a young woman who has always suppressed her disturbing psychic powers finds herself faced with a hostile witches' coven, she must embrace her power in order to save her life.

ISBN: 978-1-933769-60-8

When a struggling director chooses a haunted bed and breakfast for the location of his next film, the darkness within him turns the otherwise peaceful spirits into a nightmarish reckoning for him and his crew.

ISBN: 978-1-933769-64-6

When the spirit of a vampire is unleashed during a séance, a resident finds herself growing more youthful even as her friends rapidly age. She must find a way to stop the process before everyone she loves is dead.